FLOWERS FOR MISS PENGELLY

FLOWERS FOR MISS PENGELLY

Rosemary Aitken

This first world edition published 2013
in Great Britain and in the USA by
SEVERN HOUSE PUBLISHERS LTD of
19 Cedar Road, Sutton, Surrey, England, SM2 5DA.

British Library Cataloguing in Publication Data

Aitken, Rosemary, 1942–
  Flowers for Miss Pengelly.
  1. Lady's maids–Fiction. 2. Social status–Fiction.
  3. Criminal investigation–Fiction. 4. Cornwall (England :
  County)–Social conditions–20th century–Fiction.
  5. Love stories.
  I. Title
  823.9'14–dc23

ISBN-13: 978-0-7278-8229-5   (cased)

For my neighbours,
Angela and Pat

All Severn House titles are printed on acid-free paper.

Severn House Publishers support the Forest Stewardship Council [FSC], the
leading international forest certification organisation. All our titles that are printed
on Greenpeace-approved FSC-certified paper carry the FSC logo.

MIX
Paper from
responsible sources
FSC® C018575

Typeset by Palimpsest Book Production Ltd.,
Falkirk, Stirlingshire, Scotland.
Printed and bound in Great Britain by
MPG Books Ltd., Bodmin, Cornwall.

Part One

Autumn 1911

One

When Effie saw the policeman outside the Westons' shop, under the sign saying 'High Class Haberdashery and Subscription Library', she almost turned and ran. Her heart, which had been pit-patting happily under her neat grey housemaid's uniform, lurched suddenly to the bottom of her buttoned boots. She knew what this meant, of course she did. They'd found out about that business with Lettie and the books.

So what would happen now? They wouldn't send you to prison for a thing like that, would they? Or would they? Even if not – think of the disgrace! Once Mrs Thatchell knew the police had been involved she'd very likely turn Effie out at once, and then whatever would become of her? It was no good hoping to go back to Aunty Madge; Uncle Joe had made his feelings clear on that. 'Girl is old enough to make a living now. You done your family duty, Madge, giving her a 'ome when her poor Pa couldn't cope, and now it's time to think about yourself. Besides, we need the bed. Young Sammy's getting that much bigger now, it's time he had one to hisself.'

And Pa couldn't have her – even now. He'd gone into lodgings after Mother died and he shared his bedroom with another miner as it was. And there was precious little hope of finding another live-in job – no-one would take a girl without a character. So would it be the workhouse? Probably it would, and that was almost worse than prison, in a way – great grey walls – and if you were in jail there was at least a chance you might get out again! Oh, glory! Why had she let Lettie talk her into this?

Suddenly her job with Mrs Thatchell seemed a precious thing. Most other girls she knew were either (like her cousins) working down the mine, breaking the tin-stone so it could be crushed; or if they were in household service, it was in humble downstairs jobs, like laundry-maids and kitchen-hands or simply scrubbing floors. But the sewing teacher had heard about the vacancy for a general maid through that same Miss Blanche Weston who was looking at her now – who kept the haberdashery and subscription library – and had been persuaded to put in a word because Effie had won the leaver's prize for 'outstanding needlework'.

It must have been a good word, because it did the trick. When a nervous Effie turned up for interview, Mrs Thatchell had asked a hundred questions (none of which Effie knew the answer to!), found a hundred faults, taken a long, hard, disapproving look at her, and then – just when Effie was sure of being sent away – suddenly decided, 'Well you're no worse than the others, and at least you're half-polite. Since you come recommended, I suppose that you will do. I haven't found anyone else remotely suitable and I hear you have one talent, if it's only sewing hems. You will be living in, of course. No drink, no followers. If you suit, I can offer you your keep, one half-day off and three and nine a week.'

It was less than lots of servants got, but Effie knew when she was fortunate. She nodded wordlessly.

'Then you can start next Monday; report to Cook six sharp and don't be late. We've got a uniform: had it for the last girl, but she didn't last a month, so it is hardly worn. It will need alteration, but no doubt you'll manage that, if you're as good as sewing as they say you are. And a good thing too. Material costs money and it's too good to waste.'

Even then Effie could hardly believe her luck. Perhaps it was because – as she discovered as soon as she moved into the house – Mrs Thatchell liked to do needlework herself. Lovely things she'd made, as well – not common things like skirts and bloomers, like you made at school, but tapestries and cushions and embroidered chairs. It was a pity no-one ever saw them, Effie thought.

She'd said as much to Mrs Lane, the stout cook-housekeeper, that very first day she was there. The cook had been rolling pastry for a pie, while Effie made a last adjustment to her uniform. It had belonged to Daisy – the one who had lasted no longer than a month – 'a flighty piece' according to the cook, and evidently a large girl, judging by the uniform she'd left. It wasn't easy doing the alterations on your own, with no-one to pin and mark the darts for you (Aunt Madge and the cousins hadn't had the time), but Effie thought she'd managed beautifully – until Mrs Thatchell saw her, said the hem was far too short and had sent her downstairs smartly to let it down a bit.

'That better?' She twirled around to show the cook.

Mrs Lane looked up from flouring her board. 'Better than on Daisy – I'll say that for you. But don't you take my word. You'd better show the mistress when you've done your chores.'

'I'm half-ashamed to show her when she sews so well herself. Lovely things she showed me that she made. I only wish the ladies from the Haberdashery could see – show them what real needlework can be.'

Mrs Lane flicked salt and pepper on her pie. 'Well don't you say so to her, my girl, that's all I can say, or you'll be out of this house quicker than you came into it. The mistress doesn't care for company.' She must have realized that she sounded sharp, because she added in a gentler voice, 'Shut herself more or less away, she has, ever since her husband was lost in the Boer War. And she never knew until his ship came in. Went all the way to Plymouth to meet the boat, poor thing – wanted to surprise him coming home, I suppose – and when she got there, just found he wasn't there.'

'And the army never even let her know?' Effie was appalled.

'Letter never reached her, see – though 'course they must have wrote. Before my time, all this was, but from what I hear of it, you never saw a body change so much. Used to be a proper beauty, by all accounts, and full of fun – lunch-parties and all sorts. And now look at her. Never a guest invited in all my years with her, apart from a yearly visit from her bank, not even for a single cup of tea. Stiff as starch, poor woman, and bitterer than sin.' She glared at Effie and brought herself up short. 'Still, she pays our wages and we mustn't judge. Now, since you have finished fiddling with that blessed hem, are you going to stand here gossiping all day or go and do the grates?'

So Effie had scuttled off to do her chores and – although she'd tried to raise the subject since – that was all that Cook could ever be prevailed upon to say. It was intriguing though.

Strange to imagine Mrs Thatchell as a lively bride, instead of a sour woman sitting in a chair, shut up in the gloomy morning room, making tapestries that nobody would see.

Even on Coronation Day it had been just the same. There were parties and pageants and dancing in the street, but Mrs Thatchell didn't put bunting round the door, like everybody else, or even stand in the window with the curtains back, to see the pageant procession and the marching bands – though she let the servants have a half-hour to watch. She herself just sat in the morning room and sewed, as usual.

But it was that same stitchery which brought Effie to the store each week, to buy new silks and also to return the books which her mistress always had from the subscription library. Improving sermons, mostly, though why she chose those, when there were hundreds of lovely things to read – Conan Doyle and that Mr Dickens whom they'd learned about at school – Effie could not see. She would have loved to borrow a few of those herself, but of course a penny was far too much to spare when she was saving every farthing towards a pair of boots, and there was a half-a-crown to give to Aunty Madge out of her meagre wages as it was.

All the same she loved to come here to the shop. Usually Tuesday morning was the highlight of her life – the Haberdashery was like a coloured fairyland: not only silks but reels of ribbon too, racks of cottons, trays of beads and sequins, hanks of wool displayed on hooks and shelves, cards of buttons hanging on a stand, spools of lovely lace and even a few bolts of plain material. It reminded Effie of a story Mother used to tell, about a boy who found a cave full of enchanted things.

And as for the little back room with all those books in it! The first time she saw it she could not believe her eyes. She had not known that there were so many books in all the world; she had only had one in her life – 'for good attendance at the Sunday school'.

That and the precious sewing-box, which had been her needlewoman's prize, were the only things she'd ever really owned. Everything else, from the camisole and nightshirt in the drawer to these much-mended boots, was a hand-me-down and had once belonged to either cousin May or cousin Peg. Not even the name 'Effie' was properly her own. Mother had named her Ethel, after her own Ma, but when Effie went to live with Aunty Madge the youngest boy was small and couldn't say 'th', so Ethel became Effie, and the name had stuck. Only Pa, when she saw him, ever called her 'Ethel' now.

She had tried to change it back when she first went to work – 'Ethel' seemed more fitting for a maid somehow – but Mrs Thatchell had waved the suggestion loftily aside. 'I was told that you were Effie, and that suits me very well. My first maid, as it happens, was called Effie, too – Ephegenia, I believe she was. So I am used to it. Besides, I like the name. It sounds "efficient" and it's easy to recall. I never could remember what half those other girls were called, Daisy and Susie and all the rest of it. No, Effie will do me very well indeed.'

'Count yourself lucky,' Aunty Madge said when she heard. 'At least it's something that you're accustomed to. There was a woman down Tresidder way called all her servants 'Rose', just so she never had to learn their different names. Anyway, what's wrong with "Effie"? It's what you're always called. It's even written on that box of yours.' Which, of course, it was.

The recollection troubled Effie now. Would Mrs Thatchell have to learn a different name again, when she had been sent off to the workhouse in disgrace and a new maid took her place? She could not bear to think about the possibility. She had known that it was naughty, the trick that she and her friend Lettie had contrived, but it had all seemed so simple at the time.

Lettie was lady's maid and dresser to the daughter of a grand house on the outskirts of the town: a pretty young lady who always looked a treat, but properly spoiled by her Papa, by all accounts. Miss Caroline was a member of the subscription library herself, but – like Mrs Thatchell – sent her maid to get her books for her, usually on alternate Tuesdays, luckily enough. That was how the two servant-girls had come to meet and now they looked forward to their little chats.

'Proper waste of sixpence,' Lettie grumbled once, taking an exciting-looking volume from the shelf. 'Only joined the library

because her smart friends belonged. Sends me in each fortnight
for her books – the latest things so she can show them off –
then scarcely even seems to glance at them. Read them myself
to save the waste, I would, except I've never been a one for
books, myself.'

'Oh, I am!' Effie said, unthinkingly.

Lettie turned to her with a wicked smile. 'Tell you what,
there is always something I could find to bring me into town
– letters to be posted or shoes to be re-soled – even on non-
library weeks. Suppose that on the alternate weeks I come and
stand outside, bringing some book Miss Caroline's decided not
to read? She'll have already paid the fee so if you take it home,
and promise me you'll get it back before the date runs out,
who will be the wiser? And don't look at me like that. It's not
as if it's stealing – it's only borrowing. And she don't want it,
so who is hurt by it?'

Effie had been easy to convince. Surely it was doing no-one
any harm? And it had worked like magic – up to now that is!
But obviously the Misses Weston had discovered it. And now
the police were here and it was too late to escape – Miss
Blanche had seen her and was gesturing her to come.

Miss Blanche was not pretty, she was too tall and thin for
that, but she was generally kind and – unlike her elder sister
– would greet you with a smile. Absurdly, she was smiling
now. 'There you are, Constable, this is Effie Pengelly – the
very girl that we were talking of.' Her voice seemed very loud
as she beckoned to Effie with a bony lace-trimmed hand.
'Come along, Effie, you are just in time. This policeman needs
to have a word with you. I was about to direct him to Mrs
Thatchell's house.'

Effie gulped. Thank heaven he had not come knocking at
Mrs Thatchell's door! Things were bad enough, without being
made an exhibition of in front of the whole street. It was all her
own fault, too, that was the worst of it. It was a mercy Lettie
hadn't yet arrived to be involved in this – though doubtless the
policeman would catch up with her as well. Effie found that she
was blinking back the tears as she stumbled down the pavement
towards Miss Blanche Weston and the waiting constable.

★　　★　　★

Blanche Weston looked affectionately at the girl as she approached. Nice little creature, she had always thought. Almost a young woman, now, and very nearly pretty if she weren't so skinny and anxious-looking, poor thing. Blanche was glad that she'd defied her sister, just for once, and recommended Effie for the maid's post at that house, even though they only knew her by repute. It was all very well for Pearl to say that she should not have spoken up.

'Just because that sewing-teacher at the school asked if we knew of any vacancies, you did not have to put our reputation at such risk,' Pearl had chided sharply, when she heard of it. Pearl had been disappointed of marriage in her youth, and had been very fond of chiding ever since. 'Simply on the basis of some stupid sewing-prize! What do we know about this Effie, anyway? Suppose she turns out to be a thief, or worse?'

But of course, she hadn't. It had worked out very well and Blanche took a particular pleasure in the fact. It was almost as if the child was her personal protégée. But whatever was the matter with the girl today? She was walking as if her legs would hardly carry her. But of course, it was the presence of the policeman at the door – the child must have realized that something was amiss.

'Come on, girl, do hurry. This poor young constable hasn't got all day!' That was Pearl now, bounding from the shop, rather like a sheepdog harrying the lambs.

Blanche smiled inwardly at her own comparison. Pearl did look rather like a terrier, the way she held her pointed chin up high. She was slightly the shorter of the two but had inherited their mother's air of effortless authority, which made her seem somehow larger than she was. And she had the looks. Blanche had no illusions on that score. She herself had a bony face and long teeth like a horse, but Pearl would have been handsome if she were not so severe, though since her 'disappointment' with that dreadful man she seemed actively to rejoice in making herself plain. Her hair was always scraped back into an unforgiving bun and her thin lips were pursed into a disapproving 'O', as if to echo the hairstyle from the front.

She was turning those pursed lips to Effie now. 'Well now

you're here, you'd better come inside. Don't want the whole town listening, do we?'

Effie had found her voice. 'If it's about the books . . .' she managed.

The poor thing was clearly frightened. Blanche said, with a smile, 'Never mind the books, dear. That can wait a little while. The constable has something he wants to say to you. Something very serious has been happening.'

The stricken look on Effie's face gave her a pang of guilt. Of course, Blanche thought, it was a terrible event – finding a dead man lying in the yard – and she should be ashamed that it had given her a little secret thrill.

It would have been a different thing, perhaps, if she had been the first person on the scene, but when she went out for water from the tap (they hadn't really needed to have it piped inside; that sort of thing was a terrible expense) there was the butcher from the shop next door saying that there was someone lying in the corner of the court. He had been cross at first because he thought it was a tramp – you did get itinerants who climbed the wall sometimes and tried to huddle in the corner out of the wind and rain. But of course, when she went over with him, it was clear this man was dead. There was no blood or anything, but the corpse was stiff and cold.

And she – Blanche Weston – had been the one to go and fetch the police. A pair of them there'd been: an older sergeant, whom she'd seen before, and this young, dark, good-looking constable. They'd listened to her story and come straight back with her.

Pearl had, predictably, been simply furious. 'Bringing the police here?' she had hissed, when Blanche got back. 'What are you thinking of? All over town by nightfall, it will be. And what will our better class of customers suppose?'

Blanche had surprised herself by finding sufficient courage to retort, 'How do you suppose that we could keep it quiet? A dead man in the yard? Did you expect to hide it? Anyway, the butcher saw it too – and he'll tell everyone who comes, in any case. At least this way we've done the proper thing by that poor dead fellow – whoever it might be.'

'Poor fellow, you call him!' Pearl had snorted. 'Well, on your head it shall be. When the police start asking questions, I shall tell the truth. Yes, we have seen him before. He came in here yesterday, as we were shutting up the shop, asking for that Pengelly girl you think so much about. What did I warn you! Now look what she's done. Bringing trouble to our door! Well, I shall tell them straight!'

And that is exactly what she did, once the body had been moved and the police had taken charge. In fact, she hadn't even waited to be asked. She collared the sergeant as soon as he came in – he had maddeningly gone and spoken to the butcher first – and told him the whole tale. He hadn't seemed much moved.

'Well then, missus, we'd better find the girl. Maybe she can tell us who he is. Nothing on the body to tell us anything. Nothing in his pockets but a single ha'penny. No initials, nothing. Just a torn bit of a train ticket, by the looks of it. Might give us a lead if we can work out exactly what that was – though in fact, it looks as if he walked a fair old way. One of his soles is almost worn right through. Seems as if he's fallen on bad times. No overcoat, for one thing – that's what did for him. Died of cold and hunger, so the doctor thinks. Not this Effie's father or brother, I suppose?'

It was Pearl who'd answered. She shook her head at him. 'Shouldn't think so for a minute. Father's a tinner down a local pit and if there were other children – which there aren't – stands to reason they'd be Effie's sort of age, not rising fifty like this man clearly was. Didn't look a tinner, either, from what I saw of him. Fancy voice he had. Wanted to know when Effie would be in. Well, I told him, not until today. She always comes on Tuesday, and I told him so.'

She sounded so disapproving that Blanche had butted in. 'He didn't even stop to ask us where she lived, just thanked us quite politely, and went off down the street. And that's the first and last we saw of him – until today of course.'

The sergeant nodded and put his book away. 'Well we'd better find the girl. I understand that you know where she is? I'll leave the constable to take down her address while I go and make some more enquiries. Someone must have seen this fellow in the town. Though I don't believe he was a local man. I've never seen him anywhere about and the butcher swears he's never set eyes on him before, though between us we know almost everyone. But perhaps this Effie can enlighten us.'

And here the poor child was, looking so terrified that it would melt your heart. But Pearl seemed almost pleased. She gave one of her rare smiles to the young policeman at her side, who was running a finger round the high collar at his neck and looking uncomfortable in his uniform. 'You can use the little back office-storeroom if you like, Constable. We also use it as a sitting-room, so you will find a chair and table and there is a fire alight in there. You won't be disturbed if there are customers.' She led the way towards it and Blanche and the policeman trooped in after her.

But Effie was lingering for an instant at the door. For a moment Blanche thought that the girl was going to run away, but then she realized that all she'd stopped to do was to pull back the cover from the basket on her arm and stuff a pile of books back on the shelf labelled 'Returns'. Wasn't it like Effie to put her duties first, even at a moment like this? Blanche gave her a small approving smile.

Effie coloured scarlet and stared down at her feet, then turned and followed Pearl and the policeman into the sitting-room.

Constable Alexander Dawes, Police number 663, looked around the poky little room where the elder of the spinsters was pulling out a chair. There was scarcely room in here for either him or it – the walls were stacked with boxes and the writing-table too – though the other woman was busy clearing off a space.

'There you are, Constable. You make yourself at home. Effie here can have the wooden stool.'

Alex ran a finger round his collar-edge again. It wasn't only nervousness: the new serge chafed his neck. Though he *was* a little anxious, if the truth be known. It was only a few months since he had joined the Borough Police and having completed the required training period of 'drill' this was the first time he'd been out on his own – up to now the sergeant had accompanied him throughout – and it wasn't going to be as simple as he'd thought.

His task had simply been to find out an address and report back to the station as soon as possible, but here the girl Effie had actually turned up. That wasn't supposed to happen. He'd have to talk to her. It was clear the shopkeepers expected it. Perhaps he could question her a bit and take her to the station a little later on and let the sergeant carry on from there. That might be best. He gave her an uncertain smile and was surprised to realize that she was even more nervous than he was himself.

Perversely, that gave him a sort of confidence. He pulled out his little notebook, took the pencil from the back and licked the tip of it. That helped a bit as well. He looked at the three lines of writing, which was all that the notebook up to now contained, and put on what he hoped was a police-manly sort of voice. 'Now, let me see. Your name is Effie Pengelly I believe?'

She nodded, swallowed, and then blurted out, 'Well actually it's Ethel, but they call me Effie, sir.'

Calling him 'sir' was oddly flattering. He nodded. 'And you work for a Mrs–' he looked down at his notes – 'a Mrs Thatchell in Morrab Road?' The girl didn't answer, so he tried again. 'Can you confirm that? It's what the ladies of the shop have told me.'

The girl Effie had dropped her head and was looking up at him with enormous hazel eyes. She would have been a proper stunner, he thought, if she hadn't been so thin. She had lovely chestnut hair, though she had pulled it back in an unbecoming twist – from which, he noticed, it was trying to escape. She gave him a brief nod. 'I suppose you'll have to tell her about all this,' she muttered, suddenly. She sounded close to tears.

'All this?' he echoed. 'So you already know what this is about?' If so, perhaps this interview would not be so bad.

She nodded. 'Yes, sir, I'm sorry . . . I'm afraid I think I do.'

Relief was spreading up his shoulder blades and he let himself lean back in his uncomfortable chair and press his fingertips together, as he had seen Sergeant Vigo do. 'So perhaps you can tell us who this fellow is?'

The downcast gaze had turned into a stare and her shock

and amazement could scarcely have been feigned. 'Fellow? What fellow?'

He took a deep breath. 'Forgive me, I thought you said you knew. There has been a stranger in the town. Came here to this shop yesterday asking where you were.'

She frowned at him. 'Well either of the Miss Westons could have told him that. They know better than anyone where Mrs Thatchell lives. But he never came there asking. Cook or someone would have told me if he had. Who is he anyway?'

Alexander took another gulp of air. 'Effie, that's exactly what we would like to know.'

She had stopped being frightened. She was merely puzzled now. 'Well, how don't you ask him?'

He didn't answer that. He looked away and underlined the writing in the book. 'You have no idea at all who this man might have been?'

She shook her head firmly. 'I don't know any men. 'Cepting for Father and Uncle Joe, of course, but they know where I live. They wouldn't have to ask . . .' She broke off suddenly. 'Here, this isn't anything to do with Father, is it? There hasn't been an accident or something down the mine . . .?'

'We don't think it is your father,' he began, meaning to reassure her.

But she was already shaking that lovely chestnut head and saying in an altered tone of voice, 'No, course it couldn't be. They'd have sent at once to Aunty Madge — and she'd have let me know. So whoever is it, to ask for me by name? And you say he isn't local.' She looked at him suddenly. 'There was a cousin of Mother's went to America, years and years ago. Couldn't be him, could it? You'd think he'd write to say. And he'd go to Father, not just ask for me.' She raised her eyes to his. 'But I suppose it might be. Sound foreign, does he?'

He said, very carefully, 'Seems to be English, from what I understand. But not a local man. No possessions, as far as we can see — except what he stood up in — and nothing about him that would help us to find out who he was.'

'Was?' The girl was staring at him disbelievingly. 'You're telling me he's dead?' He hadn't meant to let that out so soon, but she had been too sharp. Before he could say anything, she spoke again. 'Never been murdered, has he?'

'Nothing so dramatic. Died of cold and hunger, by the look of it. The butcher found his body lying in the yard. But there's nothing on the body to tell us who he was – no name, no wallet, nothing of the kind.'

'Someone might have robbed him after he was dead,' the girl said, surprising him. That was an intelligent idea. Perhaps he would suggest that to the sergeant later on.

'Maybe, though it looked more as if he'd fallen on hard times.'

'You mean he was a tramp.' Effie was frowning. 'How didn't he go to the workhouse, whoever he was? I know it's bad up there, but surely it's better'n dying, freezing on the street. And what did he want me for? Who was he anyway?'

He cleared his throat and put the notebook carefully away. 'Effie,' he said gently, 'you'd better come with me. I'm sorry to ask you, but the sergeant will want to have a word, and maybe you had better have a look – it may be that you'll know this person when you see his face. You want me to let your employer know where you have gone?'

She shook her head. 'Better not – she'll be spitting tin-tacks as it is, without having a policeman turn up on her step. No doubt the Misses Weston will stand up for me. Won't take too long, will it, looking at the corpse?'

'It won't disturb you?'

She flashed him a wry smile. 'Don't worry about me. I've seen dead folks before. Though never a stranger, come to think of it. And this must be a stranger – I can't think who else. But why on earth should he be wanting me?'

She was a resilient little creature and she looked so awfully young. He rather wished he'd not suggested this; it would have saved her anguish – but someone was sure to have fetched her in the end. Though if anyone was going to shepherd Effie through this unpleasant business, he was happy that it should be Alexander Dawes. He got slowly to his feet. 'Then, if you'll follow me.'

Another bashful smile. 'If you say so, sir. Only I'd better get these books and silks before we go – Mrs Thatchell will be livid with me, as it is.'

'I'm afraid that your errands will have to wait. Dead men are in no hurry – but my sergeant is.' He found himself adding, with a little smile, 'If there's any trouble when you do get home, make sure you let me know, and I will come and explain things to your mistress myself.'

Two

It wasn't so terrible, looking at the corpse. It wasn't mangled, like the bodies that she'd once seen at the mine, and there was none of the heartbreaking familiarity and sense of loss that had accompanied Mother's laying-out. This was just an ordinary man, looking quite peaceful although a little blue, and lying stiffly underneath the sheet which they pulled back from the face to let her have a look.

She did look, quite closely, but then shook her head. 'I'm quite sure,' she told the nice young policeman, who was standing at her side. 'Nobody I've ever set eyes on in my life.'

'It couldn't be that cousin of your mother's from America?'

She looked at the dead stranger's waxy countenance again. There wasn't the slightest resemblance to the family, as far as she could see. 'Shouldn't think so, from the look of him,' she murmured doubtfully. 'Only you'd better ask my Pa, just to make quite sure. He would have known that cousin, years ago – when they were young.' Were you allowed to suggest that sort of thing to police? She glanced at the constable to see if she had overstepped the mark.

But he didn't seem to be offended in the least. 'We'll do that!' He signalled that the mortuary man should cover up the corpse's head again and said quite gently, 'Thank you. You've been very brave.'

Even the stout sergeant, who was standing by the door, was smiling at her now from behind his thick moustache – which he hadn't shown the slightest tendency to do when he was asking her all those questions at the police-station earlier. 'This has been an ordeal for you, miss, I'm afraid,' he said. 'But you'll appreciate our position. When someone comes to town and asks for you by name, and then turns up dead of cold, naturally we hope that you will help us with his identity. But I accept that you genuinely did not know the man.'

Effie turned scarlet with embarrassment. She deserved to be

in trouble with the police, over that business with the books, and here they were apologizing to her instead! She said, in a guilty attempt to help, 'He must have heard my name from somewhere else — although I can't for the life of me think how. Perhaps he knew my second-cousin in America, for all you say he had an English-sounding voice?'

The sergeant very nearly smiled again. 'That is a possibility of course. Perhaps, as you say, your father can throw some light on it. However, that is our affair. Thank you for attempting to assist. If we need to speak to you again, be sure we'll let you know.'

Effie found she'd turned to jelly at the knees. 'Come down the police station again, you mean?' she stammered. Dreadful scenes were flashing through her mind, with Mrs Thatchell being furious. 'My mistress won't . . .'

He seemed to realize that she was upset. 'Only if we really need you — which I hope we won't. I'm sorry you've been bothered, Miss Pengelly,' he said, putting her in a little flurry suddenly. Nobody ever normally called her 'Miss Pengelly' — although of course, that's exactly what she was.

'Well, if you want my father, he'll be down the mine.' She frowned. 'Won't lose a day's pay, will he, for having to come here?' If so, it would be her fault, she thought wretchedly. 'Can't wait till he's finished I don't suppose? Early shift this week so he should be off at four.' The policemen were exchanging glances, which almost gave her hope, until an idea struck her and she added wretchedly, 'Without he's working doublers — in which case he won't be up to ground till after midnight, I suppose.'

'Doublers?' The young constable sounded mystified.

Effie stared at him. Surely everybody knew what doublers were? 'Two shifts back to back,' she explained, patiently. 'Being a tributer and working for his-self, he can do that sometimes if he likes — does his own and then stands in on someone else's team. Either they pay you extra or you exchange your time in lieu, and that's what he does sometimes — gets a half-day off and comes to Aunty Madge's for a meal. Likes to take it Thursday, if he can manage it — that's my free afternoon, and I generally go over then as well.'

The sergeant was still smiling as he held the door for her. 'Thursday? I'm afraid this matter cannot wait till then.'

She hadn't meant that and she shook her head. 'Never thought it would. I was only warning you that Pa might not be up to ground again today. Mind, he doesn't always do the double shift, even if the chance is there: he's getting old, and nowadays he finds it very hard . . .' She trailed off in dismay. She was keeping the policemen waiting, she realized suddenly – chattering on when they expected her to move. She took a hurried step towards the door.

But the young constable was already at her side. 'We'll make enquiries. And we'll see he doesn't suffer for assisting us,' he said, taking her elbow gently and guiding her out of the mortuary and back into the street. 'I'm sure his masters will agree to let us question him.'

She turned to look up at him – he towered over her. He had a nice face, though a little pink around the ears, and his grey eyes were looking into hers. She dropped her gaze at once. 'They might stop his money, that's the only thing,' she told him earnestly. 'Like my mistress will probably stop mine – or worse – if I don't look lively and get back to work. And even now I haven't got the books and threads that I was sent to fetch!'

The two policemen were exchanging looks again. The sergeant nodded. 'Well, Constable, you'd better see this young lady home. Explain to her employer what's been happening – that she's been doing her public duty and all that sort of thing.'

'Yes, Sergeant, certainly I will. Thank you, sir.' Was she imagining it or did the sergeant wink and was young Constable Dawes turning even redder than before?

Alex had an unaccountable desire to make the escorting mission take as long as possible, but of course that would hardly have been very fair – the poor girl was obviously anxious to be back and terrified she'd be in trouble as it was. He contented himself with hurrying along, while asking her lots of questions about herself, which – perhaps because of the uniform he wore – she answered in detail and without embarrassment. He quickly learned that she was an only child and that her mother had died in childbirth when the girl was only ten.

'Pa couldn't have me,' she told him earnestly. 'What with working shifts, so Aunt Madge took me in. Course he always paid her something for my keep – and now I give her half-a-crown myself. 'Tisn't much, with all those mouths to feed, but it does help a bit, especially with what the older girls bring home these days from the bal.'

'And you still feel obliged to contribute?'

She stared at him. 'What else would I do? What I would have done without that family, heaven only knows. Ended up in the workhouse I shouldn't be surprised, or taken in by strangers – which would have broke my heart. Bit of a crush in that small house of course, especially after the little ones were born – but we all managed somehow.'

She was quite without self-pity, though to him her life seemed very hard – nine people squashed into a tiny cottage, the four boys in one bedroom lying head to toe and the two girl-cousins with whom Effie shared a room, doing the same thing in a narrow bunk, while she thought herself lucky to have a tiny truckle bed to herself. 'Aunt Madge insisted,' she went on gravely, 'seeing Pa was paying for my keep. But they can't well afford the space, now the boys are growing big – Sammy keeps on falling out and keeping the other three awake. He's got my truckle now. That's how I was so pleased to get this job. Let's just hope I still have it after all of this.'

He thought of his own well-appointed home – a bedroom of his own, with handsome furniture, a wash-stand and thick rugs and someone to bring a tray of tea when you woke up, and light the fire and draw the curtains back. Even in the training quarters at the police station he had a comfortable bed, and a private locker in which to keep his things. He said, 'So you like it where you are? I got the impression that your Mrs Thatchell was a bit severe.'

Effie gave him a sheepish sideways grin. 'Well, so she is – but you've got to count your blessings, haven't you, and it's lovely having a whole attic to myself. Proper iron bedstead and a corner with a rail where I can hang my clothes – even a piece of mirror where I can comb my hair. Better off than I ever was back there – though it is a bit chilly of a morning now and then. And Mrs Thatchell isn't all that bad if you jump to it and see your chores are done – though she can be a proper Tartar if you don't come up to scratch.' She looked at him. 'In fact, it's very nice of you to see me home like this, but when we get there I shouldn't come inside if I were you. She'll likely bite your head off, constable or not – and I don't want her deciding that I've got a follower. She'd have me out of there before you could say knife – if she wasn't minded to do that anyway.'

'You heard my sergeant,' Alex said. 'I'm to take you home and explain to your superiors why you were delayed. Those were my orders – and I'll tell them so; that way they can't go blaming you for it.'

By now they were crossing the bottom of the street on which the haberdashery was sited further up. He half-expected Effie to want to go back there and get the silks and books she had been sent to fetch, and he was calculating whether he dared permit her to, or whether the sergeant would complain at him for being out so long. But Effie did not even look towards the shop, because at that moment the town clock struck the hour.

'My stars!' she murmured. 'Listen to the time. I'd better hurry on. Mrs Thatchell will have me for garters as it is.'

He took her elbow and steered her firmly straight across the road. 'I'll come in and have a word to Mrs Thatchell for you, if you like,' he offered, and saw the look of gratitude on Effie's pretty face. 'We'll see if she "has you for garters" after that!' However, when they got back to the house, he almost wished he hadn't said so much. There was a skinny woman scrubbing the front steps as they arrived, and her thin face looked up at Effie with a scowl.

'So there you are, young lady. Where on earth have you been to? Madam's been creating for at least an hour and even Cook is crosser than two sticks.'

Alex cleared his throat. 'That is what I've come here to explain – if we might just get past.'

She glowered up at him. 'Maids don't come in the front

door, in this house any road. Effie can go round the back, like she belongs to do. And you, young fellow – policeman you may be – but since you've come with 'er, I'd be obliged if you would go round that way too and don't go putting your great boots where I've just washed the step.'

Effie was already tugging at his arm, pulling him down the narrow alley to the back. 'That's Mrs Mitchell, comes to scrub for us,' she hissed. 'Don't take no notice, she's as sour as grapes.'

He nodded, 'So I see!'

Effie almost giggled. 'Well, we'd be sour as well, if we had six children and a sick man to keep. Her husband's got too weak to leave his bed, poor man, and she's reduced to scrubbing to scrape enough to eat. People make allowances – give her a scrap or two sometimes, if there is anything to spare – though you'd wait till the millennium if you wanted gratitude. Cook generally saves her a thick end of the loaf – and my dear life, here she's coming with it now!'

A large stout woman in a pinafore and cap had just rounded the corner of the house carrying a small parcel wrapped up in newspaper, but she caught sight of Effie and brought herself up short. 'Effie Pengelly! Where in heaven have you been? You've had us in confluptions, worrying!' She looked at Alex, very doubtfully. 'And now I see the police have brought you home. Never been in some sort of accident, has she?' she added, in a different tone, addressing the question directly to himself.

Alex tried to adopt a sober look, the way a policeman should. 'Not an accident exactly, I am glad to say. But there has been an unpleasant incident. A man has died – apparently of cold behind the Westons' shop – and Effie has been trying to assist us with the case.'

The Cook's face lost its stern look and became concerned. 'Find the body, did she? Poor lamb – that must have been an awful shock. Here!' She pushed the little packet into Alex's hand. 'You take that round and leave it by the corner at the front. It's for Mrs Mitchell – she knows to look for it. Meanwhile I'll take Effie in and see she gets some tea – a strong cup with some sugar – before she goes upstairs. She'll need it too, if I am any judge; Mrs Thatchell's waiting and she's in a proper stew – but I'll make sure she knows the rights and wrongs of this.'

Alex was unwilling to be parted from the girl. He said, stubbornly, 'I'll do that if you like. My orders were to bring her back to her employer and explain the reason she was late – she feared she'd be in trouble.'

The cook squared her shoulders. 'Well, so she would have been. But finding corpses – that's a different thing. It's kind of you to offer, but you leave the girl with me. The mistress don't like having strangers in the house, and very likely it would make things worse. I'll see that Mrs Thatchell knows what's been happening.'

Effie gave him an imploring look. 'I didn't actually find the body, Mrs Lane – Miss Blanche and the butcher did that earlier. It was only that I had to see it afterwards . . .' She trailed off as Alex shook his head at her.

'And that was shock enough!' he said, as firmly as he could. The girl was being offered sympathy – no point in wilfully repudiating that and he wasn't helping her by lingering. He turned to Effie. 'So if Mrs Lane – is it? – will undertake to see that you get that cup of tea, I will leave you in her care as she suggests, and get back to the station to write up my report.' He raised his helmet with a fingertip and grinned. 'Not forgetting to deliver this parcel as I go.'

He was rewarded with a grateful smile from both. But he was thoughtful as he turned away. If Mrs Thatchell was as suspicious of strangers as all that, how would she react when she learned that this strange tramp had been asking for the girl? And it was very likely that she would hear of it – Effie was too honest to conceal anything. He sighed. It seemed there wasn't anything that he could do to help: as the Cook had said, it was probably wisest to leave the matter there.

What a pity, he thought inwardly. He'd been imagining himself as knight-errant to the girl. And now, who knew if they'd ever meet again? Perhaps he could find a reason for calling here another time? Or better still . . . He could not help himself – as he paused at the corner to put the parcel down, he turned and called to Effie's now-retreating back.

'Remember! If you need me – as a witness or for anything at all – you know where I am.'

But the cook was hurrying her away and she did not turn round.

Lettie Pearson was getting really anxious by this time. She had been hovering near the Westons' shop for half an hour at least, shifting her weight from foot to foot and looking out for Effie all the while. Of course she was a little late herself today (serve her right for stopping to gossip to that good-looking grocer's boy!) but time was really getting on and there was no sign of Effie anywhere.

This was beginning to be worrying. It was a library Tuesday and in a minute she would have to go in and return the books she had, without the one that Effie had borrowed for the week. But it was due today and if it wasn't back there'd be a lateness fine and Miss Caroline was sure to come to hear of it. Miss Pearl sent out reminder letters, if the books were overdue, and besides there would be a title not crossed out on Miss Caroline's page in the Misses Westons' book, so Lettie would only be able to take five others home today. Even her mistress (who didn't even read the jolly things) would notice that! So their clever little scheme was bound to come to light – and then wouldn't hoity-toity Miss Caroline have a picnic-day!

She gave a fretful sigh. Effie would only say that this had served them right and they should never have been doing it. Effie was like that – too cautious by a mile, and left to herself she would never have dreamed up a risky thing like this. But perhaps she had been right. Was it possible that Lettie's famous luck was running out?

Because Lettie was lucky – or so people said. Lucky to have the post with Miss Caroline at all: if her stepmother hadn't been related to the cook up there, Lettie would never have had the slightest chance, despite being the cleverest in her class at school by half. Lucky to be so pretty with that long red hair. Lucky to have good brains, as well, her stepmother would say – and her stepmother should know, since she was quite the silliest woman you could ever meet: though it had to be allowed that she was good to Fayther and had done her best for Lettie, according to her lights.

'Lucky to have a stepmother who looks out for you!' No doubt, but Lettie could not help but feel that it would have been a great deal luckier if that horse hadn't run away and trampled Mother up against the wall in the first place.

The really lucky people, she had always thought, were ones like Miss Caroline Evalina Knight – spoiled and difficult and dafter than a bat, who had everything she wanted before she asked for it and had never done a hand's turn of anything useful in her life. In fact Lettie had never known her apply herself to anything at all, useful or otherwise, except occasionally to paint insipid pictures of flowers in a vase.

Miss Caroline's real talent was finding fault with things: from the way that Lettie made a clatter on the stairs to the way the breakfast tray was laid. Indeed she'd even threatened to complain to her Papa, and though Lettie took that with a pinch of salt, it paid to be specially careful for a day or two; Major Knight would probably dismiss the whole staff on the spot if his beloved daughter ever asked him to. It wasn't wise to annoy Miss Caroline so it was important that Effie turned up very soon indeed. Otherwise . . .

Dear Heaven and all the angels! There was Effie now, being escorted by a policeman, of all people, at the far end of the street – it looked as if he was marching her back home. He was clearly asking questions and Effie chatted back.

What had she been saying? It must be about the books. Was the policeman going to come for Lettie next? Her mind began to race. Perhaps she could offer to return the lending fee. She began to calculate if she had a few pence clear, but she'd spent it all on ribbons yesterday to impress the grocer's boy. She could pawn her combs perhaps? She was getting ready to promise something of the kind but the policeman did not even glance at her, just helped Effie firmly across the road and they disappeared again towards where Mrs Thatchell lived.

She sent up a silent prayer to whatever gods might be. It was obvious that Effie was not involving her. It made her feel quite guilty – would she have done as much? – though it was a great relief. But it didn't solve the problem. What about the missing book? And there was no escaping; Miss Blanche was on the step, baring her long teeth in a horsey smile.

'Ah, it's young Lettie, isn't it, come for Miss Caroline's books? I'm sorry if there was no-one in the shop. Have you been waiting? Miss Pearl and I were talking to the butcher in the court and didn't realize we couldn't hear the bell. I'm afraid there was a little incident there this morning, and we had to call the police. But it's all been taken care of and we're back to normal now. So come in, do. Have you brought back some books?'

She had of course – but only five of them. But there was nothing for it except to go inside and hand them in, before they started earning lateness fines themselves. Perhaps she could pass the missing volume off as a mistake? She put them quickly on the shelf reserved for the returns, but there was no disguising the fact that she did not have all six. There were no others – if any had come in, the Miss Westons had obviously already dealt with them.

And now Lettie must find some new ones to take home; Miss Caroline would be sure to notice otherwise. She selected five at random – hardly bothering to see which ones they were – then went up to the counter so that Miss Blanche could issue them. Lettie could hardly wait for all the rigmarole – taking the card out of the book and filing it in the little box under today's date, stamping the due date on the book itself, writing the titles in spiky script in the foolscap register under Miss Caroline's account and finally taking the penny lending fee for each.

Miss Blanche stamped the books and began to write the titles against Miss Caroline's account. She did the first two and then looked up surprised. 'Oh, you didn't need to put this through again. You could just have brought it straight up here and I'd change the date by hand. But I'm glad your mistress liked it. I've never known her take a book out twice. Or was it just that she didn't finish it?'

For a moment Lettie didn't understand.

She must have looked puzzled because Miss Blanche gave a laugh. 'Either way, she must have wanted it. If we get another by that author, I'll put it by for you!'

And Lettie, who had just recognized the cover of the book, and worked out that Effie had somehow – bless her – contrived to return the missing volume to the shelf, managed to stammer, 'That would be kind, Miss Blanche, though I think my mistress simply hadn't read it!' Which at least was true!

She and Effie had got away with it. She was so relieved she stopped to gossip with the grocer's boy again, when he happened to ride past on his bicycle, accidentally-on-purpose, with deliveries. He was a handsome fellow with a pair of laughing eyes and hair that curled around his temples like an advertisement for brilliantine. He teased her for her freckles and she tarried far too long.

Miss Caroline was very sharp with her when she got back. 'Lettie, I shall be obliged to part with you if this goes on much more. I send you on an errand and you're not back for hours. And even then you do not do it right. These titles are all boring, every one of them – and for some reason you only brought me five!' She did not even notice she'd had one of them before, though she was quick to demand the penny change, of course.

It wasn't until Lettie was climbing into bed that it occurred to her to think again about her friend, and wonder why – if it was not about the books – Effie had been walking through the town in company with a constable of police.

Three

Mrs Thatchell was still madder than a bull – Effie could see that the moment she walked in, from Madam's tight lips and the tell-tale spots of angry colour in her cheeks – but Cook had gone upstairs ahead and had obviously had some kind of word with her, so all that happened was that the mistress gave a disapproving snort and looked at Effie coldly down her long bony nose.

'Well, girl, so you've deigned to come back here at last, though I understand that even now you haven't managed to fetch my books and silks. What's all this that Cook is telling me? Some cock and bantam story that it is not your fault at all, but that a dead body was discovered in the street and you had to stop and answer a lot of questions by the police?'

Effie nodded earnestly. 'Yes, Madam, that's right. I'm sorry. I did not have the chance to get your things. I'll go down again this minute and pick them up for you.'

'Indeed you will! And I should hope so too!' Mrs Thatchell swept imaginary hair into the hairgrips which she always wore to hold her tight grey plaits in their two fierce coils just above her ears. 'I don't know what the world is coming to, when an employer can't expect to have her errands run without her servants being called upon to get involved with matters that are no concern of theirs!' She made a tutting noise. 'Who was it anyway? Some tramp, I understand.'

Effie was about to say that she had only been 'called upon' because the dead man had asked for her by name, but one glance at Mrs Thatchell's beaky face was enough to tell her that was not a good idea. Instead she said, 'That is the problem, Madam. They don't know who he is; he seems to be a stranger – they were trying to find out.'

'So why ever would the policemen want to talk to you?' The angry red patches in Mrs Thatchell's cheeks looked even brighter now. 'What could they possibly suppose that you would know? You don't consort with vagrants, I suppose?'

Effie closed her eyes. She would be for it now! Mrs Thatchell hated anything that 'smelt of trouble'. She said, carefully, 'From something that he said before he died, they think he might have known my mother's cousin in America, perhaps. That's why the police thought that maybe I could help, but when I looked, I'd never seen the man before. So they're going out to Penvarris and they're going to ask my Pa.' She waited for Mrs Thatchell to exclaim that since the Pengelly family brought problems to the door by knowing down-and-outs it would be better if they parted company.

But there was no such outburst and when Effie dared to look, Mrs Thatchell was calmly threading her needle up again to stitch at the chair-back that she was working on. 'Well! A good thing too! I don't know why they didn't think of going to him at first,' she said. Her voice was sharp, but the angry flush was gone. 'It might have saved us all this inconvenience. However, I don't want to be unfair. I'm a Christian woman and Cook says you've had a shock. We shall let it pass, this time. But I warn you, Effie, if such a thing occurs again, I shall have to reconsider. Is that understood?'

It was no good protesting that it wasn't likely to, and that it wouldn't be her fault if it did! Effie could only stand and nod her head and – as soon as she was freed – rush back to the Miss Westons' to get the silks and sermons as required. She did glance at the bookshelves, while she was in the shop, to make sure the Scarlet Pimpernel book was safely in its place, but she couldn't see it anywhere. That was alarming, but she dared not linger long and she could only hope it had been taken out again. Otherwise poor Lettie would be in the soup! And all so that Effie could have a bit of a read! It made her feel quite dreadful, particularly when Miss Blanche was especially nice to her.

'My dear Effie! How are you feeling now? Such a dreadful shock all this has been to everyone! That poor man dying in the cold and wet! I'm sure I shall have nightmares about it for a week. Now you're sure you've got all the coloured silks you want? Then that will be a shilling – one and fourpence with the books.'

Miss Pearl was more direct. She came in while Effie was counting out the coins and said, 'You going to tell us who that fellow was? After all he only came here asking after you and, next thing we find him lying dead out in our back court – on our premises without a by-your-leave.'

Effie shook her head. 'Never seen him in my life before. I can't imagine how he got my name. That nice young constable is going out to see Pa, see if he can help.' She scooped her purchases into her wicker frail and added quickly, 'And that is all I know, myself. Good-day, ladies! Thank you very much.' She beat a quick retreat before Miss Pearl could ask her any more.

But it seemed that Pa was just as mystified. When she saw him, Thursday afternoon at Aunt Madge's house (he had been working extra, other times, to get there, as she'd told the police) he took her immediately to one side. He led her to the little lean-to garden shed, which was Uncle Joe's but where Pa liked to work sometimes. He was good with making things. This time he'd been using his pen-knife to fashion a small top out of a piece of birchwood for one of Madge's boys. He picked it up again and starting whittling, but after a minute he looked up at her.

'Now see here, Effie,' he said in his bluff way, 'don't think I'm blaming you. But you can tell me, if there's anything amiss. That tramp, for instance, that was found dead in the town – if he was something to you, you'd better let me know.'

She stared at him, amazed. 'To me? Of course he wasn't anything to me. Surely the policeman must have told you, Pa? I haven't even the slightest notion who he was.'

He looked away and started shaping the body of the top, easing out the indentation where the string would go. 'That so, Effie?' He wouldn't meet her eyes. 'Yet they say he went there asking for you by your name. How do you account for that then?'

She frowned at him. 'I can't account for it! That is why the policeman came to you. We were hoping that you could help us – that perhaps you or Mother had known him years ago?'

She realized that she'd allied herself with the constable and felt a surge of pinkness in her cheeks. Drat it – Pa was sure to read the wrong thing into that. 'I certainly hadn't! I kept saying so.'

He met her eyes then. 'Well, if you say that, my maid, I daresay it's true. But don't you be surprised if others take a different view.' He jerked his head in the direction of the house.

'Uncle Joe, you mean?' she queried, but of course he did. Her uncle always thought the worst of everyone and Aunt Madge generally went along with him, for the sake of house-hold peace.

Pa nodded. 'Made his mind up there'd been shenanigans, the minute that policeman turned up at the mine and asked to talk to me.'

'Shenanigans?' Effie had often heard the word, but she had only the faintest notion what it meant – except that it was something not-quite-nice that men and girls got up to now and then. 'How could I be having shenanigans with him? I keep on telling you, I'd never seen or heard of him before.'

She was relieved to see Pa actually smile. 'And I believe you – even if your uncle won't. Not a girl for lying – never were.' He met her eyes. 'But you can't blame people for jumping to conclusions over this. It is peculiar, when you come to think. A perfect stranger turning up and wanting you.'

'So you didn't know him either? You're quite sure of that?'

Pa shook his head. 'I can't answer for your mother, naturally – but he wasn't anyone that I could recognize. Not from round here either, by the look of it. They've found a faded label in his shirt which said it came from someplace in the London area, and they're going to ask the police up there to make enquiries.'

'But how can they make enquiries about a shirt? Must be thousands of them sold up in the capital. Hundreds of them, even in Penzance.'

Her father gave her a sideways look. 'But this one looks as if it was bespoke. Obviously made a little time ago, but it's possible the shirt-maker might remember who he made it for.'

Effie was positively goggling by now. Nobody that she knew

had ever even owned a shop-made shirt, except for going to church, and as for made-to-measure! That sort of thing was just for gentle-folk. 'But I thought he was a tramp?'

'And probably he was. The police think it likely he was wearing hand-me-downs – everything was half worn-out and clearly made for someone twice as wide. No doubt given to him out of charity, but if the police can discover who used to own the things, maybe that person could tell them who he gave his cast-offs to.'

'But would he remember?'

'Very likely not. It's only a faint hope. More likely there'll be a missing person on the books, somewhere in the country, and they'll match him up, much to the distress of his grieving family. If not, there isn't much that they can do. It's not a pressing matter – not as if the fellow met a violent death: they'll keep him in the morgue a day or two, I expect, and give him a pauper's burial if they can't find out his name. Sad, of course, but don't concern yourself. I was only worried, just in case there was anything you hadn't told me of – I know it's difficult sometimes and I'm not your Ma – but if he was nothing to you, I shan't fret any more.' He held up the top he had been working on. 'Now, if you'll pass me that little pot of varnish over there I'll get this finished for Sam to take to school. He's been longing for a whipping-top like all the other boys. I thought I'd make a couple for the feast. You coming home for that?'

She shook her head. Penvarris Feast Monday was quite a festival – brass bands and fancy dress parades and dancing in the street. Special services and cream teas at the Vicarage for the churchgoers, and saffron buns and teacakes for the Methodists, followed by sports and races and fair booths in the street; it was the only day, apart from Christmas, when they shut down the mine and only a few men went underground, for safety's sake. Any girl in service who could possibly be spared would try to come home Friday evening and stay the whole weekend – there was a special horsebus laid on Monday night, to take them back to town.

But Effie Pengelly would not be one of them. Mrs Thatchell would never let her off – even if Effie had the nerve to ask.

'Shan't be able to. But you could save me a bit of ginger fairing, afterwards.'

Pa said, 'Course I will, my lover. And I'll try to fetch you a bunch of flowers from the procession too, when the girls on the decorated carts start to throw them to the crowds.' He gave her a wicked grin – catching a posy from the feast queen or her maids was supposed to bring the catcher luck in matters of the heart. 'Not that it's likely to do me any good, but I know you always loved to have one when you were living home! Now pass me that bit of emery and let me finish off this whipping top.'

And that was that. Sammy came out to call them in to tea, and Pa didn't speak of the dead man again. Uncle Joe and Aunty Madge looked questioningly at them when they came in, but Pa just shook his head and talked of something else – and though they exchanged glances, they didn't say anything about the incident.

In fact, they said nothing very much at all – at least to Effie – right the way through tea, and when she said anything to them they were noticeably cool. It was the same thing afterwards: her uncle hurried the younger children quickly up the stairs without the story which Effie generally made up for them, and then when she went to give Aunt Madge her usual parting hug, her aunt picked up a tea-towel and evaded her. 'Get on, Effie, you will miss your bus!'

Effie was hurt, but she recognized the signs. Her uncle still suspected her of those 'shenanigans' – whatever they might be.

Alex did not have the time to think of Effie much. Even when he was not busy accompanying a colleague on the beat, or being given impromptu quizzes by his sergeant on aspects of police procedure and the like ('It is one thing to learn things off by heart for an examination, young Dawes; it is quite another to have them at your fingertips'), he was in the living-quarters with his Instruction Manual and his hand-written notes brushing up on how to write reports or tender evidence. At least there were a lot of other things that he had learnt by now: how to press his uniform and sew a button on, or simply make his bed and polish up his boots – none of them things he'd ever had to do before, not even in the years when he was away at school. He had found it very difficult at first.

Not that his family would sympathize, of course. They had never wanted him to join the police. Father had been a Major in what he called 'the Regiment' (the Duke of Cornwall's Light Infantry, of course, but it was always spoken of as if there was no other in the world) and expected all his sons to follow him. 'Why not the Regiment, lad, for heaven's sake? The army – that's the ticket, for a clever lad like you . . .' And on and on he would go about how Great-grandfather had served with Wellington and won a gallantry medal at Quatre Bras. 'The Thirty-second Regiment of Foot, it was called in those days, but the Cornish were famous for their bravery even then. And there's been a Dawes as an officer in the regiment ever since. It's in the blood, y'see! Unless it's been diluted in the last few years.'

That was a dig at Mother, who was his second wife: both Alex's half-brothers had signed up long ago. But she said nothing – she hardly ever did, except to murmur that Daddy mustn't be upset. But Alex still ventured to voice his own dissent, remarking that few of those illustrious ancestors had died peacefully at home.

'So I have spawned a sissy!' The Major could be relentless when he tried. 'Well, if the army's too red-blooded for your taste, why not the church or – at the very least – the law? Though I did expect a son of mine to be prepared to serve his king and country, I confess!'

'And what am I proposing, if not to serve "my king and country" as you say?'

His father thumped his cane upon the floor. 'Don't be cute, young fellow. You know what I mean. All this policeman business. It's not our sort of thing. In fact I well remember my mother telling me that she was horrified, when she was young, to see the sort of men who were first recruited to the force – half-illiterate the lot of them, and apt to be caught out drinking and slovenly at the local pub. Not that apparently they lasted very long. Half of them dismissed before the month was out, she said.'

Alex kept his temper. 'But that was long ago. Things are

quite different now. There is a test before they'll even take you on and as for character, look at our local constable – two commendations from the King for bravery!'

'Indeed!' A snort. 'But the principle still holds. Of course our local bobby's a good fellow, and all that – but he doesn't have the sort of background that you have been fortunate to have. He was the son of some labourer on a farm.'

So it was no good explaining that it was this very man who had inspired Alex to join the force, by making headlines in the local press: first by stopping a panicked horse that bolted with a cart and then, a few months later, diving straight into the sea – still in his boots and tunic – to rescue a young woman who had fallen in and would otherwise have drowned. The only kind of heroism Father recognized was the military kind.

'Besides, lad, you must see it's an unpleasant sort of life. Dealing with people of the lowest kind, criminals and desperados and women of the street. And dangerous, to boot. A lot of these fellows carry arms and knives and wouldn't think twice about attacking you. You read about it in the papers all the time.'

Never mind that Father had lost a leg himself – smashed to smithereens when some Boer sniper had shot a horse from under him – and was now reduced to limping round the house and grounds. Or that the family finances were running rather thin because an army pension was not enough to keep up the estate, and they were using up all Mother's capital. All that was waved away. The police force was simply not for gentlemen. It had taken all Alex's determination to persist.

But persist he had, despite his father's best attempts to press him into other occupations. There had been a year or two of grace-and-favour placements here and there (including a humiliating term as a junior tutor at his old boarding school, which Father had arranged and Alex had cordially detested from the start) before at last the Major capitulated in a rage. 'Very well, I suppose that now you're turning twenty-one, I can't stand in your way. I still think it's folly, but you won't be told. Go and be a policeman, if you're so set on it, but then you're on your own. Don't come whining back to me because you want to quit. Though I'm convinced you will. I give you a month or two at most.'

So Alex was doubly determined to succeed and would not have admitted if he'd hated it – but, truth to tell, he liked it very much, from the moment that he went away to train. There was something about the ordered life which did appeal to him and he took a certain secret pride in wearing uniform and the conviction that he was of use – perhaps the Major had been right about there being something in the blood. He threw himself into the training course with everything he had and felt a quiet triumph when he came top of all the new recruits at the end-of-course examination.

Taking up his proper duties was a little different, especially since Penzance was half-a-day away from home, but it was interesting work and he'd even earned a medal that Mama could boast about – though it was only for being part of the police procession on Coronation Day. So even Sergeant Vigo's constant jibes and jokes, and the continuous quizzing on the Instruction Manual, did not dismay Alex in the least; he had endured a great deal worse at school. Besides, he was almost certain that by now he'd won himself a measure of respect: surely the sergeant had manipulated things so that Alex could walk that girl Effie home the other day?

He put his foolscap notebook down upon the bed, feeling a little guilty under the accusing eyes of the new King in the picture on the wall. But there was time enough a little later to brush up on the classifications of a felony. Instead he thought about that strange business with the corpse.

There had been little progress on identifying it – it had no distinguishing marks of any kind, apart from one mole on the left buttock, which was no help at all! Letters to nearby work-houses had given them no leads, there was nothing useful from the London shirt-maker, and none of the local landladies had taken in a visitor remotely answering the description of the corpse. A pity, Alex thought. He had been rather hoping to have something to report. It would have given him a reason for calling at the house again – if only to offer reassurance to the girl.

He sighed. Funny sort of business, but the girl was nice.

Effie Pengelly. He hadn't seen her since, though he'd made a special point of walking down that way, any time he got the chance – even when his duties didn't strictly take him there. But there had been no sign of Effie, nor indeed the cook, nor even of that snappy woman who was scrubbing down the step. Alex had been ready to have a word with her, at worst, but there had been no opportunity even to do that. Would it be improper for him to call there openly, just to let Effie know there'd been no further news and that the parish had agreed to give the body burial? Or would that simply make more trouble for the girl? Maybe . . .

'Well, young Dawes, you intending on sitting up all night?' It was Jenkins, the police administrative clerk with whom he shared the room, who was already dropping his braces down his arms and loosening his collar so that he could wash. 'Time will come when I'll be told to put you down for duty over-night, to man the place, then you'll be wanting a mattress on the floor downstairs, no doubt – so you can take your forty-winks if you're not wanted in the town. Half a mind to put you down for night-duty tonight, teach you to keep proper hours like the rest of us.' He buried his face in the cold water from the jug, came up scarlet and towelled himself dry, then emptied the washbowl into the pail of slops. 'Now, you going to blow that candle out, young fellow, or shall I?'

Alex started. He hadn't realized how the time had passed. 'I've got the snuffer, I will see to it. Just give me half a mo!' He found himself scrambling to prepare for bed. The classifica-tions of a felony, like Effie and the proper polishing of boots, would have to wait until another day.

'What do you mean, the Westons found a body in the court?' Lettie gave the grocer's boy a playful push. 'Get out of it, you silly thing! I don't believe a word.'

He was standing, leaning against his bicycle, balancing the weight of the basket on the front, but he freed his right hand from the handlebars. 'Cross my heart and hope to die!' He made a vague cross-shape across his chest with one finger, then raised it to his mouth. 'Slit my tongue if this should prove a lie! It was even in the paper, just a paragraph.' He rolled his eyes at her. He was better-looking than that Rudolf Valentino was, and his name was Bert – she'd got that fact out of him. He was an awful tease, as she was well aware, and he was grinning now, but he seemed to be earnest about this. 'Why don't you ask your pretty little friend – Effie is it? She can tell you more.'

Lettie frowned. Of course it was not surprising if he noticed Effie's looks, but all the same she didn't like him saying that. 'Effie? She's all right, if you admire that sort of thing. But what's she got to do with it?'

Bert laughed and chucked her underneath her chin. 'Now, now, don't be jealous. You know that I've got eyes for you, my 'andsome, and for no-one else. Wouldn't have noticed 'er if it hadn't been for you, but I have seen you with her once or twice. Far too thin and peaky for my taste, and anyway it's obvious I wouldn't stand a chance. Smitten with that policeman, that's as clear as day.'

Lettie stared at him. 'What policeman?' she began, and then remembered what she had seen. 'Oh! I think I know the one. I saw them in the street together Tuesday fortnight gone.' Truth to tell she felt a little bit betrayed. Lettie was supposed to be the daring one who had admirers, not mousey little Effie, with her timid ways. Come to think of it, in fact, she'd not seen Effie since, though she'd looked out for her both Tuesdays at the shop. Obviously her so-called friend had found other things to do! But Lettie wasn't going to say as much to Bert. She tossed her thick auburn curls and said, dismissively, 'I don't believe there's anything in that. Effie would have told me and she's never said a word.'

'Course she wouldn't,' Bert retorted with a smile. 'Anyway she might not have had the chance. From what I hear they'd never met before that day. He took her down the station to ask about the corpse – and next thing you know they're walking up the street, gazing at each other like a pair of lovesick swans. Saw them with my own eyes, when I was coming to meet you.'

Lettie was still frowning. 'Took her down the station? About the corpse you say?' Up until that minute she'd been sure that it was about the books, although of course she'd never mentioned that affair to Bert. 'Why in heaven's name would they want her about that?'

'Seems the fellow came asking for her in the Westons' shop. Butcher's son told me, and he ought to know − his father was the one who looked across the wall and saw the dead body lying in the court. When they called Miss Pearl out, the first thing that she said was that the man had been hanging round the door the day before, enquiring if she knew an Effie Pengelly in the town. Though why he went there asking is a mystery to me. Think he'd ask a policeman or something, wouldn't you?'

Lettie tossed her hair back from her face again. 'He must have known she was keen on needlework. Effie won a prize for sewing, you know, at school − donated by some ancient biddy who approved of seamstresses. Prouder'n a peacock, Effie was of that − though it was only an old sewing-box, when all was said and done.' She wrinkled her brow into a prettier frown. 'Here, Bert, you don't suppose this man had some connection with all that?'

Bert shrugged his shoulders. 'Search me, me 'andsome − I don't know, or care! I just heard there'd been a dead man found behind the shop, and I knew you often go there, so I thought you'd like to know. I'm only surprised you didn't hear of it before.'

'Miss Blanche did say there had been trouble in the alleyway, that day − but I thought she meant the wretched urchins had been throwing stones again. Never crossed my mind it might be more than that.'

He was giving her his broadest grin. 'Trust the Miss Westons to try and hush it up − but they really couldn't hope to keep it secret very long, especially when the papers got a hold of it. Anyway the butcher's boy had seen the corpse, so the news was all round town before the day was out.'

'Well, never reached me then.' Lettie gave a flounce.

'Too busy running after your Miss Caroline?' Bert gave a knowing wink. 'Too busy to meet me for weeks, I do know that!'

Lettie gave him another little punch. 'Well, so I was. She keeps me on the run. Harder than a trapped badger to please,

she is, as well. Half a minute late and she wants a full report
– everywhere I've been and everyone I've met.' She gave him
a little smile. 'Not that I necessarily tell her everything. I'd
only have her keeping me indoors and scolding me for having
followers. Which reminds me, I suppose I'd better hurry now,
before I'm late again.'

'Poor Miss Caroline! That would never do.' Bert seized the
handlebars with both his hands again. 'So perhaps it's better if
I don't wait round for you like this. Someone will see us and
then she's sure to hear.'

'Bert Symons!' Lettie's tone was playful, but she was really
hurt. 'Don't go saying things like that. That isn't what I meant.
You know I'd hate it if we never met.'

He pushed his laden bicycle along an inch or two, till the
top pedal was where he wanted it. He planted his right foot
on it and paused. 'Who said anything about not meeting you?'
he said. 'Get a half-day, sometimes, don't you? Maybe we could
get together then – go for a walk around Mount Misery or
something of the kind, if you aren't doing anything else
particular.'

Lettie always went to see her stepmother that day, and stopped
to tea with Pa, but she wasn't going to say so and seem to
turn Bert down. She found herself saying, 'I get off at one
o'clock on Monday afternoon. I'd have to meet you up there,
or we'd be seen for sure. And no good if it's raining.' It sounded
rather grudging – which she hadn't meant.

He shook his head at her. 'Won't be next week, either. I'll
have to work around it, organize deliveries to make sure I can
be free – but the week after, that should be all right. Can't
say for certain right away of course, but I'll look out for you
in town and try to let you know.' He dropped one eyelid in
a fearsome wink. 'Make sure you wear your thickest boots,
though, if we're going to walk. Can be very muddy at this
time of year, especially if you happen to wander off the path.'

'Off the path? You cheeky blighter!' she called after him,
but he was already gone, leaving Lettie with a fluttering heart.
It was official then. Lettie Pearson was really 'walking out'.
Now that was something to tell Effie when they met!

She could think of nothing else as she hurried back to work.

She wasn't keen on walking expeditions as a general rule, but this one promised to be quite different! And one thing was certain – wandering off the path or not – she was going to wear her Sunday best and not her clumsy boots. She was already planning what excuse she'd give to her stepmother and Pa.

Four

The story about the body was in the newspaper. Effie actually saw it for herself, on a piece of the Evening Tidings that the green-grocer had used to wrap the swedes and carrots in the week's delivery – Mrs Thatchell didn't take a paper as a rule. But there it was. Great big letters in the middle of the page.

'Unknown Man Found Dead in Alleyway,' the headline said.

That wasn't quite the way of it, she thought. Actually it had been found in the little court behind the haberdashery shop, but probably the Misses Weston wouldn't want that noised abroad – it might put people off coming there. It had quite put Effie off calling there herself! She still had to go, of course, but these days she hurried to make any purchases and hunt out the sort of books that Mrs Thatchell liked, then got away as fast as possible – she hadn't lingered to see Lettie once since the incident. No more sneaking off with Miss Caroline's borrowings! The very thought of all that made her go shaky at the knees.

In fact, the memory of the fright she'd had that day still made her wake up sometimes in a sweat, and she kept dreaming of that policeman standing outside on the street – but that was not surprising. He was in her daydreams too, though that was obviously different and she did not mind at all.

She had actually glimpsed him once or twice, that nice young constable. Well, more than once or twice! He seemed to be patrolling regularly up this very street – perhaps his new beat was taking him this way. She'd even wondered about calling out to him, one day when Mrs Lane was busy with a cake, but he was clearly doing his duties at the time, pausing every now and then to gaze carefully around. Probably on the look-out for thieves and vagabonds – and you must not inter-rupt a man when he's busy with his work, she'd learned that lesson long ago from Uncle Joe.

She shook her head and turned her attention back to the

piece of the Evening Tidings and the rest of the report. The paragraph was lengthy but it did not tell you much. Extensive police enquiries had been made but no-one had come forward to identify the man, who was believed to come from London (which was news to her) but this had not been proved. A witness had been found who thought he 'might have seen the subject on a train' but could not swear to it or say exactly when, and a railway ticket discovered on the corpse was indecipherable. Finally, since all normal channels had been exhaustively explored and death by natural causes officially confirmed, the body had been released and subsequently buried by the parish charities.

So at least it was all over, Effie thought.

The 'Tidings' had done their best to make it sound sensational – 'foul play was not suspected' and all that – but in the end it was simply rather sad. A man that no-one knew or seemed to care about, dying a lonely death and now lying unmourned in an unmarked pauper's grave. Poor fellow! She couldn't help wondering who he might have been and how he came to be asking about her, but now, presumably, nobody would ever know. Thank heaven there was no mention of all that. Effie wondered if she had the constable to thank for keeping her name out of the report; there would almost certainly have been trouble otherwise.

She sighed and put the paper to one side – it would be used for wrapping peelings and passed on to Mrs Lane's cousin for the pigs – and tried to concentrate upon her chores. The first task was to put the vegetables away. That meant going into the larder-room. She had never really got accustomed to town-ways of doing things – potatoes and carrots that went on open racks instead of being kept in straw-heaps in a barn, and apples in a fruit-bowl instead of in the dark – but she was learning fast. Just as she was learning how to polish knives and leather boots, black-lead the range or coax a tiny heap of coals into a fire – jobs that Uncle Joe or Pa had always done at home. She shook the loose earth from the root-crops into a kitchen-pail, then arranged the items neatly with the onions on the rack.

'Effie!' Cook's voice from the kitchen summoned her.

'Coming, Cook.' She scuttled up the three steps and back through the scullery.

Mrs Lane was standing by the cooking range, wielding a heavy saucepan and a slotted spoon. She gave a nod to Effie. 'Bring that basin here – I'm boiling up this mutton-end to make a drop of soup.' She lifted up the saucepan and strained the liquid through as Effie held the bowl up to the light. Mrs Lane liked to 'watch the stock run through, make sure it's the proper colour and the right consistency'.

It was a chore that Effie hated. It always worried her. The basin was the biggest china one, heavy to start with and much heavier as you went – apart from becoming uncomfortably hot. You held it with the thick cloth pot-holder throughout, of course, but all the same it never felt quite safe. Effie had to grit her teeth and hold on for dear life.

'There!' Cook looked approvingly into the sieve and poked at the remaining bits of bone. There were a few scraps of mutton still adhering here and there. 'I've got the best of it, but there's goodness in it yet. You can wrap up these scraps d'rectly and put them at the gate, so Eileen Mitchell can have them when she comes to scrub. I 'spect she'll make a drop of broth herself, poor soul. Let that get cold a minute first, and see that it's well drained. Out the front corner by the path – you know where it goes. Use that bit of newsprint from the green-grocer – I'll find a paper bag or something you can put it in.'

'Yes, Mrs Lane.' Effie put down the basin with relief.

Cook nodded. 'In the meantime you can take the tea-tray up. I've made some Albert biscuits, the sort the mistress likes. You'll find them in the biscuit barrel, give her two or three and some of those ham sandwiches I've cut for her. You've been lucky there, my girl. There's an odd end left over and a crust of bread that we can have ourselves. And I think there's a bit of pickle in the jar.'

Effie grinned. Cook always saw to it that there was some-thing nice: the bread and ham were freshly baked that day – the kitchen was still full of cooking smells – and that pickle that she made was always beautiful. 'Yes, Cook,' she said, and hurried to obey.

It did give her an odd feeling later on, when the mutton-bone was cool and patted fairly dry, to use that piece of newspaper to wrap it in: almost as if the story was shamefully her own, and she did not want the world reading it – Mrs Eileen Mitchell in particular. She placed the bone exactly where it covered the report, and she was pleased to see that it was damp enough to wet the paper through.

Then she hurried out to put it where the poor soul would look for it.

When he saw Effie coming from the house Alex could hardly believe his eyes. He had been this way so often without a glimpse of her that he was beginning to believe she was avoiding him. In fact he was almost certain that she was: he was sure he had seen her at the basement window once, a day or so ago, and from the way she coloured up she must have noticed him – but though he had loitered much longer than he should, pretending to look up and down the street and taking an interest in every garden wall in order not to look conspicuous, she had not come out or even looked again and given him a wave. He was beginning to think he ought to give it up.

And then suddenly, there she was today, pretty as ever and blushing like a rose. But even then she would not meet his eyes. She had a paper parcel in her hand and she stooped to put it down, exactly where he'd been told to put his own the day they met.

He seized time by the forelock – it was a phrase that he remembered vaguely from a book at school – and stepped towards the girl. 'Morning, Effie. What do you have there?' It made an opening, although of course he knew the answer perfectly. 'Another present for your scrubbing woman, I suppose?'

She nodded, crimson-faced. 'She'll be here d'rectly. In fact, if everybody had their rights, she should be here by now, but her poor husband had been took quite bad again, and she hasn't been quite punctual this last week or two. Arrive here any minute, I expect, all hot and bothered 'cause she's had to walk for miles – hasn't the money for a horsebus, with her 'usband like he is.'

'But you do expect her?' Alex had a wild notion of offering to take the parcel round – he could come back when off duty and report success.

But Effie's answer was too quick for him. 'Oh, Mrs Mitchell always gets here in the end. She's no charmer, but you can rely on her for that. She won't cut corners, either, when she does arrive. She'll scrub until the place is sparkling – until it's dark if that is what it takes. That's how we always . . .' She broke off suddenly, and said, as if she thought she'd been gossiping too much, 'But I know I mustn't keep you; you're a busy man yourself.'

She was already turning back towards the house. He said, to prevent her, 'By the way, there's been no other news. That dead man who seemed to know you. We did send to London to ask about his shirt – I don't know if anybody told you about that – but though we found the maker it didn't lead us anywhere. The man that it was made for has gone away abroad. Apparently his wife had not been well and wanted to visit South Africa again before she died.'

Effie was listening, her clever little face full of lively interest – just the way that he'd remembered it. Her comment was intelligent as well. 'I suppose that's how he came to give away his shirts? Couldn't pack them all, I shouldn't be surprised.'

He nodded. 'Exactly the conclusion that we came to, ourselves. And no-one could tell us where it was he'd gone. So . . .'

'You gave it up and the body's been buried on the rates?' She must have realized that he was surprised, because she added, 'I read it in the paper, only just today. In fact, it's on this very parcel I've got here. I'll show you if you like, though it will be all damp by now . . .' She made as if to unwrap the paper all the same, and he was edging closer on the pretence of looking at the paragraph, when the basement window was flung open and a loud voice called, 'Effie! What in heaven are you up to now? Put that parcel where I told you and get back in here at once – I've got this galantine to make and God only blessed me with a single pair of hands.'

Effie wrapped the parcel up again and threw a glance at him. 'I'm some sorry, Alex – Constable Dawes, that is – you can see I'm wanted. I can't stop here, chatting, any more than

you.' She paused a moment, and then blurted out, 'Though
it's been some nice to see you.'

That gave him courage and he caught her arm. 'Nice enough
to want to do it on some other day? I know you go to see
your family on your half-day off – Thursdays, isn't it? But
maybe, if I could arrange my shifts . . . Could I meet you for
a little, first?'

She had turned redder than a beetroot now and she pulled
away from him. 'Don't be so daft. We'd never have the time.
Besides, I got to go. Though . . .'

He caught his breath. 'Though . . . what?'

'There might just be an opportunity next week. We're going
to have a caller – a fellow from the bank, wants to talk to Mrs
T about her bank affairs. She wants me on the Thursday, to
be on call while he is there, though I'll get a day in lieu.
Friday, most likely, if that is any good?'

Any good? He could have kissed the fellow from the bank.
'I'm off-duty from one o'clock that day. I could come . . .'

She shook her head at him. 'Better meet you somewhere.
You know Mount Misery?'

He looked perplexed. 'I think I've heard of it – not a name
you easily forget. Isn't that out somewhere on the road towards
Land's End?'

She nodded, grinning. 'Just where it branches out towards
St Just. Not far out of town – it gets its name from the fever
hospital. But don't worry, it's a lovely place – with footpaths
out to Devil's Rock or up around the lanes. Two o'clock
Friday, I'll do my very best. Though, the way things are, I
make no promises.' And before Alex could say another word,
she'd pushed the parcel in under the hedge and hurried round
towards the back again.

He stood for a moment, gazing after her, until a sharp voice
at his elbow brought him to himself. 'Now look here, young
constable, I'm sure you're on your beat and you've got good
reason to be standing here, but when you've quite finished I
needs to wiggle past and get me cleaning tools. I got the steps
to scrub and I'm already late.' Shrew-faced Mrs Mitchell was
glaring up at him.

He reminded himself about her husband being bad and

managed to mutter 'Please excuse me!' with some grace before he went back to resume his street patrol. He walked the beat with what he thought was proper diligence, but when he got back he found that there was nothing to report. Perhaps his mind had not been wholly on his task.

His mind was racing forward to the roster for next week, but there was nothing he could do to find out what it was – or alter it – so after tea he went back to his notes, and tried to occupy his wayward brain by revising how to make a plaster cast of footprints at a scene. He'd never done it, but he hoped to have the chance. Sergeant Vigo said it was the surest way of catching thieves.

Lettie was not in the sunniest of moods. Come to that it wasn't the sunniest of days – the clouds were gathering and it looked as if there would be rain by dusk. Already her hair, which she'd carefully put up in rags last night (though the torment always stopped her sleeping properly) was being blown out of its artful curls and into rats' tails by the rising wind. And then she'd be expected to tramp about for miles on what Bert always called his 'favourite walk'.

Drat the fellow! Why couldn't he take her to the pictures for a change? There was a film of Valentino showing in the town. She would have loved to see it – she'd been dropping hints – but it never even seemed to cross his mind. Course it cost money, that was probably the thing, but all the same! Bert must be earning ten and six a week, though he worked for his father, so perhaps he kept him short. Still, they could have gone into the tuppennies – surely to goodness it wouldn't hurt for once! But no, it was Mount Misery and the walk as usual. And even then he hadn't met the bus. Why could he never be anywhere on time?

She frowned and stood back in the shelter of the trees, huddling her best green hooded cape around her. She should have worn the brown one, it was far warmer, but it was getting old and she'd had to mend one corner where she'd caught it on a twig. She could hardly wear it when she was walking out with Bert. Still, he'd kept her waiting. Serve him right if she had turned up in that!

The sound of a footfall on the path disturbed her thoughts and she stepped forward, ready with a smile. 'Oh, there you are . . .' She tailed off in surprise. 'My dear life! Effie Pengelly! If it isn't you!'

Effie was looking at her in what looked like mild dismay, as if she wasn't especially pleased to find her standing there. 'Well, I never! Lettie! Fancy seeing you.' Her face had turned an alarming shade of red.

Lettie wasn't stupid. She realized what it was. Effie was still ashamed about the books. They'd never really spoken since that awful day, though she had lingered at the Westons' library once or twice. The only time that their paths had crossed in town there'd been a quick, 'Hello, how are you?' and Effie had hastened by, obviously in a hurry to get somewhere else. Lettie said carefully, 'And a sight for sore eyes you are. Sorry that I haven't seen you at the Westons' all these weeks. I've missed our little chats.'

Effie turned more scarlet still, if that were possible. It gave her face a colour which was flattering. She was wearing blue – a thick shawl and heavy skirt which did nothing for her shape but of a shade which drew attention to her eyes. 'I'm sorry,' she was murmuring, 'I haven't stopped to wait. After that policeman gave me such a shock, I didn't want to . . .'

Lettie nodded. 'Course, I understand. We would have had to stop that business soon in any case – if we'd gone on much longer they were sure to catch us out.' She was aware that this wasn't what she had said before – she'd always told Effie it was as safe as possible – but obviously things were rather different now. 'Clever of you to get that book back on the shelves that day.'

Effie looked first startled, then relieved. 'You saw it then? I haven't seen it since. I'd begun to wonder what had happened to the dratted thing!'

Lettie laughed. 'Saw it? I should think I did! I managed to take it out again – by accident. But Miss Blanche didn't tumble to it, even then.'

Effie had put on a determined face. 'I aren't doing it again, though, Lettie. Too dangerous, by half.'

'Aren't doing what?' a voice behind them said, and there

was Bert at last – looking a picture in his second-best Sunday suit, a bit too short and tight for him these days, and a little shiny round the cuffs and trouser-seat, but a proper suit for all that. He had a scarf and hat on and his boots were fairly clean – though he hadn't brought his cycle and he must have walked for miles. Nice-looking as ever and grinning at them in that cheeky way of his. Lettie felt proud of him. She was about to introduce the two of them, but Effie had turned that lobster pink again, and had begun to speak, obviously in answer to what Bert had said.

'Nothing!' she said quickly. 'We were just gossiping. And I mustn't keep you. I know you want to walk.'

Bert looked at her. His eyes were twinkling. 'Only a little stroll around the lanes. There's no hurry – no need to rush away. Lettie, introduce me to your pretty friend.'

Lettie found – rather to her own surprise – that she was furious. 'This is Effie,' she muttered gracelessly. 'Works at Mrs Thatchell's down Morrab Road.'

Bert did the twinkle that she liked so much, but it was aimed at Effie. 'Then that is where I've seen you. I knew I knew the face. No doubt we've spoken when I brought the groceries.'

What a sweet-talker the blighter was, Lettie thought crossly. He knows her perfectly – he was the one who said that he'd seen her on the street with that confounded policeman. She forced herself to smile. 'Effie this is Bert. My beau. We've started walking out – only of course we can't let Miss Caroline find out. Strictly, I'm not permitted to have followers.'

Effie was looking admiringly at Bert. Lettie was impatient. This would never do. She stepped out beside him and slid her arm through his – something that she never generally did. Bert was always grumbling that she kept him at arm's length, though of course she didn't really: she let him take her hand when there was nobody about and even give her a quick peck on the cheek each time they said goodbye. This time, though, she hugged his arm against her side. 'Nice to see you, Effie. We must meet again. See you at the Westons' shop perhaps. Nothing to stop us having a chatter, is there, now and then?'

Effie shook her head. 'Well . . . only a chat mind! I'll look out for you. Now I mustn't stop you walking with your beau.'

Bert gave a little bow. 'And I see that yours is coming to claim you,' he said.

Lettie whirled around. A young man was walking towards them down the path, a young man so handsome that it took her breath away. He was tall and fairish, with broad shoulders and long legs and in his smart Norfolk jacket, flannel trousers and tweed hat, even Valentino could not hold a torch to him. She found that she was boggling, and it took a tug upon her arm from Bert to bring her to herself.

Even Effie was looking quite surprised. 'Why if it isn't Alexander Dawes. I hardly knew you in those clothes!'

The newcomer was smiling down at her. He was so handsome that Lettie felt quite feeble at the knees. She extricated her right hand again and held it out. 'Mr Dawes. I'm Lettie Pearson, Effie's friend. I'm so glad that we've met.' She was going to add something about having heard of him, but Effie was listening so she left out that. 'And this is Bert Symons, from the grocer's shop.'

Bert nodded vaguely. 'Glad to meet you, sir, I'm sure.' He turned pointedly to her. 'Now Lettie, do you fancy a walk along to Devil's Rock, today? I think we've just got time before it comes to rain.'

Lettie was reluctant to leave Effie with that vision of a man. 'Would you like to come with us?' she heard herself saying. Bert looked at her surprised, but she ploughed desperately on. 'I haven't seen Effie for simply weeks and weeks – to talk to properly.'

Bert was looking daggers. 'It's a nice thought, Lettie. But I'm sure this young man would prefer to have Effie to himself – and I feel the same. We haven't had much chance to talk for weeks, ourselves.'

'Besides,' the vision gave her a slow smile that knocked Bert's cheerful twinkle into a cocked hat. 'We don't have much time – not enough to go as far as that – and I'm not really dressed for muddy paths. Some other time, perhaps.' He tipped his hat and – bold as you like – offered his arm to Effie, who took it with a blush.

'Nice to see you, Lettie. I'll look out for you next week.' And she was gone.

'Well!' Lettie muttered. 'I'll be blowed. She's a dark horse that one, and no mistake.' She turned to Bert. 'Imagine Effie with a man like that! He couldn't be a cousin, or something, I suppose?'

Bert laughed. 'Don't be so daft! Do you mean to say you don't know who it was? It's that constable I saw her with the other day. I told you I'd seen them walking down the street, gazing at each other like a pair of fools. Mind, I'm not surprised he fell for her – a pretty girl like that.'

'Pretty is as pretty does,' she muttered with a sniff. 'Don't know what Mrs Thatchell would have to say, I'm sure.'

Bert pulled her round to face him. 'I do believe you're jealous, Lettie Pearson!' he exclaimed. 'Not enough for you to be Bert Symons' favourite girl?' He attempted to kiss her on the nose, but she resisted.

'Don't be daft, what are you playing at!' She pulled away from him. 'I've half a mind to leave you here and go back home again!'

'And miss the chance to go and see the film with me next week?' he grinned. 'I can't believe you mean it. Prettiest girl for miles and you'd walk out on me?'

She hesitated. The pictures? And Valentino was on another week. 'You really think I'm pretty?'

He hugged her to him. 'Course I do. Don't they have no mirrors up there where you work? Prettier'n a picture. I've told you that before.' This time he did manage to land a little kiss.

She stepped away and slipped her arm through his. 'In that case I forgive you.' She didn't say for what and Bert did not ask her – which was fortunate, because she wasn't sure herself. 'Let's go down to Devil's Rock if that's what we're going to do.'

This was her beau, she told herself. A proper beau who took her to the picture-house. Effie might be pretty, but Bert liked Lettie best. And one day he had prospects of a business of his own, with a little flat above the shop and everything. Lucky Lettie! Really, she didn't envy Effie in the least.

Bert's voice broke teasingly into her reverie. 'Now then, Lettie, what are you frowning at? Can't have that, can we? A penny for your thoughts?'

This time, when he kissed her, she met him with her lips.

Part Two

April to July 1912

One

Alex's meetings with Effie had become a settled thing. He waited for her on the outskirts of the town every second Thursday of the month. When it was not actually raining they still went for walks, though they tended to avoid Mount Misery for fear of meeting Lettie and her beau again. (It could have happened too, Effie told him earnestly, because Lettie's household sometimes varied her half-day.)

When it was wet – or even hailing, as it had been once – he and Effie found a sheltered place to sit (usually the covered bandstand in the park) and simply chatted till it was time for her to go. He had suggested going to see the 'flicks', as people were calling the modern moving-picture shows – there was a brand-new picture-drome in town that had a matinee – but she was too afraid of being seen.

'If Mrs Mitchell happened to come by – and she might do, 'cause she cleans for other people in the town – she'd report me to Mrs Thatchell sure as eggs. Besides, it's a terrible lot of money, isn't it? Twopence each and nothing to show for it afterwards!'

He would have paid much more than fourpence for the privilege of sitting close beside her in the flickering warm dark, but he didn't tell her that. He tried another tack and lured her to a country tea-shop for an hour – thinking that a pot of tea and toast would be a treat – but she'd still been so nervous about being spotted with a man (and news of that reaching her uncle, this time!) that it was no treat at all and he hadn't bothered to suggest it since.

But it did not really matter to Alex where they went; talking to Effie was a pleasure in itself. She was so different from the other girls he knew: she had a freshness and a frank good-heartedness which was lacking in the well-bred daughters of his parents' friends, to whom his mother seemed peculiarly intent on introducing him on the rare occasions when he dined

at home. These young women were always perfectly polite and
tried to talk about the weather and the world, but they had
nothing much to say and seemed much more concerned with
how they looked and what they wore. Effie was pretty, but
too artless to be vain.

He would not have minded if she'd met him every week,
however cold it was – in fact he had proposed it several times
– but Effie remained quite adamant that she dared do no more.
He tried again today.

'Couldn't we meet more often? Now that I have got my
duty roster for the next six weeks and can rely on Thursday
afternoons to spend with you? It wasn't easy to arrange you
know, and it might not work out so well another time.' He
spoke with feeling there – no-one asked a junior policeman
what shifts he would prefer. He'd managed to wangle it, three
six-weekly rosters in row, by offering to work a regular late-
evening shift that day.

Manning the police-station at night was not a favourite with
his peers – a senior man stayed on duty and awake while the
junior tried to snatch what sleep he could on a lumpy mattress
on the back-office floor, ready to be called on if required.
Most of his colleagues hated it, but Alex volunteered – in
order to earn himself the precious afternoon – and there had
been an unexpected bonus too. On the quarterly appraisal, for
the powers-that-be, Sergeant Vigo had written 'Constable
Dawes (Police No. 663) has shown ability and should be
particularly commended for his willingness to take on extra
and demanding duties.' Policeman No. 663 found himself
smiling at the recollection even now.

'Pity to waste the opportunity, when I've arranged it all,' he
said now to Effie. 'Might not be so lucky next time round.
Besides, think of all the lovely days like this we'd have to miss!'
He spoke as if the day was bright and warm, but in fact it was
a chilly afternoon, with a stiff little April breeze in off the sea.
They were walking on the country lanes round the back of
Gulval, where the high stone hedges gave them shelter from the
wind but kept the thin spring sunshine from really reaching them,
though it gave a special lustre to the new leaves on the trees.
'Couldn't we make it every fortnight, perhaps?'

Effie had taken a fancy for picking violets and had brought a basket with her so she could take some home – doubtless to give herself a visible excuse for wandering down lanes if ever Mrs Thatchell got to hear of it. She turned away from him on the pretence of plucking another fragile bloom from a tiny crevice in the wall. 'Alex, I can't – I keep on telling you. If Mrs Thatchell gave me any other afternoon – like she did the first time that we met – of course I'd jump at it. But she doesn't usually have meetings with the bank, so it has to be a Thursday and they expect me home, and even as it is I often miss my only opportunity of seeing Pa. Besides, if we met more often,' she turned slightly pink, 'I'd never hear the last of it from Uncle Joe, he's always asking questions as it is, wanting to know where I went and what I did.'

'And what do you tell him?'

'The truth – that I have been out walking with a friend, although,' she giggled, 'I let them think that it's a girl. That's bad enough, to hear my Uncle Joe go on, grumbling that I haven't brought my money home that week.'

She didn't say so, but he was fairly sure that her aunt and uncle scolded her to death every time she 'wasted' an afternoon like this. She did make a contribution to the family purse, he knew – and no doubt they were concerned if that was late.

'Why don't I come out with you? Then you could do both – spend some time with me and see your Pa and give the money to your aunt at the same time. Anyway, I'd like to meet your relatives.'

Effie laid the violet with the rest and looked at him scornfully. 'Get along with you! You don't know what they're like.'

'Well, whose fault is that?' he said, half-jokingly. 'You keep them from me, though I go on asking you about them all the time.'

That was true. He often asked her questions, though she didn't notice it, just to start her prattling about her life at home. It seemed so entirely different from his own. That tiny cottage – he had seen it once, of course, when he went with Sergeant Vigo to interview her Pa, and he still retained a vivid picture in his mind. All that crowd of people packed in like sardines! He'd often tried to visualize living in that way, but imagination failed. Effie said that when she was living at the house, the other children all slept head to tail – one bed for the boys and another for the girls – and ate in relays if someone came to call, because there weren't sufficient stools and settles to go round.

Perhaps that's why she shook her head at him. 'Couldn't take you out there. You don't know what it's like. Proper mayhem sometimes. You're not used to it.' She coloured, in that pretty way she sometimes did. 'You were brought up with pianos and fancy ornaments. It's different out the Terrace: earth floors in the kitchen and wet washing everywhere and always someone squabbling somewhere in the house, mostly because wherever you sit down and start to sew or draw, within five minutes you've got to move because somebody wants something the other side of you.' She paused and went on in an altered tone. 'And Uncle Joe would give you such a time of it – he doesn't care for policemen and he'd very likely call you rude things to your face. I would be ashamed to take you there.'

He looked down at her. 'Meaning – really – that you're ashamed of me?'

Her eyes flashed hotly. 'Of course I aren't! Don't be so bally daft!'

It was not like her to speak so sharply, and he realized that, although he'd only meant to tease, his remark had genuinely touched a nerve. He put his hand out to her, but she pulled away.

'It's just – I can't explain it – you're from a different world. You must know what I mean. Would you feel comfortable if you took me home and had to introduce me to your Ma and Pa?' She shrugged him off and went back to looking for her flowers.

He said, 'But that's quite different, Effie. You know it can't be done – not while we've only got an hour or two to spare. It would take us all that time to get there – let alone get back.' He saw the look that she was giving him and he added, rather lamely, 'Anyway, I'm sure my parents would like you very much.' But it lacked conviction and he knew it did.

Secretly, he was aware that she was right. Mother would be charming, as she always was to guests, and would take pains to make Effie feel at home – no doubt offering sandwiches and tea. But afterwards, he knew, it would be a different thing.

He could almost hear his mother saying, outraged and aggrieved, 'What can you have been thinking of, Alex, to bring that poor girl here? Can't you see that you've embarrassed her? Didn't know what on earth to say to us. And talk about a lack of breeding! Can't hold a tea-cup properly and when offered sandwiches helps herself to a whole handful at a time! I can't imagine what your father's going to say!' But Alex could, and he was squirming at the very thought of it.

Effie seemed to read this in his face. 'There you are,' she said triumphantly. 'It's clear as daylight that you know exactly what I mean!'

But he would not admit it, not out loud at least. 'Well, I'll have to meet your people sometime,' he said stubbornly. 'If we're going to . . .' He tailed off in dismay.

She was looking at him strangely, raising her head so that her bonnet slipped right back. 'If we are going to . . . what?'

'Go on walking out,' he said lightly, realizing that he'd nearly said something far more serious. 'And move on to doing this.' He leaned over and brushed his lips against her hair. 'I can't be on kissing terms with just anyone, you know.'

'Get off, you great lummox.' She ducked away and laughed. 'Whoever said you could be on kissing terms with me?' But she didn't seem displeased and – although she did not allude to it again – she kept on smiling at him all the afternoon, as they wandered down the lanes collecting violets.

They had gathered quite a number by the time they turned for home. 'Going to bunch and sell them?' He knew that people did, to earn a few pennies from the townsfolk on a market day. He wouldn't have blamed her if she'd planned on doing that – though their walk together seemed a funny time to choose.

But she simply laughed. 'Never make my fortune, will I? I never thought of that. No, I generally pick something, when I'm out with you. I like to take it back with me – remind me of our walks – but violets are too fragile to carry in my hand, or put into the pocket of my shawl like I b'long to do . . .' She flushed and turned away.

He put a hand beneath her chin and turned it gently so that she was facing him again. 'Do you really do that? I've seen you pick a piece of something now and then – ferns and berries and that sort of thing – I never thought about you keeping them. Anyway, I shouldn't have thought they'd last above a day or two.'

'I've kept a bunch of wildflowers for better than a week!' she protested with a grin. 'I put them in a jam jar right beside my bed, and look at them to cheer me up whenever Madam's cross as sticks with me – which seems to be happening more and more these days. Anyway,' she shook the basket of violets at him, 'even when these are wilted I've got a use for them. I'll put them in the rinse-jug when I wash my hair. It takes away the smell of vinegar.'

'Vinegar?'

She giggled. 'I always use it when I wash my hair. Mother used to say it made it shine.' She gave him a playful push. 'Though I can see I'll have to give up doing that, if it's going to make you start taking liberties, like you did just now.'

'Like this?' he said, and bent to kiss her hair again, but as he did so she turned her face to his and almost accidently he brushed against her lips.

It was a fleeting moment but he realized that it embarrassed her. She would not take his arm again, even on the field-paths, and she talked nineteen to the dozen all the way back to the town, about Mrs Thatchell and the cook and anything at all – except themselves. Even when they parted she did not look at him.

Effie did not mean to lie awake that night and think about that kiss, but she found she could not dismiss it from her mind. Of course he hadn't meant to – it was half an accident – but it was the first real kiss that she'd ever had, if you didn't count a peck from the Kellow boy next door when they were six.

Well, except that Alex had brushed his lips against her hair, this very afternoon – but that hardly counted now, though it had seemed sufficiently exciting at the time. And that had been no accident at all!

She was both excited and alarmed – there were stories about

girls who let themselves be kissed – but there wasn't anyone that she could tell. It was moments like this that she missed her mother most. It was not the sort of thing that you could say to Aunty Madge; you certainly would not want Uncle Joe to know, and it was difficult to get to talk to Pa alone. She could try confiding in her cousin Peg, who had always been the friendliest of the family, though she'd done that once before and it had not altogether turned out as she had hoped. They'd been upstairs together wrapping Christmas presents in December-time, and Effie had mentioned the 'real nice policeman' she had met.

But Peg was not especially impressed. 'A policeman! You can't mean you're sweet on him? My dear life, Effie, have you got no sense at all! You know what Fayther thinks about the police – never had time for them since that lock-out at the mine.'

Effie nodded; she had heard that story many times from Uncle Joe himself. The miners had been threatening to strike, after a dispute about the cost of candles for their hats, and in the end the owners locked them out. Then, after having no work or wages for a month, a party of them came clamouring at the gates demanding to be let in and listened to: so the owners called the constables, who baton-charged the men – including her uncle, who'd been tumbled to the ground. Of course it had all been settled in the end – in fact the miners had won a sort of compromise – but Joe had been wary of policemen ever since. 'Knocked down by some young bugger in a uniform, simply for trying to get what should have been me own in any case,' as he never tired of telling everyone.

Effie shrugged. 'I know. But that was years ago. Alex didn't take any part in that. Besides, if someone came and burgled Uncle Joe he'd be the first to want the police to help.'

Peg looked scornful. 'If someone stole from Fayther he wouldn't call the police. He'd go and find the culprit for himself, and knock the living daylights out of him.'

Effie had to own that this was likely to be true, but she did not give up the argument. 'But supposing that he couldn't find out who the culprit was? That's where the police come in. They've got all kinds of modern ways of finding criminals.

Alex spends hours looking out for clues – I've seen him do it outside on the street – and he can make a plaster cast of foot-prints and all sorts. He's very good at it, apparently. He says his sergeant is impressed with him, and he's hoping to be made up to the second grade.'

'Well, so he may be, but what use is that to you? It wouldn't work out, Effie. Surely you can see? No doubt he really likes you, but it won't be serious. It will be years and years before he even thinks of settling down. Take him all his time to work his way up through the ranks.'

'It isn't like that,' Effie muttered in dismay. She hid her misery by folding a piece of tissue paper round the knitted socks she'd made for Uncle Joe. (By saving a penny from her wages every week she'd managed to buy wool enough for gloves or socks all round. She wasn't as good with knitting as she was with stitchery, but it was easier to manage when you worked by candlelight and by doing an inch or two each night she'd done them easily.) 'I'm sure that he'll go far. His family have a lot of influence. The father was some sort of hero in the cavalry. And you should hear him talk about his home – gardens and stables and cook and everything.' She tied her parcel with a piece of coloured string and picked up the gloves for Pa. She had embroidered a pocket-handkerchief with 'A' to give to Alex, but she hadn't brought that here.

Peg put down the pot-holder that she had made for her Ma, and whirled round with a frown. 'Well, Effie Pengelly, you're more fool than I thought. Never thought this constable of yours might be halfway to gentry! Not a bit of good you mooning over him. Don't you go letting him lead you into anything!' She must have seen the hurt on Effie's face, because all of a sudden she leaned forward with a smile. 'You'd be better off finding some young fellow from the mine – like that nice Peter Kellow who used to live next door, when you lived down the Narrows with your Ma and Pa.'

Effie turned away. 'Don't be so bally daft!'

'I mean it. I see his elder brother now and then, and I know that Pete's been mad about you since the pair of you were small. I never see him without he asks for you and I've even met him sometimes moping in the lane – though he's got no other reason to come up this way. How don't you talk to 'im? He's on men's wages now and he'd have you like a shot, give you a home and family as soon as he'd saved up. Proper man's job too. Not like this poli—' She broke off as her father came clattering up the stairs and stuck his head around the bedroom door.

He was scowling at them, as he often did. 'What's all this whispering? And what are you two doing, hiding yourselves away upstairs like this? We don't have secrets from other people in the house.'

Peg looked at Effie. 'I was saying to Effie about . . .' But Effie cut her off.

'Only wrapping Christmas presents, Uncle Joe.' She waved the little parcel at him as she spoke. 'I've just done one for you. Don't look at the others or you will spoil the surprise.'

Her uncle glanced at the unwrapped pile remaining on the bed, then gave a grumpy 'Harrumph!' and went away again.

Peg turned to Effie. 'Good for you! That was a close-run thing! I only hope he's satisfied, otherwise he'll wait until you've gone and chivvy me till he gets it out of me.' It was obvious that, if he did, she would soon spill the beans and there and then Effie made a private vow that she would not confide in cousin Peg again.

Perhaps she could find a moment to be alone with Pa, if he was there next week – though it seemed a long, long time to wait. And what would she tell him? That she had been kissed, and by a member of the police? The same one that had come out to the house to question him? What would he say to that? Tell her the same as cousin Peg had done, most like – to smile at Peter Kellow and have done with it.

She tried to think of Peter as a potential beau, but she could not manage it. Poor Peter with his ginger hair and gently baffled look. He was a pleasant-enough fellow, hard-working and sober and honest as the day, and she'd known him all her life (he was the one who'd stolen that kiss when they were young) but there was nothing in him that would stir the heart. He wasn't bad-looking, though his teeth stuck out a bit, but his stocky frame could not compare to Alex's tall, athletic grace. Of course, she knew what cousin Peg would say – romantic love was very fine in books but it did not pay the rent. And that was true, of course.

Among the bal-maidens at Penvarris mine, Peter would be regarded as 'a catch'. He'd make someone a splendid husband, Effie had no doubt – it was just that she did not want it to be her. Tied down in a tiny cottage with a herd of little ones, washing and scrubbing all the hours God sent, fretting about stretching the purse to pay for food and worrying all the time in case the mine-alarm went off and there had been some sort of accident. Surely there must be something else in life?

But what? Generations of her family had done exactly that, and she could hardly suppose that she was different. She sighed. As she'd said to Alex, they came from different worlds and that was all there was to that.

She punched her bolster-pillow as though it were at fault, and pulled the bed-clothes firmly up around her nose – but it was no good. She was far too restless to settle down to sleep. She got up in the darkness and pulled back the blind. The moon was up and bathing everything in an unearthly light.

It reminded her of something that she'd read once in a book. 'A cold moon was floating in a milky sky, and the trees had turned to silhouettes against the silver night.' Some lovely picture that painted, didn't it? She'd thought so the first time that she'd seen it written down – in one of those unwanted stories of Miss Caroline's, that Lettie had lent to her.

Lettie! Why had she not thought of it before? Lettie would listen – she knew about these things, and she would be certain to have some good advice. Effie shivered and pulled her thin nightdress round her knees: the room was rather draughty and the night was chill, but she went back to bed with a much lighter heart. On Tuesday she would linger at the Westons' shop again and have a talk to Lettie, if she could.

Ten minutes later she was fast asleep.

Walter Pengelly was also lying sleepless in his bed. He had spent the evening a disappointed man. All that walk to go to Madge's house for a meal – only to find that Effie wasn't there. That was the second time since Christmas, and he'd worked doublers specially to be there tonight.

The thought must have affected him more than he supposed because he was unwise enough to mention it to Joe, when they were sitting together on the settle after tea. Madge and the older girls had gone upstairs, putting little ones safely into bed, and for a brief ten minutes the two men had the kitchen to themselves.

Joe was on about the meetings at the mine about setting up a Union. 'There's a group of us meeting at the Worker's Institute tonight. That fellow from London is going to talk about the benefits of setting up a branch.' As he spoke he was filling his evil-smelling pipe with his peculiar brand of Virginia tobacco – what he called his 'little weakness' – and tamping it down firmly with his thumb. He cocked an eye at Walter. 'You want to come and all?'

Walter shook his head. 'I don't hold with all these unions and their "workers' rights". Likely to stir up trouble as far as I can see. Look what 'appened last time. Damned near starved us out.'

'But we won a concession from them in the end.' Joe could be downright cussed when he tried: earlier he had been grumbling about the London man, himself. 'And the Union's only about trying to get a decent wage.'

Walter stood his ground. He could be as stubborn as anybody else. 'We tributers have always had a contract with the mine – so much per ton for what we bring to ground. These blighters are urging that we get a settled rate – so much an hour – where's the skill in that? What do these London Johnnies know about it anyway? Bad enough they've got us paying for that dratted stamp, when we already pay our Friendly dues.' Joe was looking ready to argue half the night, so he added peaceably, 'Different for you fellows up to ground, working in the sorting sheds, p'rhaps, but I got better things to do than sit in draughty meetings at this time of night. No, I'm going home early, seeing Effie isn't here.'

'Well, you knew she wasn't coming. She said as much last week.'

Walter pushed his empty cup aside. 'Yes, I'd forgotten that. Going to go out walking with a friend, she said. Course it is nice for her to have a pal, but I don't half miss her when she isn't here. I suppose it's that maid Lettie that she's with – the one she talks about.'

His brother-in-law looked at him with a peculiar knowing air. 'Well, if you believe that, Wally, you're dafter than I thought. You'll tell me next that you believe the moon is made of cheese.' Joe leaned forward to light a taper from the fire and lit his pipe, then sat back, sucking happily and sending up little clouds of pungent smoke. 'It's clear to me there's some young man involved. Far too busy to come and see her family, and never mind that we're relying on her bringing her four shillings in.'

Walter allowed himself to be quite stung by this – as Joe no doubt intended. 'Effie told me that she always gave her wages in, and if she didn't come out here she paid it off the butcher's bill in town, save Madge from having to traipse in there every week. Are you telling me that isn't true?'

Joe poked at his pipe-bowl with a bit of stick. 'I suppose it's true enough. But when she doesn't come, Madge doesn't have the money in her hand that week, and that is what she likes. Give her a bit of flexibility. Mind, I blame Peg. She was the one suggested that Effie could pay it off that way. And didn't your maid bite her hand off at the suggestion too! You could see that she'd much rather not come home. No there'll be some fellow – you can bet your boots on that. They'll be hanging round her, like wasps around the jam. Too pretty and she knows it, if you ask me, old son.'

Walter peered at him through the pipe-smoke. Joe always thought the worst of everyone. He supposed that he ought not to be surprised at the idea of his daughter having some admirer – after all she had her mother's looks – but all the same! 'Not Effie, surely? She wouldn't go encouraging anyone. Not without telling me about it, any road.' He was about to add that Effie was not much more than a child, when it occurred to him that his own Susan had been younger still when he started wooing her, so he just said unhappily, 'You don't really think she would?'

Joe had got his pipe alight again. 'I did warn you, Wally. You know I've had my private thoughts about that girl, ever since they found that fellow that she swore she didn't know.

Course, I know that she persuaded you – and if you are happy, who am I to judge? But it's a funny business – that's all I will say. I'd keep my eye on Effie, if I were you, old son. I'd worry about the company she keeps, if she were mine, especially when we are not around to see . . .' He broke off as Madge and the elder girls came clattering downstairs.

Walter would have liked to ask him more – it was hard to let this painful matter go, like putting your tongue into a sore place in a tooth – but Joe was on his feet, off to talk Unions at the Miner's Arms. Walter lingered for a little, for politeness' sake, while Madge and her girls were washing up the cloam, and the conversation turned to a story Peg had heard in town – some fancy new liner that had hit some ice and drowned the passengers.

'Very first time it went to sea! And it was supposed to be unsinkable!'

So he listened for a moment but that was all she knew, and shortly after it was time to leave. But for that night and many afterwards he had uneasy dreams – not about the liner, but about what Joe had said. Next time he saw Effie they would have to talk.

Two

'My dear life! Effie!' It was Tuesday and Lettie was amazed to see her friend waiting for her in the Westons' Haberdashery, just as she used to do. 'A sight for sore eyes, this is, and no mistake! I'd given up all hope of ever seeing you again. And here you are, more 'andsome than you ever were!' It was no more than the truth. There was a sparkle about Effie that had not been there before. Lettie was not given to paying compliments, but she was disposed to be magnanimous today, since there was no Bert to make comparisons. She noticed her friend's embarrassed blush and added wickedly, 'Thought you'd forgotten me! Too caught up with that young constable of yours to have time for your old friends.'

Effie was looking even more embarrassed now. 'Course it isn't like that! It was just . . . there was so much trouble last time with those bally books, what with that dead man and everything – I thought it was better if we didn't meet here for a bit. I didn't want to be caught up in all that again.'

Lettie laughed. Effie took everything so seriously, it wasn't fair to tease her. All the same she could not resist the impulse to say, 'Should have thought you would have been quite pleased about the way that day turned out. How would you have met your policeman otherwise?'

'Here! Don't talk so loudly. Miss Pearl will overhear.' Effie glanced nervously around the shop, but Miss Pearl was out of earshot, sorting books out in the office at the back.

Lettie grinned. 'Afraid she'd tell tales on you to Mrs T? Well if that's the case you want to be more careful where you go. Don't think I haven't seen you, sneaking round the lanes – you two were at Gulval only just last week.'

Effie had turned pinker than the skein of sewing silk that she was taking from the stand. 'How do you know that?'

'Oh, Bert and I were out there, but we didn't stop to speak. Obviously you two did not want to be disturbed.' She didn't add that she had not wanted to be disturbed herself. She had wangled an excuse to go out that way, taking some samples to a private dressmaker, and so snatched a few minutes in a disused shed with Bert, where he had proved to be extremely passionate.

'Well I never saw you!'

'Too busy making eyes at him, I 'spect!' Lettie said, not altogether truthfully. And then, in case Effie started asking awkward questions about her vantage point, she added teasingly, 'Wouldn't care to have a policeman for a beau myself – you'd always be thinking that he's checking up on you. But he seems quite smitten, I'll say that for him.'

Effie selected another skein, pretending to match it to a sample that she'd brought. After a moment, in which she did not raise her eyes, she muttered, 'Actually that's why I waited to talk to you today. I wanted to ask for your advice.'

Lettie looked as grave as possible, though she was grinning inwardly. She loved to have a secret and it was flattering to be turned to in this way. Of course she did know much more about the world than Effie did, and had a good deal more experience with boys. She said, in a whisper, 'Naturally I'll help. Not in the shop, of course. Miss Pearl's got bigger ears than Farmer Crowdie's mule. Perhaps outside on the corner, when you've finished here?'

Effie nodded and turned away to fidget with her silks, while Lettie went over to the shelves of books and selected another half a dozen volumes for Miss Caroline to ignore. She took them to the counter for Miss Pearl to issue them.

Miss Pearl gave her usual thin-lipped smile. 'Ah, I see that my sister has put a book aside for you – or for your employer, I suppose that I should say. Another Scarlet Pimpernel that has just come in – apparently Miss Knight has shown a predilection for those tales.'

Lettie had no idea what a 'predilection' was, but she nodded anyway, although she didn't like the sound of it all. She knew what 'dereliction of duty' was – she had heard it thundered at a butler once, when the man was discovered in the scullery much the worse for wear on the Major's favourite port. A 'predilection' sounded rather similar – perhaps it meant that somebody had found you out – so she was decidedly nervous as she took the proffered book and swapped it for one that she had chosen from the shelf. To her alarm she recognized the writer's name: the one that had nearly got her caught out once before.

But Miss Pearl said nothing, only pursed her lips and entered up the borrowings as usual. Lettie was quite relieved to make a quick escape and go to wait for Effie round the corner of the street. But the more she waited, the more Effie didn't come, until after ten minutes by the town hall clock, which you could see above the rooftops, Lettie was about to give her up and go.

But, thank heavens, here she was at last, with her basketful of books and the little paper packet with the silks in it.

'My life, Effie!' Lettie said as she came up. 'What took you such a time? I'd begun to think that I was going to have to go without that chat that you were looking for. 'Ere!' she added, gazing into Effie's flushed and troubled face, 'You're looking all peculiar. Is there something wrong?'

They were standing directly outside a house, and Effie put her basket down and leant against the wall. She looked quite shaken as she shook her head. 'Sorry to keep you waiting – I'd have finished long ago, only Miss Pearl kept me back. Wanted to ask me questions about that man again.'

Lettie said, unnecessarily, 'The one Miss Blanche found lying in the court?' She realized she was frowning. 'I thought all that was dead and buried long ago.' She tried a little joke. 'Just like the man himself.'

Effie was in no mood to be amused. She gave a little sigh. 'And so did I! I'd almost managed to half-forget that day. I don't know why she wants to rake it up again.'

'What did she want to know, in any case?' Lettie was intrigued.

'Was it true I didn't know him – or was there something that I hadn't told the police? Or any little thing that I'd remembered since? I told her that there wasn't, but she wouldn't let it rest. On and on, as though by asking the same thing in a dozen different ways, she was going to make me change my mind.'

'So what did you tell her?'

'The same thing I told the police. That I'd never seen the fellow and I don't know who he was. I'm not sure that she believed me, but I know that Alex does, so I finally suggested that she took it up with him.'

'You never!' Lettie giggled. Effie could be more daring than she had supposed. 'What did she say to that?'

Effie's tense face softened to a reluctant grin. 'Nothing very much. Made a sour face as though I'd pricked her with a pin, then changed the subject and issued me my books – all with an air of outrage as though I'd told her lies.' She shook her head. 'I don't know what she expected me to say.'

Lettie shrugged. 'Wonder what started her on that again? Must have been something happened, to have reminded her.'

'I didn't think of that.' Effie seemed to be considering this idea. 'I suppose there might have been. But if there was, she didn't say anything to me.'

Lettie looked down at the books that she was carrying. There was that 'predilection' volume on the top – perhaps that was what had jogged Miss Weston's memory. But she did not share the thought with Effie. 'Can't have been anything important, or the police would know,' she said lightly. 'And your constable would tell you – so don't let that worry you. Perhaps it was just seeing us together in the shop. Reminded her of something she'd been mulling in her mind – you know how suspicious Miss Pearl can sometimes be.' Effie nodded but she was still looking unconvinced so Lettie changed the subject, purposely. 'But don't let's waste what little time we've got. That wasn't what you wanted to talk to me about. You said you wanted to ask for my advice?'

It worked. Effie picked up her basket and perked up at once. 'Actually, it is about that policeman . . .' she began.

When she had finished the story, there wasn't much to tell. Her young man had kissed her, half by accident, that's all – and Effie wanted to make a drama out of it. If she only knew what Bert and Lettie had been doing in that shed, then there might have been something interesting to say! But here was Effie asking for advice.

'What would you do, Lettie, if you were in my shoes? Should I break it off before it gets too serious?'

Lettie did her best. 'Didn't you like it when he kissed you?'
'Yes of course I did; that's why I'm asking you. And I'm
sure that he likes me. He gave me a little notebook as a present,
Christmas-time. But, as my cousin pointed out to me, I can't
hope for any future with a man like him.'

Lettie stared at her. 'You got another suitor?'

Effie shook her head. 'Not one I care about. No-one I'd
want to marry, that's for certain-sure.'

'Then what's the worry with this policeman? You like him
and he likes you. What's a kiss or two? I can't see that there's
any harm in that. You're not hurting anyone as far as I can
see and it doesn't stop you finding someone better later on. If
you decide you really want him, that's a different thing.'

'My cousin doesn't think that it would work out, anyway,'
Effie said. 'His family would probably not permit it for one
thing, and for another Uncle Joe would hit the rafters if he
knew — very likely forbid me to come home at all.'

Lettie laughed. 'Your policeman doesn't need permission,
he's over twenty-one. It's true you might have to change your
uncle's views a bit — though there might even be ways and
means of doing that, supposing this Alex is the sort of decent
fellow that you say, and would stand by you if . . . well, if it
really came to it.'

Effie could be peculiarly dense sometimes. She said sharply,
'If it came to what?'

'If you . . . you know . . . got yourself into the family way,'
Lettie prompted with a grin.

Her friend looked puzzled. 'Don't you have to be married
to do that?' She wasn't fooling, it was clear she didn't understand. She probably thought you had to send a message to the
stork!

Lettie said impatiently, 'Oh, for goodness' sake! You have
lived in the country all your life. You must have noticed what
was happening in the fields!' But Effie still looked baffled. Of
course she had no mother to tell her anything, and for all her
reading there was obviously lots she didn't know. Probably they
didn't put that sort of thing in books. Lettie sighed. 'I'll have
to tell you some time, but I can't do it now. Miss Caroline
will give me a jawing for lateness as it is. I'll see you in a

fortnight, if you can manage it, at the Westons' shop as usual. In the meantime, enjoy that young policeman's company while you've got the chance. Lots of girls would give their eyes for him.' And with that she hurried off.

Bert would have a giggle when he heard – they had not required a book to work it out – but there wasn't even time to wait for him that day. She was already late and braced for trouble as she hurried home, but she need not have been concerned. Miss Caroline just glanced briefly at the books, as usual, then put them down and fussed about a wine-stain on her favourite dress.

'You haven't managed to get it out at all,' she said, as though Lettie had not spent half an hour sponging it carefully with vinegar. 'You'll just have to sew on a silk rose spray to cover it. The one I had on last year's old tulle toque will do; you'll find it in a hat-box in the attic, I expect.'

Lettie was inwardly horrified, though she dared not let it show. A lady's maid was expected to deal with simple alterations and repairs, but she did not have Effie's talent for that sort of thing, and was rarely called on to attempt such tasks. 'The regular sewing-woman will be here tomorrow . . .' she demurred.

Her mistress shook her head. 'This can't wait for the sewing-girl to come. I want that dress tonight. I'm going to a charity supper for the Titanic Fund.'

So Lettie had to do it, which took her simply hours, but at least there were no 'predilections' – then or later on.

It was a relief to talk to Lettie, in a lot of ways. She had said exactly what Effie hoped to hear: there was no harm in seeing Alex and permitting him a kiss.

Effie hugged that notion to her, all through the next few weeks, repeating it like a verse of poetry that you had to learn for school. She muttered it when she was cleaning brass and setting fires. She was not hurting anyone at all. She had no other suitors and, as Lettie said, this friendship did not stop her finding 'someone better' later on – though (here she paused in the act of polishing the stairs) it was hard to imagine finding anyone that she liked half as well! 'More suitable' of course was what her friend had meant.

'Effie!' Mrs Lane's voice brought her to herself. 'Don't just stand there idling, put some vim in it. And when you've finished, get yourself downstairs. Mrs Thatchell has a letter to the bank she wants to post. You'll have to take it, and be quick about it too. I'm up to my ears already making pastry for a pie and there's a dozen things that I'll be needing help with later on.'

'Yes, Cook,' she mumbled and set to work again. When she concentrated the polishing did not take very long, and half an hour later she was dashing down the street, taking Mrs Thatchell's letter to the Post Office – since of course it lacked a stamp. Mrs Thatchell did not keep a stock of them because she very rarely wrote to anyone at all, except her bank, and she probably would not even had done that if it had not been a fancy private one which did not have a local branch. (According to Cook it was an up-country one that her father and her husband used to use, and Mrs Thatchell had simply stuck to it.) But she wrote so rarely that even the stationery which she kept for the purpose was beginning to turn slightly brown with age, like the ink which formed the spidery writing on the envelope.

Effie didn't mind the extra errand in the least. It gave her a rare excuse to leave the house, but she didn't see Alex on his beat, although she looked out for him. She did see the sergeant at the top of Tolver Road: he was on his bicycle, puffing and blowing as he struggled up the rise, but he slowed down when he saw her and gave a cheery wave. 'Morning, Miss Pengelly! Not so cold today!'

She nodded vaguely. 'Morning!' She gave him a quick smile. But he wasn't Alex and she did not pause.

Alex! She had not meant to think of him but there it was again, the name that filled her mind. Yet things had not been easy since he had snatched that kiss. Last time they had met it had been awkward all the time. If only she could do what he had said and take him home with her – let the family see him. They would like him then. Pa would try to, she was certain, if only for her sake. But as for Uncle Joe . . .

What could Lettie possibly have meant about there being 'ways and means' of persuading even him to change his views? Something about getting 'in the family way'. Well she knew what that meant, of course she did, because of Aunty Madge. It meant having babies, but how you achieved that she had no idea. Unless you were married, she was pretty sure, it had something to do with those 'shenanigans' that Uncle Joe had always been so scornful of, and how could Lettie think that they would help? They were shameful, weren't they, whatever they may be? And Uncle Joe would like that even less.

And what was that about seeing what happened in the fields? Muck-spreading and harvest and grazing cows. Couldn't be that though, could it? So what had Lettie meant?

She shook her head. She'd have to ask her the next time that they met – after all Lettie had promised to explain. Or perhaps it would be better to ask Pa, if he happened to be there one Thursday soon – as Effie hoped he would.

Well it wouldn't do to loiter; she'd be wanted back. Mrs Lane was making pastry for a pie – that would mean the knives would all want sharpening, and the chopping block would have to be scrubbed down afterwards. But first there was this letter which she had to post.

Effie sighed and hurried along St James Street and down the arcade steps into the busy town. Scores of people were jostling in the street: errand-boys on bicycles and horses pulling carts, women with baskets hustling into shops, and shop-assistants standing by their colourful displays – cabbages and shoes and no end of other things, piled on racks and spilling from the doorways of their stores. She kept a careful look-out till she reached the Post Office, but there wasn't any sign of Alex anywhere.

It was Thursday again, but there was no Effie to look forward to today and Alex was sitting in his room, whiling away an hour by studying a book about the main types of tobacco generally on sale and the slightly differing types of ash that they produced. He had told his room-mate Jenkins that he was 'studying', and that was true, perhaps – but this was not anything that would be required in the police examination in a month or two; this was prompted simply by a story he had read. Mr Conan Doyle's great detective, Sherlock Holmes, had identified a criminal entirely by this means, and Police Constable 633 was keen to do the same – although it was proving to be a great deal more complicated than it had been in the tale.

So he was not altogether sorry when there was a gentle knock and Jenkins put his head around the door. 'Proper little book-worm, aren't you, Dawes?' he said. 'Your head will split with all that learning, if you don't look out. Anyway – I know it's your day off and all – but I'm sent to tell you that you're wanted at the desk.'

Alex put his book down with a snap. 'But I'm not on duty,' he protested. 'I'm going out this afternoon.' He had been proposing a constitutional, out in the lanes where they had been last week. 'I am not even in my uniform.'

Jenkins grinned. 'That's what I told her, but she insisted all the same. Said she wanted to take you into town, and that you'd want to see her, if you knew that she was there.'

Effie! Alex felt his heart begin to pound. It had to be Effie – who else would it be? Perhaps she had decided that she'd spend that extra half-day with him, after all, and never mind her family for once! 'Tell her I'll be there. I won't be very long.' He was reaching for his tie and jacket as he spoke, and looking round for his civilian shoes. Jenkins gave a wicked smile and disappeared.

Alex did his tie up with indecent haste. Imagine Effie coming! That was wonderful. He had begun to worry that he had spoiled things. Many a time since that April afternoon, he had gone over and over the events of it. He was almost certain she hadn't minded at the time – but she had avoided looking at him all the way back home and last time they'd met she'd hardly said a word, just turned bright scarlet every time he even spoke to her.

Yet here she was again, so obviously he had not embarrassed her too much – though he would have to warn her not to come here to the police station like this to look for him. His superiors would not stand for it, any more than hers would – but Effie being Effie, she would understand. Though he'd have to find a way to hustle her outside before he mentioned it because that dratted Jenkins would no doubt be listening in, with ears stretched bigger than an elephant's.

He was rehearsing how he'd phrase it, as he hurried down the stairs and into the front office. 'My dear Miss Penge . . .' he began, but the words died on his lips. The woman waiting was not Effie after all. This was a much older woman, dressed in a fashionably narrow dove-grey coat and skirt and a tall hat with artificial cherries on the crown. She had her back to him and for a moment he could not think who it was. Then she turned to face him, a look of mild impatience on her handsome face.

'Alex. Thank heaven! There you are at last. Did you not get my letter? Weren't you expecting me?'

'Mother!' Alex gave a little inward moan. She had written to say that she might come down 'since you do not seem to have much time to visit us these days', but no date was mentioned and he'd supposed that his reply – that he was busy studying for his promotion test – had been successful in dissuading her. 'You did decide to come!'

'Of course I did, dear, it's been simply weeks!' She offered him a powdered perfumed cheek to kiss, ignoring Jenkins and official protocol. 'Now I know you are studying and all that sort of thing, but I simply had to come and take you out to lunch. You don't have any other arrangements, I assume?'

He didn't, and he said so, though rather grudgingly. If this impromptu visit had occurred on a second Thursday of the month, it would have caused him acute embarrassment. 'Though you are very fortunate to find me here at all,' he added, pompously. 'Better to give me prior warning if you come another time.'

His mother gave a little girlish laugh. 'Oh, it was such a frightful journey, I don't know if I shall bother to come all this way again. But I am doubly glad to find you, because – you'll never guess – on the station I ran into an old friend of mine, Priscilla Knight – I used to know her in your father's army days – and when she heard that you are working here and that I'd come all this way to visit you, she insisted on inviting us to lunch.'

Alex felt his heart sink to his civilian shoes. He'd met the wives of regimental friends before, and knew what such a luncheon was likely to be like: a lot of reminiscences about people he had never heard of in his life, places he had never visited, and incidents that happened years before he was born. But it was too late to plead a prior engagement now – he had already admitted that there wasn't one. He made the best excuse that he could find.

'But, Mother, I'm not dressed for formal visiting. I've only got what I am standing in. Most of my better clothes are still at home.'

His mother smiled. 'Well I'm not exactly dressed for lunching, either, dear, but it doesn't signify. Priscilla knows that I was travelling on the train and this is quite impromptu. Of course she'll understand. It won't be a formal thing in any case – Priscilla says there won't be anybody else, except the family, but she is sure the cook can make it stretch.' She gave him a sidelong glance. 'There's only three of them. Her husband's there, of course, I knew him years ago, and I understand there is a daughter too – so there will be some company for you.'

Alex's heart was already in his boots but it sank still lower at this last remark. So that was the reason for this rendezvous – another young woman to be introduced. He wondered if the fortuitous meeting with this friend had been altogether the accident that his mother claimed – he would not have put it past her to have planned this all along. But he was aware of Jenkins listening in and he said, 'I'm sure she will be charming,' as etiquette required. 'At what time are we expected?'

His mother smiled again. 'In half an hour or so. We are to be waiting in the railway-station yard, where I am promised that their coachman will come and pick us up. And after luncheon he will drive us back. I understand the family has a large estate somewhere on the outskirts of the town. Major and Mrs Knight. Perhaps you know the place?'

Alex nodded. 'I have heard of it. The Knights are very well known in the town.' That was an understatement. Everybody who was anybody in Penzance would know the Knights. He should have recognized the name before. Even Jenkins, tapping at his newfangled typewriting machine, was looking quite impressed. And he was to go there – dressed unsuitably – and make small talk to the daughter of the house, who would no doubt think him terribly ill-bred and be as reluctant for this enterprise as he was himself. 'Well I'll make myself respectable and see you at the door. It will take us a few moments to walk back down the street.'

It occurred to him, as he trailed back to his room, why his mother had settled on the railway terminus as a place for the carriage to come and pick them up – she was embarrassed by the idea of the police-station. It promised to be a very awkward afternoon.

It was not, in the event, as dreadful as he feared. The food was good and it was plentiful – no question of anything 'made to stretch' – and there was much less army reminiscence than there might have been, perhaps because his father was not there.

'Knew your father many years ago. Fine soldier he was too. Not intending to enlist, yourself, young man?' The Major, who was small and bluff and red of face, fixed a monocle into his eye and looked at Alex very searchingly.

'Only the civilian arm, sir,' Alex said. 'I've enlisted in the police.'

The monocle was dropped to dangle on its cord. 'Policeman, eh? Don't know many police, though I think we've entertained your chief man occasionally. Know old Broughton, do you?'

'Old Broughton' was the Chief of Penzance Borough Police, by far the most senior officer in the local force, and thus – in Alex's eyes – not far removed from God. He said, 'Not personally, sir, though I have met him once or twice.' Exactly twice, in fact – once when Alex was first admitted to the force and again when he'd got that commendatory report. On both occasions he'd been required to salute and nothing more.

But it seemed that the Major was entirely satisfied and the conversation moved to other things – in particular the gallant 'Titus' Oates, whom Knight had served with briefly in South Africa, before the ill-fated expedition to the Pole.

Miss Caroline, the daughter, was agreeable enough and attempted to engage the visitor in talk – though she had nothing of any consequence to say. She was smart and pleasant-looking, if you did not mind the pronounced capacity to flounce if one did not immediately agree with what she said – and at least she was not vapid, as so many of his mother's other girls had been.

So the occasion might have been a mild success if it had not been for what happened just before they left. Mrs Knight had pressed them to a cup of tea, and Alex and the ladies were in the drawing-room – the Major having excused himself and gone away to meet his land-agent. Alex was making small-talk to Miss Caroline, who professed an unexpected interest in books, and he was telling her all about tobacco and its ash, when a little maidservant came in with the tray.

She put it down with such a clatter that Mrs Knight remarked, 'You must excuse the maid. We weren't expecting visitors and it's the parlour-maid's day off. Never mind, Lettie, you may serve the tea.'

Lettie! Yes, of course it was! Effie's bouncy friend, though in this setting she seemed very different: awkward and cowed and insignificant. And she was staring at him crimson-faced, as though he were an apparition of some kind. When she saw him looking she made him a little bob. 'Constable Dawes! You gave me quite a turn. Good afternoon, sir. Didn't know that it was you.'

All eyes turned to him. He said 'Good afternoon!' politely, and tried to pass it off by turning back to Caroline and going on conversing about the books she liked to read. Nothing more was said about the incident, but it was awkward all the same and on the way back to the station in the carriage, his mother tackled him.

'Who was that frightful creature who called you by your name? How presumptuous! How did she come to know it, anyway?'

'I met her briefly once. I was called upon to interview another maidservant who was a friend of hers and who was an important witness in a case – that's all.'

'Really all?' She looked at him intently. 'Your father is convinced that you do not come home, and you try to dissuade me from visiting you here, because you have some quite unsuitable young girl in view. Promise me that he is wrong and that Priscilla's awful maid is not a secret fling.'

'I have told you, Mother. I have met her once, that's all – and only for a fleeting moment then. I doubt that we exchanged a dozen words, and besides she had a young man with her at the time. I promise you I have no interest in the girl.' He felt like a traitor to Effie as he said these words but his mother seemed relieved.

'I suppose as a policeman you would be obliged to deal with people of that class,' she observed. 'And no doubt you made an impression on her at the time. All the same it was unfortunate. She should know better than to speak to you, uninvited, when you are a guest. No doubt her mistress will have words with her.'

'I hope she does not scold the girl on my account,' he said, and meant it too. He did not want Lettie giving details as to how and when they'd met. 'After all, she's not a parlour-maid at all. She's really the lady's maid to Miss Caroline.'

He had blurted out that information before he stopped to think, and he braced himself for questions about how he came to know, but his mother simply smiled and sat back in the carriage-seat. 'Ah, yes, Miss Caroline. I think you made a little conquest there. What did you think of her?'

He said something non-committal, and his mother said, 'Well, despite your unfortunate acquaintance with the maid, you have obviously made a good impression on the Knights. The Major says you're welcome any time and he would be delighted to let you have a horse, if you care to come to lunch. I suggested next Thursday, since that's when you are free. He'll drop a note to you confirming it, of course.'

'But I've got to study some time,' he heard himself declare. 'I can't be going to luncheon out there every week.' He wasn't interested in Miss Caroline, but the offer of a horse was a very tempting thing. Perhaps he would go out there, just once more, and ride – but visiting the Knights must not become a ritual.

Next week there would be no Effie, but it was important that the following Thursday was kept free.

But somehow he could not bring himself to confess that to Mother. And that was worrying.

Three

Jenkins ragged him mercilessly when he got back. 'Wafted off by carriage to have luncheon with the gentry, eh?' he teased. 'And there's a daughter too! What would your other young friend have to say to that?'

'What friend?' Alex challenged. He had never told anyone about his meetings with Effie and had fondly supposed that his colleagues didn't know. However, Jenkins raised a pitying eyebrow at him, which convinced him otherwise, and he went on weakly, 'Anyway, that was a private conversation with my family. You had no business to be listening.'

'A good policeman keeps his ears and eyes open at all times,' Jenkins replied good-humouredly, quoting Old Broughton's favourite motto from the Manual. 'Anyway, you don't suppose the station doesn't know about your little outings on Thursday afternoons? Why do you suppose that Sergeant Vigo arranged the rota as he did? I think your Miss Pengelly, or whatever she is called, made quite a good impression when she came here that day.'

The remark left Alex speechless. He had supposed he'd wangled that himself, by volunteering to work that extra night a week – which, of course, he was very shortly going to have to do today. It was rather embarrassing to think he'd been indulged, and still more embarrassing if everybody knew. Besides, he thought with irritation, what he chose to do with his free afternoon was surely his affair – provided that he didn't bring the police force into disrepute.

But before he could think of any suitable riposte, Jenkins spoke again. 'Talking of Miss Pengelly – you've missed all the fun. While you were out we had a strange enquiry about that corpse of hers. Some firm of debt-collectors or something of the kind – seems they have been attempting to trace a missing man, and our London people put him on to us in case our body turned out to be the one. They'd already seen a copy of the newspaper report, and thought that it might possibly just match up, so they were writing to ask if we could tell them any more. Sergeant Vigo had me type a letter back at once, to say that the man was buried now, the matter had been closed and we had no further information as to who he was.'

'You didn't mention that he asked for Effie?' Alex was alarmed.

Jenkins shook his head. 'Wasn't my responsibility. It was Sergeant Vigo's letter. He dictated it. I just took it down and typed it up for him to sign. But I can assure you that it didn't mention anyone by name – just confirmed the details in the newspaper: where the corpse was found, what he was wearing, that he appeared to have died of natural causes, and that sort of thing – and that we were sorry we could be no further help. Nothing else at all. But – as old Vigo said to me himself – the fellow's dead and buried and they cannot touch him now, however much he owed. And besides it seems a long chance that he was even the man that they were looking for, so it served no purpose dragging other people into it.' He grinned. 'So your Miss Pengelly's safe. I told you the sergeant thought a lot of her.'

'She's not "my" Miss Pengelly,' Alex said ungraciously, though he was relieved.

Jenkins laughed again. 'I don't suppose she will be, either, now that you've started lunching with daughters of the gentry. But I knew you used to have an eye for her and I thought you'd like to know.'

Alex muttered something and went back to his room. He was rattled by Jenkins' last remark. 'Had an eye' for Effie – what a thing to say! It made him sound a real Lothario. But then he remembered that April afternoon. Was he really being fair to Effie, doing things like that? A kiss would mean a great deal more to her than it would to one of Mother's socialites.

And looking back, it wasn't just the kiss. His tongue had almost run away with him. 'If we are going to . . .' he'd begun, and almost mentioned something permanent, though he had stopped himself in time. But he hadn't promised anything, just talked of 'walking out'. Surely there could be no harm in that?

All the same he'd kissed her, and that altered everything. Effie would still be justified in having hopes of him.

Even when he went on duty, later on that night, he couldn't put the question of Effie from his mind. Mother's suspicions of his knowing the Knights' parlour-maid today had shocked him into facing up to things. It was obvious, to anyone with sense, that marriage to Effie was not available to him. Their respective families would never stand for it. Yet he was not the sort of man to offer less – or Effie the sort of girl who would agree to it! He remembered what she'd said about visiting his home, and she was obviously right. Mother had proved it. They came from different worlds.

So what was he doing, walking out with her? He mustn't 'lead her on', as the unpleasant saying went. He would have to talk to her about it, that was all – face her next time, and tell her the truth: that he was getting far too fond of her and it would be better if they did not meet again. He would try to find a way to put it tactfully – that he had years of training to look forward to and he could not expect her to save herself for him. Better, if she had a follower at all, for it to be some decent fellow from the mine.

It was such an awful prospect that he couldn't sleep. He told himself that he was mostly anxious about hurting her – it had been so sweetly touching the way she kept the flowers as a memento of their little walks. Naturally a parting would be very hard, but it was for the best, and no doubt her family would be actually relieved if she started going home every week again. He was being very sensible, he assured himself, and was only sleepless because the floor was hard.

But the more he tossed and turned the more it dawned on him that actually the truth was something else. What kept him wakeful was the thought of losing her – of weeks and weeks of empty summer days without her cheerful prattling and artless happy laugh. None of her swift smiles, no upward glance, no gentle Cornish burr. Mother would try to match him with one of those ghastly girls whom she kept inviting for his benefit. Or – worse – Miss Caroline!

He was almost relieved when the duty sergeant roused

him from his bed and sent him with his bull-dog lantern
out into the rain, looking for a burglar who had robbed a
house nearby.

'My lor', Effie! You will never guess!' Lettie was almost bursting
with her tale. It was Tuesday and they had met up in the
haberdashery again, but there were others in the shop and
there might be listening ears. Miss Blanche was busy with a
customer, so Lettie pulled her friend into the corner by the
knitting wool where they could not be overheard. 'I swear you
could have knocked me over with one of the feathers from
Miss Caroline's new hat. Went in with a tray of tea and there
he was – sitting in the drawing-room and looking quite at
ease.' She glanced slyly at Effie from underneath her lids.

He friend was looking appropriately mystified. 'Who was?'

'Why, your constable of course!'

Effie had turned a gratifying shade of red. 'Alex! Whatever
was he doing there?'

'Having luncheon with Miss Caroline, it seems – though
they had finished eating by that time. Cook says she thinks
the mothers dreamed the party up – apparently the two ladies
have known each other years and they ran into one another
in the town – accidentally for the purpose, Cook appears to
think. Mrs Dawes was naturally invited to luncheon at the
house and practically begged to bring her son as well – the
coachman says she dropped all sorts of hints – and courtesy
obliged the Major to agree, even if your Alex is just a constable.
Mrs Knight was practically in ecstasy when she got home, I
hear. She would love to find a husband for Miss Caroline –
most of the other suitors haven't lasted long. There was some
scandal with a cousin of the house, who was involved in a
divorce – a lot of better families back away from things like
that – and Miss Caroline is as wilful as a nanny-goat herself.
But no doubt a policeman would know how to handle it.'

Effie said, 'I see!' a little woefully.

Lettie did not wish to cause her friend unnecessary grief
but there was an odd pleasure in passing on this news. It gave
a sort of power, in a peculiar way – and what she was saying
was no more than the truth. Besides, the sooner Effie knew,

the less she would be hurt and the better it would be for everyone. That's why Lettie added, with a little smile, 'Miss Caroline seemed very charmed with him.'

Effie said nothing.

After a moment, Lettie had to speak. 'You could have knocked me down for sixpence when I saw him sitting there! I almost dropped the tea-tray with the teapot and the sandwiches and all and before I thought I'd blurted out "Hello, Mr Dawes!" Well, you can imagine! The mistress nearly bit my head off for taking liberties and Miss Caroline was frowning fit to burst. I was expecting a right royal dressing-down after the visitor had gone – but when she got me on my own, all she did was ask me how I came to know his name.'

'I hope you didn't tell her? Or I'll be in the soup!'

Lettie shrugged. 'I said that I had met him when that corpse was found and he came asking questions at the Westons' shop. That seemed to be enough. In fact it made Miss Caroline go all dewy-eyed. Went on about how brave and clever he must be, dealing with such things – as if looking at a dead man was something terrible. Proper taken with your Alex, that was clear to see. Anyway, the upshot of it is, he's coming back to lunch again next week – and they two are going out riding. Your Alex is going to have her father's horse.'

Effie was looking slightly stricken as she said, 'Not "my" Alex, really, is he then?'

Lettie felt rather guilty, but she said cheerfully, 'Well you did tell me you thought you weren't well suited, anyway. And it solves your little problem for you, doesn't it? No need to worry that you let him kiss you, now. Just be glad he did it while he had the chance. No harm done; just a pleasant memory.' She picked up her pile of books. 'Now I'd better get these back and find some more to take.'

Effie said dully, 'Won't matter much, I suppose.'

Lettie gave a laugh. 'That's what you think, Effie. I'll have to be a lot more careful what I choose this week. Miss Caroline is very likely going to look at them for once. Your constable has had a strange effect on her. This lot was piled up in the drawing room, and he saw them and asked her if she liked to read. Well, to hear her talk you'd think she'd read the lot, though of course she'd never glanced at them at all. But ever since she has been doing nothing else – though even then she doesn't read them properly. Seems to look at the first few pages and the last – and leave it go at that.'

But Effie wasn't listening. She simply muttered, in a strangled voice, 'I'll have to go, myself. Bye-bye, Lettie.' And she hurried from the shop.

Lettie found that she was secretly relieved. It was a shame about the policeman, naturally it was, but all this had saved her an embarrassment. She'd promised Effie to tell her the truth about the stork, and now she wouldn't have to – which was just as well. Mind you, Bert could give some lessons! She gave a little laugh and took her selection of volumes to the desk.

It was not really anybody's fault – even Captain Maddern said so, and he'd been shift-captain at the mine a dozen years and ought to know. It was just an accident – a weakness in the rocks.

It wasn't even as if they had been blasting at the time, only preparing the places to put the charges in. More than likely there had been a hidden fault and boring the shot-holes had just struck into it and caused the 'run' of stone. There was always a possibility of a rock-fall in a stope, especially when you were working 'overhand', digging out the ore above your head. Walter knew that, but he still blamed himself. He was the leader of the little team – the 'pare' – and it was his decision where to place the drill. If he had not had half his mind on other things – what Joe had said to him about his girl – perhaps he would have spotted the signs of weakness in the stope and the whole catastrophe would never have occurred.

He lay there on the makeshift stretcher and tried to shake his head. He still could not believe the suddenness of this. Two men injured and another dead. Not that he had been all that badly hurt, himself. He might have felt less guilty if he had. But the sight of Tommy Richards' legs sticking out from under half a ton of rock – all that was visible of his oldest friend and mate – and the retrieval of the crushed corpse afterwards would live with Walter for ever, he knew. And even that was not the worst of it. Tommy's son Jimmy, the youngest member of the team, who was only just thirteen and only recently come down to underground, was badly hurt as well. Walter had managed to pull him back in time to save his life, but a piece of flying granite took him in the eye and it would be a wonder if he ever saw again.

What was Walter going to say to Mrs Richards now?

He had seen her just this morning, standing at her gate, laughing as she gave her son and husband their 'crowst-bags' for their lunch and waving as they all three walked down to the mine. Beautiful fine morning, with the sun bright on the sea – you could not have guessed that it would end this way. Poor woman, Jimmy was the only child she had: it would be a long time before she laughed again.

Yet it had begun like any other shift: changing into their flannels and fustians in the 'dry', where they had been left drying overnight: each man kneading a lump of clay into a candle-holder, and sticking a lit taper to his felt 'tull' hat, and hanging the remainder of the candles from a button of a working coat – waistcoat or jacket, as the case may be. Then joshing and joking with the other men as they walked over to the 'ope', and singing as they went down the half-mile of ladders to the level they were working at. Walter's choice of level – that was the tragic thing.

Like all the other pare-leaders at Penvarris Mine, he was a 'tributer' – meaning (as he'd said to Joe) that he had a contract with the mine for so much per ton of tin – so that his earnings (and the earnings of his team) depended on how much ore he won. He had the choice of where his pare would work: that was the skill of it – judging where the seams were and which way they would run – and Walter's judgement had generally been among the best, though there had been some lean times, as there always were. Of course, he'd started like everybody did, being a part of someone else's pare – still did if he was working doublers in place of someone sick – but he was proud to be the leader of his team. It made you feel a proper man, he often said – almost as if you were working for yourself, because you were the only one responsible.

It was that responsibility that hurt him most today – much

worse than the smashed ankle and the bruising on his back. He had chosen to open up that stope – working from the bottom level first. It had looked promising when he prospected it. He had seen the green of copper shining in the stone, and where there was copper there was often tin below. And he had been right, as well – this last week or two the stone they'd sent up in the trolleys to be crushed had been assessed as being rich in ore. Jimmy and Tommy would be owed a day or two's good pay – and they'd both paid into the Miners' Friendly every week so there'd be something to help the widow for a little while.

The widow! Even now it was impossible to believe the truth of that. One minute there was Tommy, taking turns with him at hammering in the bore-bit while Jimmy held it in position in the hole, the next there was a shouted warning from the stope above, then a rumble from just above their heads. Walter had a recollection of a shout – 'She's going to run! Take cover!' – as he seized the boy and thrust him bodily into the tunnel at their backs. It was a narrow tunnel and they had to bend as a report like gun-shot echoed through the mine. He looked around for Tommy but he could not see for sudden dust. The walls around them trembled and the very air appeared to shake, blowing out their candles to leave them in the dark, as with a roar like thunder the rock began to fall. Instinctively Walter had thrown himself full-length, covering his eyes and ears to shield the blast, but Jimmy did not have a miner's instincts yet and he must have raised his head to shout out 'Father!'. And the rest was history.

It had seemed a long, long time before the help arrived, and with it the candles that showed the dreadful truth: Tommy's twisted bloodstained legs emerging from the pile and the dreadful gash where Jimmy's eye had been. Even now, as he was carried on the stretcher to the winze, where they could winch him to the surface, Walter could see that nightmare picture in his mind.

'You've been lucky, Walt Pengelly!' Captain Maddern was at his elbow still. 'I'm sure they'll fix that broken ankle good as new. And that back will quickly heal – only surface cuts and bruises where bits of rock have hit. Only small stuff, but it makes a mess. Good thing you had the sense to shield your head – you've only got a little gash from flying stone – not like poor Jimmy who took it in the face. But it's down to you that he's alive at all. And if you hadn't thrust that boy away and lain yourself across him, he very likely would be dead as well.'

He was only trying to be comforting, as Walter was aware – but somehow, as he was jogged along the tunnel, by the flickering flames of candles stuck on projecting rocks, he found that he was clinging to the reassuring words. They emerged into the larger space beside the winze, and the cool clean air descending from the shaft – after the heat and dust of further in – worked on Walter like a draught of medicinal wine.

He took great gulps of it, and for the first time since the accident he found his voice. It sounded very hoarse and faraway, even to his own ears, and his lips were dry with dust but he did manage to say, 'Someone tell my daughter and let Joe Martin know.'

But then they put the stretcher in the cage to winch it up and the pain of his leg and ankle came wafting over him. He tried to raise his head, but found it hurt too much. He must have been more injured than he thought. The world went black and he did not speak again. He must have been uncon-scious – or something close to it – for several hours, for he knew nothing further until he found himself propped up in an unfamiliar bed with Effie at his side and the mine doctor bending over him.

Four

Effie was in the empty breakfast room with a pile of sheets and towels and pillowslips spread out in front of her. The room was chilly, since it was rarely used (Mrs Thatchell always had her breakfast sent up on a tray); no fire was ever lit and it smelt shut-up and musty, and even with the shutters back the light was very poor. Effie hated being in there, but she had to check the laundry marks on everything to go to the Sanitary Steam Laundry before the boy with the cart arrived to pick them up.

It was a job she cordially detested, too. Some of Mrs Thatchell's linen had once been poorly marked in a patent ink that had not proved to be 'indelible' at all, so that the initials 'J.K.T.' in the corner of the hem had half-washed out with time. Effie's task was to 'refresh' the stamp, by covering the letters exactly as they were with proper Indian ink: a fiddly business, made more difficult because the steel nib that Mrs Thatchell provided for the job was old and scratchy and easy to get crossed. (Rather like the owner of the sheets herself, Effie thought wickedly, but it was no joking matter.) Besides, the wretched pen inclined to smudge.

She was just struggling with a lace-edged bolster case when she was aware of a sudden commotion at the door downstairs, followed by Mrs Lane's voice muttering to a man.

Dear Heaven, surely the laundry cart had not already come? If so this re-marking would have to wait until next time – it was only to be hoped the items came back home all right. Effie jammed the lid back on the ink bottle and hastily cleaned the offending nib on the pen-wiper. She would have to bundle up the laundry as it was, and she hadn't yet double-checked to make sure that all the items were written on the list. She began to do so, hastily: bed sheets (linen) 2; pillowslips (embroidered) 2: calico single bed sheets . . . She would never get it done.

She was interrupted by the breathless arrival of Cook.

'Effie! You are wanted. There's a man here from the mine.'
Mrs Lane came hurrying across and did the strangest thing –
she put her arms round Effie.

It was as well that Effie had put the ink-pot down, or she
would certainly have dropped it with the shock. 'What's
happened?' It was clearly something terrible.

'There's been some sort of accident and your father's hurt.
Still alive, mind – though it seems there's others dead.'

Effie heard her own voice saying, 'Badly hurt?' though she
had no consciousness of framing any sound.

'Couldn't rightly say, my handsome. Bad enough, I think,'
Mrs Lane said, in a gentle tone. 'Seems as how he passed out
with the pain and they had to have the mine doctor to have
a look at him. Best you get down there and see him for
yourself.'

'A doctor!' Effie caught her breath. It must be really bad.
You didn't call the doctor if it wasn't serious. Of course they'd
had one come when Ma had been so sick, but it had done
no good, and afterwards Pa had had to pawn his watch to pay
the man his fee. And now he was the one they'd called the
doctor for! She pulled off her working apron and was halfway
to the door, when a thought hit her. 'But Mrs Thatchell . . .'

'No doubt she will grumble, but she'll let you go, once she
hears what's happened, I am sure. She was good to me a year
or two ago when my brother Fred was ill. Tell you what, you
go and get your coat on and I'll go to see her first – put in
a word for you – then she'll be prepared and won't snap your
head off before she's heard you out.'

Effie swallowed and did as she was told. Afterwards she could
not properly recall how she climbed the staircase and changed
her working clothes, but she must have done it because a little
later on she found herself standing outside the parlour in her
cloak and bonnet, and her outdoor boots.

'Come in, Effie!' Mrs Thatchell's voice, almost before she'd
had the time to knock.

'Excuse me, Mrs Thatchell. It's my father, see . . .'

Her employer waved an impatient hand at her. 'Don't bother
with all that. Mrs Lane has told me what the problem is. I

understand you want time off for the remainder of the day. Indeed I see that you have dressed accordingly. Well, in the circumstances, I do not object, though of course I shall expect you to make up the time. Fortunately that is easy to arrange: you can simply work one Thursday afternoon in lieu. Next week, perhaps, when your father is a little more himself. I hope that's satisfactory?'

It was more than Effie had been hoping for, in fact: she had expected at least to lose her wages for a day. It would mean no Alex on that afternoon – but perhaps that didn't matter, after what she'd heard. Maybe she ought to get a note to him. But she'd think about that later. Seeing Pa today was the important thing. She managed to stammer, with genuine relief, 'Thank you, madam. You are very good.'

Mrs Thatchell gave a thin-lipped little smile. 'I know my Christian duty, I should hope. Now don't just stand there. I have given my permission and you are free to go. I understand there's someone waiting in the street with a cart to take you to your father straight away.'

It was the first that Effie had heard about a cart, but the information came as a relief. She had been fretting about how long it would take to get to Pa on foot. There was no horse-bus to Penvarris at this time of day (there would not be another one for hours) and, though it was only a matter of five miles and in this fine weather it was obviously possible to walk, with all the worry about the accident it would have seemed to take for ever, she could see. Thank heavens the fellow from the mine had brought a cart – though she could not imagine whose cart it would be. Most probably a friend of Uncle Joe's who had lent it to him for the trip, she thought, as she hurried down the kitchen steps and out into the yard.

But it was not Uncle Joe who was awaiting her. This was someone taller and much stockier, but for a foolish moment she did not recognize the man who was standing on the pavement, dressed in filthy working clothes. He must have come directly, not even stopping to rinse off at the dry, because he was still covered from head to foot in red dust from the mine, with only the moistness of his eyes and mouth making a living contrast with the dusty mask. When he saw her his wet lips opened in a smile and he grabbed off his grubby cap and began to twist it between his grimy hands.

When he took off the cap Effie saw ginger in the hair and realized for the first time who the caller was. 'Peter!' she cried, astonished.

He nodded, his face quite solemn suddenly. 'Sorry to be the bringer of bad news, but I thought you ought to 'ear as soon as possible. Came to fetch you the minute I was free – your cousin Peg told me where you were working to – and I went t'see Crowdie from the farm, and he obliged by offering to drive me into Penzance hisself. Said he 'ad an errand in the town in any case – but I don't believe it, 'cause he's not been gone five minutes and here he is again.' He gestured to the farm-cart that was lumbering up the street. 'You know Crowdie, don't you?'

Effie found that she was nodding, rather tearfully – partly from gratitude and partly from relief. Everyone knew Crowdie, and if he was on the cart there could be no awkwardness with Peter as she had briefly feared. She said, with a gush of genuine gratitude, 'Hello Crowdie. Thanks for driving in. You have both been angels. But about my Pa . . .'

'They've taken him by stretcher to your Uncle Joe's – he couldn't have managed in his lodgings on his own,' Crowdie was saying as he bent down to help her into the cart.

She scrambled up beside him. He smelt of straw and cows, which she somehow found extremely comforting. 'I hear they fetched the doctor. Is he badly hurt?'

Peter Kellow was climbing up onto the seat and sitting close to her, though he placed a piece of sack between them, not to soil her clothes. It was rather touching, the way he thought of that and when she felt the pressure of his arm against her own she did not flinch and shuffle further off. Not that there was anything romantic in the contact, she assured herself; it was simply comfort, that was all.

Peter smiled at her as the wagon moved along. 'Done something to his ankle, it's gone an awful shape – they nearly brought him here into Penzance, so he could go up to the hospital and have one of they clever photographs they do these days of bones, "exerays" or something, and have that plaster

of Paris on his leg. But they didn't do it – it would have cost
no end, and anyway the doctor didn't think that he could stand
the trip.'

'My lord!' Effie whispered. 'That's never just his ankle. How
didn't you say?'

'They think that something must have hit him on the head.
Nobody realized it at first, 'cause he seemed as right as rain,
but a little later on he passed out cold and hasn't come around.
Or hadn't, when I left, half an hour ago.'

'He's gone unconscious?' Effie was alarmed. 'Going uncon-
scious' was a famous danger sign.

Peter nodded. 'Mind, they're clever nowadays, they can do
all sorts. This doctor says he's seen this kind of thing before
and not to worry, old ways are just as good. Most likely your
Pa will come out of this and be as right as ninepence in the
end – although it might be weeks before he's fit to work.'

Effie stared at him. 'But what's he going to live on, if he
can't go to work? And how are we ever going to pay the
doctor's fee?'

It was Crowdie who answered. 'Don't you fret 'bout that,
my handsome. Time was it would have been the workhouse
for him, or someone's charity. But that's all altered now. There's
that new Act of Parliament they passed last year has just come
into force – they take fourpence weekly from your wage
packet to what they call the "stamp" and if you're sick or
injured you still get a bit of pay. Ten bob for the first month
or two, I believe it is.' He gave her a sideways grin. 'And
they'll pay the doctor for a wage-earner. You could almost
say that he'd been lucky there. It was all in the papers. You
hadn't heard of it?'

She shook her head. 'I haven't seen Pa for a week or two
and he wouldn't worry me about it anyway – any more than
Uncle Joe would do.' She rarely talked to Joe at all, she thought,
except about the weather and who's dying and who's dead.
'But I'm glad you told me; it's like a miracle.'

Peter gave her arm a little nudge. 'I'm surprised your family
never mentioned it. There was quite a stir about it down the
mine and the owners had to hold a meeting to explain. I know
your father wasn't keen, for one – people already paid into

the Friendly fund, he said, and this will mean that they were paying twice.'

Effie had to swallow hard when she heard this. 'No doubt he's changed his mind by now. A bit of money coming in will be a blessing to us all, and no mistake. Pay his rent and have a doctor come for free— Whoops!' She broke off as they hit a pothole in the road.

They had left the outskirts of the town by now and were lurching along the narrow country lanes. Crowdie was doing his best to urge the horse, of course, and the heavy cart was bouncing like a light-weight gig.

Effie did not talk much after that. She found she was obliged to clasp her bonnet with one hand to save it falling off and, with the other, to hold herself onto the narrow seat. Peter was doing something similar and there was an awkward moment when their fingers met.

She felt herself turn scarlet and snatched her hand away. Peter looked embarrassed and a silence fell. Indeed, if Crowdie had not kept up a cheerful commentary – he knew every wood and farm and village that they passed along the way – there would have been no more conversation until they reached the house.

Effie was so pleased to get there and so eager to get down that she almost forgot to thank her two companions for their help. But as Peter helped her to the ground, she recalled herself enough to give him a smile of gratitude.

'God bless the pair of you,' she murmured, turning at the door. 'Without you I don't know what I should have done. It would have taken simply hours getting home.'

Crowdie nodded at her. 'Don't give it no more thought, my handsome! Only wish there was more that we could do. But don't you hover there and chat to us – you go and see your father. He'll be wanting you.'

Aunt Madge was in the kitchen, her face as pale as chalk. 'You're here then, child? He has been asking for you in his sleep. Doctor's still with him, but he says to send you up. We've put him in our room for the time – we'll have to sleep down in the front room chairs, meanwhile.'

Effie nodded. The best front room was hardly ever used, in

any case, 'cepting for Christmastime and funerals. She hurried up and found her father lying in Aunt Madge's bed, whiter than the sheets. The doctor was still doing something to his leg but indicated a stool where she could sit. There was a funny, strong carbolic smell about the room.

She sat down and took her father's hand between her own. It felt as cold as ice, and it seemed a lifetime before he stirred at last.

Alex was in St Clare Street with his notebook out, interviewing an angry farmer about a stolen pig.

'Brought it in 'ere, I did, tied up on my cart – going to sell 'un, see.' He gestured to an ancient wagon standing in the road, drawn by an equally decrepit-looking horse. A large open crate was lying on the cart, upturned but still containing the remains of a nest of trodden straw, while a short length of broken rope was all the witness that remained of the former occupant. 'But when I got here, the beggar wasn't 'ere, and while I was round the corner asking questions in the street, he must have come round 'ere and pinched it off the cart.'

Alex licked his pencil. 'Private arrangement, was it? It isn't market day.'

The man looked shifty. 'Didn't put 'un through the market. Met a fellow here on market-day, told me he had a little small-holding out towards Newbridge, and was looking for a farrow sow. Well, o' course, I said I had one home, and he promised me a decent price for it.'

'The name of this gentleman?' Alex felt every inch the constable.

The farmer pushed his cap back on his head and ran his fingers through his thinning hair. 'Well, that's the trouble, see. I aren't exactly sure. He wrote it down – I'm damty sure he did – but I'm no real hand at ciphering, and anyhow I can't remember where I put the paper to.'

Alex tried to keep his face composed. 'And I suppose, you don't have an address?'

The complainant shook his head. 'Well, I didn't need it, see. I arranged to meet him on this corner here, ten o'clock this morning, but he never came. Leastways, if he did, he left before I came – I was a minute or two late meself, cause I couldn't get the damty creature in the cart. Well, I know a woman keeps that corner shop and I went to ask her if she'd seen him anywhere, but of course she hadn't – and blow me down for sixpence, when I got back 'ere again the damty rope was broke in two and the damty pig was gone. Beggar must have stole it while my back was turned.'

Alex stifled a wild desire to laugh. 'This was a valuable animal?' he enquired with gravity.

An energetic nod. 'I should damty think so! She was in farrow too . . . Worth every penny of the three pound ten that I was asking for.'

'So when . . .?' Alex was saying when a cart bowled up the road. He broke off and glanced towards it. 'Is this your fellow now?'

The farmer shook a fierce, indignant head. 'Don't know much, do 'ee?! Course that isn't him. That there's Crowdie from out Penvarris way – should have thought that anybody could have told you that – and he's got Peter Kellow and that Pengelly girl up there with him, by the look of it. I told you, this blighter that has took my pig comes from out Newbridge – or at least that's what he said. If you can trace him, I'm sure you'll find my sow! Here, are you listening to anything I say?'

'Of course I'm listening,' Alex said, untruthfully. In fact his attention was mostly on the cart. He had only glimpsed it, but the farmer was quite right. It was clearly Effie on the cart. Alex would have known her anywhere.

But what was Effie doing at this time of day? And who was that Peter Kellow she was snuggling up against, and smiling at in that familiar way? It couldn't be her cousin – the surname wasn't right, and she had assured him that she had no other family in Cornwall any more. Besides, the way that boy was making eyes at her, he did not look the least bit like a relative!

'What the blazes is going on?' he heard the farmer say. 'What on earth is she doing there with him? He's got no right to have her!'

It was so exactly what Alex had been thinking himself that he found himself staring at the farmer stupidly. 'You think so?'

'Course I damty think so,' the man said angrily. 'Don't you think I recognize my own damty pig? Well don't just stand there looking, aren't you going to take him in?' He gestured down the street.

Alex followed the direction of the hand and saw what he had not noticed up to now – he had been so busy thinking about Effie and the cart that he had not seen the little drama further up the street. An aged gentleman was standing by his gate, cursing and hopping angrily from foot to foot, while gesticulating at Alex with his stick, and a younger fellow – possibly his son – was putting his whole weight against a rope, attempting to tow back out onto the street a fat, reluctant and extremely ugly pig.

'You tell them, Constable!' the farmer urged, following Alex as he strode towards the scene. 'Look at him scraping her along the path – shouldn't be treating a prize sow like that. If he's not careful she'll get her dander up, and then he'll be sorry. More than a hundredweight of pig – you don't want that charging at you, I can promise you.'

Alex had come to that conclusion for himself and was careful to keep the wall between him and the sow as he strode towards the garden. 'Well now, what's all this? This man is complaining that you've got his sow.'

The younger man gave a scornful snort and let go of the rope. 'His pig is it? Well, he ought to keep a better eye on it. Look what it's done to Fayther's cabbages!' He gestured to the garden, where the pig – released from tugging – had risen to its feet and was now munching pansies with a contented air, a length of broken rope still trailing from its neck. The man turned back to Alex and said, as though the farmer wasn't there, 'Dratted animal broke down the fence as well. We shall want paying for the damage, you can tell the owner that.'

The farmer was almost sputtering by now. 'You mean to tell me that it just escaped . . .' He broke off as another horse and cart came into view. 'Well, 'ere's the man you want to talk to about that. Wouldn't have happened if he'd been on time . . .'

'No such thing! You let the beast escape.'

'Is that my pig? I'm sorry to be late.' The cart driver pulled up outside the gate and everyone began to talk at once – except the pig, which went on serenely chewing flowers. Alex left them to it and went back to his beat.

It was a funny story and it would make Jenkins laugh, but somehow Alex couldn't raise a smile. All he could think of was Effie on that cart and the boy who had been looking so protectively at her – and she didn't seem to mind, though the boy was red with mine-dust from his forehead to his toes!

Of course he had been resolving to have it out with her – tell her there was no future, and that sort of thing – but it would have caused him so much pain that he was not quite sure that he could bear to give her up. It was only for her sake that he might have managed it. He had been half-rehearsing that sorry little speech in which he urged her to find 'some nice fellow from the mine' – but he hadn't wanted her to do it, especially not so soon! Or was this someone she had secretly cared for all along?

His mood was so sombre when he reported back that day, that even Jenkins didn't try to tease, just said baldly, 'There's been a message left. Major Knight will send a carriage if you like, and pick you up on Thursday so you can go to lunch. Take some clothes for riding – he has arranged a horse.'

Alex nodded glumly and went back to his room. It was not an appointment that he was keen to keep – but it wasn't Effie's Thursday, and even if it were, it didn't look as if she'd miss him very much. One might as well take such pleasure as one could. He took the trouble to write a little note, thanking the Major for his hospitality and accepting the kind offer of a carriage-ride.

Walter swam up from a deep, uneasy sleep. For a moment he could not work out where he was. His head was aching and he could not think. He didn't recognize the framed text on the wall, or the crooked chest of drawers beside the bed. Or the knitted patchwork bedspread, come to that. But Effie was beside him, so it must be all right.

He tried to move but there was something odd about his leg. It hurt; he couldn't shift it and it seemed to weigh a ton.

He raised his head a fraction and tried to look at it, but all he could see was a sort of wooden plank.

'Now then, Walt, you take it easy or you'll disturb the splint. Are you awake again? Don't matter if you're not. You've had some chloroform. The doctor said that you might sleep for hours, but if the pain gets bad, he's left some laudanum.'

Through a kind of dizzy sickness, he recognized the voice. It was his sister Madge. Of course, he'd had some kind of accident. Slowly recollection floated back to him. He'd been lying on the table in the kitchen – hadn't he? – and somebody had held a cloth of something wet against his mouth and nose. Now he seemed to be lying in a bedroom in her house.

He tried to speak but found his mouth was dry. Only a sort of strangled sound came out, and a moment later Effie was holding a cup of water to his lips.

'Have a bit of this, Pa. It will do you good.'

He raised his hand and squeezed her fingers with his own. He seemed to have no power to do more than that. But she was delighted.

'Well, thank the stars for that! I think you're really with us, this time, and I'm some glad of it. You've been drifting in and out for simply hours. The last horse-bus back is due in just a little while and I was afraid that I would have to leave before you came properly awake – and then I would have worried about you all the night. But I can see you know me, so you must be clearer now.'

'Course I know you, Effie!' It came out as a croak but it obviously touched her – there were tears on her lashes.

She raised the cup again. 'Don't try to talk too much, you'll only tire yourself. I'll be back here Thursday; we can talk longer then. Mrs Thatchell has been very good – she's letting me have an extra afternoon this week.' She gave a feeble grin. 'Mind, we shall have to make the most of it – she wants me to work all day next week in lieu. Now, have another sip of this. It seems to do you good.'

He took a tiny mouthful, obediently. It soothed his throat. 'Back to work by that time,' he managed, with a smile.

'Don't be so damty stupid.' That was Madge again. She'd been standing out of sight beside the door and he'd forgotten she was there. 'The doctor says it's likely to be weeks before you walk and even then your ankle may never be quite right. Don't look so gone-out, Effie – he will have to know some time. It's no good pretending. At least it seems he's going to turn out all right in the head. With that great thump he's taken on the bottom of his skull, there was a time that we weren't even very sure of that – and Lord knows how we would have managed with him then.'

She was talking about him as if he wasn't there and he made a feeble motion to protest. 'Can't expect it all to fall on you,' he said. 'Get me to my lodgings and I'll make shift somehow.'

'Walter Pengelly, you are dafter than a brush! It's clear as rainwater you're not going anywhere. How would you manage up two flights of stairs? I told you, you won't be able to walk about for weeks. And Old Ma Hitchens is nearly seventy; you can't expect her to be running after you. No!' She gave a short affronted sniff. 'You are my family and I know my duty, I should hope. You'll stay here with us until you're on your feet.'

Walter leant back on the pillow. He was going to be a burden to his sister, he could see, but all the same her offer came as a relief. He made a feeble effort to do the proper thing. 'That's handsome of you, Madgie, but what's Joe going to say?'

She snorted. 'I don't suppose he'll like it, but he'll put up with it. He put up with your Effie living here for years.' There was nothing sentimental about Madge. 'And when you're feeling better you can lend a hand; there's a few shoes need mending and that sort of thing. You're clever with your hands. Save us a few coppers and help to pay your keep. Joe can do anything with a piece of stone, but he was always helpless when it came to soling shoes.'

It was her attempt at leaving him some pride, though he could see that Effie was a little hurt at hearing that she'd been 'put up with' all these years. He said, 'Well, we'll see about all that. I'd be glad to stay a little while at least.'

'And as for helping with your keep,' his daughter said, 'Crowdie says there's sick pay for the first ten weeks, these days. And I 'spect the Miners' Friendly will be round as well – after all, you've paid your dues all these years.'

Madge gave another snort. 'Came while you were sleeping,

or whatever else you were. Told them to come back tomorrow, see how you were then. Going down to see the widow and the boy that's lost his eye. They're the ones who'll need it, as it seems to me.'

Walter felt a wave of grief and guilt break over him. He hadn't thought about poor Tommy Richards and his son – almost as if his brain refused to take it in. 'Poor soul – I don't know how to make it up to her. I was pare-leader; she'll hold me to blame.'

'Don't be so daft, Walt! Everybody knows you hit a faulty seam. The man from the Friendly even told me that they're saying down the mine that if anyone could have avoided it, you would have been the man. Mrs Richards may be bitter against you for a while, but these things happen and in time she'll come to see it was an accident.' His sister came and stood beside him, looking down at him. 'Now you're looking tired again – I think you've had enough. You say goodbye to Effie and she can catch her bus, and when you've had a little sleep I'll bring you up some tea, or perhaps a bit of chicken if you could fancy that?'

She was making an effort to look after him. Chicken was an expensive luxury. He tried to thank her but she had already gone downstairs. Effie was bending over him to kiss him on the cheek and he gave her a smile. 'Thursday then!'

Suddenly, though, he felt immensely weak. Weariness swept over him and he was asleep before she closed the door.

Part Three

August – October 1912

One

Ever since that awful business with the corpse (who had come in asking questions the day before he died), Blanche had felt a little anxious dealing with casual clientele. She dared not mention her concern to Pearl, who would only have scoffed at her timidity, but she did try never to be left alone when there were any strangers in the shop. Of course there weren't usually many of them in any case – a occasional miner's wife on market day who wanted darning wool, or the servant of some visitor looking for fresh lace – but always for the haber-dashery, as naturally 'passing trade' could not be wanting books.

So she was horrified one day, when Pearl was in the town and she herself was kneeling by the shelves, putting the returns back where they ought to be, to hear the shop bell ring and to look up to find a strange man in the library area. She was in quite a taking as she scrambled to her feet.

They did not often have male customers at all. There were one or two subscriptions to the library held by people of what Pearl described as 'the other gender' – but there were not very many, and any case, Blanche knew all of them by sight. But this man she had never seen before.

He was not quite what you'd call a gentleman – a bowler hat with an open Ulster overcoat, showing a lounge suit with a double-breasted waistcoat and what was clearly a false high collar on his shirt – and besides, as she told Pearl afterwards, 'he walked into the shop, no horse-cab waiting or anything like that.'

He was not a servant either, you could tell that at a glance (no servant ever wore a collar quite like that!) but it was clear at once that he was respectable from the way he took his hat off as soon as he came in, and from the courteous nature of his first enquiry.

'Have I the honour of addressing a Miss Weston?' he said

good-naturedly, bowing slightly across his bowler hat and peering at her through his gold-rimmed spectacles.

She hastened to correct him. 'That would be my elder sister, Pearl. She isn't at present on the premises, but I am Miss Blanche Weston, if that is any use?' His formality had transferred itself to her, and she found herself quite flustered and answering in kind. Lovely manners, she thought, approvingly, though it was not a local voice. Sounded more up-country, like their late Papa.

The stranger reached into an inner pocket and produced a silver case from which he drew a little printed card. 'Josiah Broadbent, at your service.' He presented it to her. It was embossed, she noticed. Pearl would be impressed.

She ran her eyes over the wording on the card. 'J. Broadbent – discreet enquiries. Tracing defaulters and creditors a speciality.' And an address in London, of all things. She gave him a quick, embarrassed smile. 'I'm sorry, Mr Broadbent, I fear there's some mistake. You've had a wasted journey, I'm afraid. I don't know who might have told you otherwise, but we are not in need of the kind of service you are offering.' She tried to speak with confidence, but her mind was in a whirl. There was a bit of money owing to them here and there. Surely Pearl had not written to this firm without mentioning the fact?

Josiah Broadbent shook his head at her. His gingery hair was thinning a little at the top, she noticed, though there was nothing thin about the rest of him. He was plump and portly, his waistcoat buttons pulling tight against the strain, while his round face was reddish, with veins around the nose. 'On the contrary, Miss Blanche. It is I who come to you.' His pink forehead obviously tended to be moist because he dabbed at it constantly with a pocket-handkerchief. 'On behalf of a regular client of mine in the capital. Indeed I believe we have already written to you about this matter once – over a week ago, in fact.'

Blanche was absolutely mortified. 'I assure you that we always pay our bills on time!' she snapped. It wasn't quite true, she thought guiltily – they had been a little late this month settling the account with one firm that supplied them with their knitting-wools. 'If it's about that batch of mismatched skeins they sent, I assure you that the dye was different . . .'

He shook his head again. 'I assure you, Miss Blanche Weston, there's no need for alarm. This does not concern your excellent establishment at all – or only indirectly. The fact is, I am searching for a man, whom I believe to have had dealings with you once. There is nothing to be feared. I have news to his advantage, if he can be found.' He reached into the pocket of his overcoat and took out a folded, faded photograph. It showed a young man dressed as a Hussar, standing proudly by a potted palm, his military headgear in his hand. Mr Broadbent handed it to her, saying, 'Is it possible you recognize the face?'

She stared at it. It was a handsome face, framed by a dark mop of curly hair and sporting a fine moustache and side-whiskers, but it bore no resemblance to anyone she knew. She shook her head. 'Who is it, anyway?'

'His name is Artie Royston,' she heard Mr Broadbent say. 'Does that ring a bell with you?'

She handed back the photo and looked up at him, confused. 'I have never heard the name as far as I'm aware. Royston is not a common surname around here.'

He smiled again, a reassuring smile. He had good teeth, she noticed. White and neatly matched – she wondered idly if they were his own. They did such clever things with false sets nowadays. She was suddenly conscious of her own enormous ones and pulled her mouth down firmly over them.

That seemed to convince him that she was displeased and he went on earnestly. 'All the same I have a reason to have called on you. The police in London made enquiries about a certain shirt – apparently it was discovered on a corpse, which in turn had been discovered here.'

That terrible affair again! 'But I understood it wasn't his at all!' she almost wailed. 'There was something in the paper and my sister asked the police – seeing that we had a sort of interest in the case. They told her that the shirt-maker could offer no account – he had made it for a customer who had since gone overseas and he had no idea of how the dead man came by it.'

Josiah Broadbent twinkled. 'That is quite true, my dear, but the shirt-maker in question mentioned it in passing to another customer – a certain Joseph Simms – because Royston had left without settling his account, and he knew that Simms had been a gambling friend of Royston's long ago. Simms passed the information on to me when I approached him in relation to my own enquiry and he offered what may be an explanation of a sort. He tells me he remembers Royston at the races once, after losing heavily and drinking far too much, getting into conversation with a tipster at the bar, and finally staking everything he had – including a shirt of this description – on the outcome of the final race.'

Blanche swallowed, trying not to show how shocked she was. Gambling, like drinking, was the devil's work: the very idea would have her father spinning in his grave; he would never permit playing cards or dice games in the house. But such immoral conduct brought its own reward. 'And losing?' she enquired, remembering that Mr Broadbent's card suggested that he specialized in collecting debts.

Mr Broadbent smiled. 'On the contrary, I understand he won, and after that the shirt became a kind of talisman in Royston's eyes. But he got into betting very heavily, and took violent offence when other people tried to intervene, so he very soon lost touch with all his former friends. The last time my informant saw him, he was down at heel, separated from his wife and child and living off his wits in some dismal attic where he owed the rent. Says he gave him ten shillings for a meal – for old friendship's sake – but could not be sure that Royston would not gamble it away. And when I called at the address there was no Royston there – he'd disappeared a few weeks afterwards, and of course he hadn't paid the landlady. After that I lost the trail.'

Blanche nodded. 'So you came down here? You thought the corpse was Royston?'

'Given that he had the shirt, it did seem probable. But you don't recognize him, so I'll have to think again. It's possible your corpse was indeed some sort of gambling friend who'd won the shirt from Royston in a bet – after all, we know he'd used it as a wager once before.'

'If so, it wouldn't help you, would it?'

'I'm not so sure of that. Royston would not have staked his lucky talisman if he weren't destitute. I doubt he's really gone abroad – he wouldn't have the money for his passage, anyway, and Simms has seen him since – I think that's just a rumour that he put about himself, in order to escape his creditors. If I can trace the dead man's movements in the days before he died, it might give me an indication where to look – he must have been with Royston to have won the shirt from him. I wrote down to make enquiries, both to you and to the local police, but they knew nothing and you did not answer when I wrote – so in the end I came down here myself.'

Blanche was feeling very foolish by this time. It was clear that Pearl had seen this letter and had chosen not to mention it to her – treating her, as usual, as though she were a child. The realisation made her volunteer more information than she might otherwise have done. 'You know that he came here the afternoon before his death? Asking for a maidservant who lives in the town – though she swears she doesn't know him.' The moment she had said it, she regretted it. She was annoyed with Pearl, but her thoughtless words might bring down trouble on poor Effie's head.

But Broadbent was only nodding soberly. 'So I understand, from the butcher's shop next door. Miss Pengelly, isn't it? I expect that I shall have to talk to her, though I believe they didn't meet. Do you know if he spoke to anybody else? We are trying to establish what his movements were that day.'

She was about to answer when the inner door was opened suddenly and Pearl came striding in. 'Ah, here is my sister . . .' Blanche said, helplessly, but attempting to be civil and to keep her manner bright. 'I'm sure that she can be more use to you. Pearl, this is Mr Broadbent. He makes discreet enquiries, apparently. He's got a proper card and everything.'

Pearl's face was like thunder and her eyes were furious, but she bowed the merest greeting. 'Mr Broadbent. I'm Miss Weston, the chief proprietor. May I ask what you are doing in my shop? Blanche, you may leave us.'

Blanche surprised herself by staying where she was, and saying mutinously, 'He says he wrote a letter to us, but of course I had not seen it, so I did not know who he was. It seems he's come to talk to us about that dead man again – although I suppose you know that, since you saw the note. But I think perhaps that I should stay here, Pearl dear, all the same. After all, I was the one who found the corpse.'

She had never defied her sister in this way before and she braced herself for outbursts, but Pearl only snapped, 'As you wish, my dear. On your head be it, if you have nervous palpitations afterwards. I only hoped to spare you suffering.' She turned to Mr Broadbent with an acid smile. 'My sister has an anxious disposition, as you see. I'm most displeased that you have troubled her. I had assumed that, by not responding to your presumptuous communication several weeks ago, I had signalled my unwillingness to entertain you here. In any case there is nothing whatever to report. What we know we have already told the police, and following your letter I asked the girl again and she assured me, with some vigour, that she did not know the man concerned. So, Mr Broadbent, since neither Blanche nor I can be of the remotest assistance with your case, I would ask you to be good enough to leave.'

Blanche was almost speechless with embarrassment, but Mr Broadbent was made of sterner stuff. He bowed politely, smiled and said, as though he were not offended in the least, 'But I am sure that if anything at all should come to light, you two ladies will be good enough to let me know. I am staying for a few days at the Anchor Inn. The matter is important, as I said before. A considerable sum of money is at stake. So if you think of anything – anything at all – be good enough to get in touch with me. Miss Blanche already has my card, I think.'

It was true. Blanche discovered that she was still clutching it, which was rather impolite – she should have returned it to him long ago. She flashed him an apologetic grin. 'Of course we shall be pleased to do anything we can.' She flushed. It was ridiculous. Not ten minutes earlier she'd been upset to find him there but now she was positively loath to let him go.

'We shall mind our own business!' Pearl said snappily. 'And I advise you, Mr Broadbent, to do the same! Now if you have quite finished, we have work to do.'

And Mr Broadbent said, 'Of course! Good afternoon,' and

turned away — but not before he'd given one last private glance at Blanche. She wasn't certain, but she was almost sure he winked! She did not, of course, say anything to Pearl about that, in any case — though her sister wanted to hear every word that had been said and wore her sour face all the afternoon.

'Very well,' she said to Blanche at last. 'We'll say no more about it. I suppose you're not responsible if he comes barging in.' However, she did not demand to see the card, and when Blanche went to bed she put it carefully away in a private hiding-place, behind the photograph in Mother's frame.

'Artie Royston?' Effie stared at the strange man on the doorstep in dismay, shaking her head and handing back the photograph. 'Never heard of anyone of that name in my life. There's an Artie Kellow used to live next door when I was small — I don't suppose it's anything to do with him?' She felt herself turn pink. Arthur Kellow was Peter's pa, of course. She went on hastily, 'I run across his son sometimes, I could give you the address. Come to think of it, he's got your colouring.' She looked at the caller with more interest. His hair, or what was left of it, was much the same colour as Peter's and his dad's — and he was rather stocky like the Kellows too, though he was not much like them round the face.

The stranger shook his head, giving off a faint odour of bay rum and brilliantine. 'You misunderstand me, Miss Pengelly,' he said solemnly. 'I am not enquiring on my own account. This is a business matter.' He moved his bowler to his other hand and felt in his coat pocket to produce a card. 'I specialize in tracing people, that is all, especially where money matters are involved.'

Effie took the proffered card and glanced at it before she gave it back. 'Well . . . Mr Broadbent is it? I don't know why on earth you've come to me.' The mention of debt-collection was a shock to her and she was keen to shut the door. 'You'll get me in trouble with the mistress, next. She doesn't care for callers at the best of times, and she'll start to say that I bring trouble to the house.'

Mr Broadbent took a backward pace, and almost toppled down the steps on to the street. 'My dear Miss Pengelly! Of course I do not wish to cause alarm. But surely your employer would permit me a moment of your time . . .'

She shook her head. 'You don't know Mrs Thatchell. She'll threaten to dismiss me, if she sees me chattering.'

He looked at her oddly. 'Yet I understand there was another man who was enquiring for you, too, the day before he died? Sometime in the middle of last year?'

She felt a rush of panic. 'I don't know who told you, but it's true enough – though at least he never came knocking at the door! And I don't know who he was either.'

Mr Broadbent gave a little bow. 'But that is precisely why I've to see you now. Miss Blanche Weston mentioned it to me.' He had not actually put his foot in the door, but he stood so close against the sill he might as well have done. But he was smiling and the mention of Miss Blanche made her feel less anxious, too. If he knew the Westons he was probably respectable. He was saying smoothly, 'You see, I believe that the man who died was either Captain Royston or a friend of his.'

'Well, what about it?' she said ungraciously. 'Either way, I didn't know him – so if he owes money you will have to look elsewhere. The police know all about it – perhaps you should ask them. Now, if you will excuse me . . .'

He did not move an inch. 'I assure you, Miss Pengelly, there is no need for alarm. And as for owing money, it is quite the opposite. Captain Royston had a wife and child – estranged – who died quite recently. Mrs Royston has no surviving relatives, and as they were not formally divorced her estate would pass to him. If he's alive, that is. I am trying to trace him to inform him of the fact – otherwise the money will go to Chancery. The Captain would be very glad to see me, I am sure – the sum involved is more than adequate to pay his debts – and I in turn would like to find him and so ensure my fee.'

Effie found that she was nodding. Suddenly this business did not seem so terrible. 'I see! So let's hope that it wasn't Captain Royston lying dead in the court. It could be, I suppose – though if so you wouldn't know him from that photograph. That must have been taken years and years ago. Poor fellow – it would be awful, wouldn't it, if it turned out to be him?

Starved and frozen to death, when a bob or two would certainly have saved his life and he had money coming to him all the time! Let's hope it wasn't him, and it was just his friend.' She frowned. 'Either way, it doesn't tell us why he wanted me.'

Broadbent looked at her. 'It's possible he didn't. Have you thought of that? It may be that it was just a feint—'

'A faint?' she interrupted.

'An excuse for asking questions round the town. Going into shops, for instance, where it was warm and dry. Starving people do get desperate. He may have hoped to look around for things to steal and pawn – or even hawk around the villages. I've known such things before. And I notice, Miss Blanche says that he did not ask for your address – and you say he did not call here. Don't you think he'd do so, if he really wanted you?'

Effie stared at him. She hadn't thought of that – but it was obvious when you considered it. 'But where would he get my name from? He must have known it – to do this "fainting" thing and ask Miss Blanche for me.'

Mr Broadbent nodded. 'Overheard it somewhere in the town, perhaps, and simply seized on it. These fellows can be crafty when they try. And that's where you can help me with my enquiries. I am trying to trace his movements earlier in the day, and this may be a clue. Who knows your name and might have mentioned you? Any of the tradesmen, for example, in the town?'

Effie shrugged. 'I can't imagine who. Mrs Thatchell has accounts, of course, with the grocer's and the laundry and that sort of thing, but if they were talking about us they'd use her name, not mine. I suppose that my Aunt's butcher might have mentioned me – I go in there from time to time to pay money off her bill – and I've got boots for mending in the shoemakers; they'll be in my name.' She thought a moment. Was it fair to mix Lettie up in this? But then she added, 'And I do have a friend, in service in the town, who's very friendly with the grocer's boy. They might have talked about me, I suppose.' She was about to mention Alex Dawes as well, when it occurred to her that it was not relevant. She had only met him after the unknown man was dead.

But Mr Broadbent seemed already satisfied. 'Well, that gives

me several openings to try. And I'll call in at the police station
as well, in case they have more information since I wrote.'

She felt herself turn scarlet. 'The police station!' She glanced
behind her, but there was nobody nearby to overhear. She
took a step towards him, and said in a lower voice, 'If you are
going down there in any case, would it be possible for you to
take a note for me? I've nearly written it.' She fished into her
pocket for the little notebook which Alex Dawes had given
her at Christmas time. 'I haven't quite finished but it will have
to do – I don't know how I'm going to get it to him else. I
was hoping to be sent on some errand to the town, but nobody's
wanted anything today.' She tore out the sheet and was handing
it to him, when it occurred to her she had no envelope and
she didn't want people reading what she'd said. She half-
withdrew it, adding sheepishly, 'Though I haven't even signed
it, when I come to look. And I haven't got an envelope to
put it in.'

'But I have! I've been carrying the photograph in one!' He
produced it from his pocket, shook Captain Royston out and
put her little scrap of note inside. 'It is a little dog-eared and
we don't have sealing-wax for it, but it will serve I'm sure.'
She tried to thank him but he waved her words aside. 'Glad
to be of service. Just tell me who it's for?'

Effie knew her face was even redder as she said, keeping
her voice as low as possible, 'Constable Dawes, his name is,
Alexander Dawes. I'm sure he'll guess who wrote it, but can
you tell him that it came from me?'

He nodded, but he did not put it in his pocket as she'd
hoped, but stood there looking at it doubtfully. It made Effie
nervous. 'This is nothing to do with the Royston case, I
suppose?' he said at last.

'Nothing at all.' Oh my stars, there was someone on the
stairs! How could she put this when she might be overheard?
She leaned forward and muttered in an undertone. 'Thing is,
my father's had an accident and this is just a note to let the
policeman know . . .' She broke off as a strident voice came
from the passageway behind her. Mrs Thatchell was by the
stairwell, leaning on her stick.

'Effie! What are you doing out there on the step? I won't

have you gossiping to people on the street. I'm not expecting callers. Come back here at once!' And she went into the morning room and slammed the door.

'The mistress,' Effie half-whispered. 'I shall have to go.'

Mr Broadbent nodded and, to her relief, pocketed her note to Alex with a smile. 'And if there's a reply?'

She shook her head. She hadn't thought of that – but Alex would know better than try to reach her here. 'Tell him there's no answer.'

A nod. 'Then I shall leave you. Perhaps we'll meet again. If I have any information I will pass it on to you – and perhaps you would be good enough to do the same. Miss Blanche knows where to find me, if you need to be in touch.'

He bowed, put his hat on and set off down the street.

Effie hurried back into the morning room, where Mrs Thatchell was already picking at her embroidery. She looked up, her face like thunder and her voice like ice. 'And who, pray, was that? Surely not another message from the mine?' Then, as Effie shook her head, 'I trust you are not about to tell me that you have admirers?'

'No, madam,' Effie said as humbly as she could. 'It was a man from London. He seems to know Miss Blanche. Said he was on business . . .'

Her employer cut her off. 'Well, I am surprised at you. You should have sent him packing instantly. We don't encourage hawkers! If I want silks I shall buy them from the shop. And I expect all tradesmen to call around the back. So you can tell him so, if he's impertinent enough to call again.' She turned away to match a piece of thread.

Effie was sufficiently flustered to exclaim, 'Not that sort of business, Madam. He was asking for a man – some missing man I'd never heard of in my life. Something about money that was owed to him.' She was on the verge of mentioning the connection with the corpse, but thought better of it.

Mrs Thatchell's face was white with anger as it was. 'Indeed? And what has that to do with you?'

'Nothing, Madam, and I told him so.'

Mrs Thatchell pursed her lips a little more and nodded curtly. 'And I should think so too! So, we'll let that suffice. I don't imagine that the man will call again – but if he does, refer him straight to me. I will not have my servants enter-taining strangers on the step. Is that understood?'

Effie murmured that it was.

'Then if you have quite finished with these interruptions, you may go down and fetch my tray!'

Alex had just finished on the beat and was returning to report when a man in a bowler hat accosted him.

'Ah, Constable! The very man I need.'

Alex looked at the speaker with distaste: an oily person with a florid face, smelling of sweat, bay rum and cheap cologne, wearing once-slick city fashions but rather down at heel. His policeman's eye took in the tell-tale signs – worn elbows on the jacket, well-mended boots and travel-stains on the Ulster overcoat he carried on his arm. He braced himself for the sort of hard-luck tale of theft that ended with a plea for sixpence for the bus. But he recalled his training and said, with courtesy, 'How can I help you?'

The answer surprised him. 'I'm looking for the police station, Constable. Can you direct me? I'm a stranger here.'

'As it happens, I'm returning there myself – so if you would like to follow me?'

'That would be most kind,' the man replied, trotting after Alex with alacrity. When they reached the door the stranger paused. 'There's a man called Jenkins that I'm looking for. He sent me a letter, I have got it here.'

'I'll see if I can find him,' Alex said. 'If you would be kind enough to wait?'

'The name is Broadbent,' said the stranger, handing him a card. 'I wrote some time ago. I think your colleague will remember me.'

Alex nodded. 'I'll tell him you are here.' He put his head around the inner door where Jenkins was tapping at the type-writing machine. 'There's someone here to see you.' He handed him the card.

Jenkins glanced at it. 'You'd better show him in.' But it was obvious that he did not recognize the name, because as Alex ushered in the visitor, Jenkins said to him, 'Constable Dawes informs me that you've asked for me by name.'

Broadbent turned to Alex with a smile. 'You're Dawes?' he murmured. 'Now that is fortunate. I can give you this directly.' He produced from his pocket a dog-eared envelope and handed it to Alex with a bow. 'I have not had the opportunity to write your name on it, but it's from Miss Pengelly. I promised her I would deliver it. She says she is not wanting a reply.'

Alex took it from him and beat a swift retreat under the mocking eyes of Jenkins – who was certain to rag him later on. He tore it open. It was written in indelible pencil on a piece of lined paper, torn from the notebook he had given her himself.

'Dear Alex, I don't know if you were expecting us to meet this week in any case, as I understand from Lettie that you usually dine at Major Knight's on Thursdays nowadays, but this is a note to say that I can't be there. There has been a nasty—' – there was a fragment missing where she'd torn out the page – ''cident' (did that mean 'incident' perhaps?) 'at home, so I had to take an extra day last week, and now I have to work this week to make up the time. Even if I was free, I'd want to go back home, the way things are at present, as I'm sure you'll understand. Hoping that this finds you well as it leaves me.' There was no signature.

For a moment he just stared at it. From 'Miss Pengelly', the bowler-hatted man had said. And she wanted no reply. It seemed that Effie had turned the tables on him, properly. There had clearly been some sort of incident at home – probably her uncle nagging her again – and she had decided that she would not meet him any more.

And one could hardly blame her. He had forgotten that the Lettie girl would have been telling tales, and would know that he had been out riding with the Knight girl several times and dining with her nearly every week. Of course it was not serious – or so he told himself – but how could Effie be expected to know that?

No wonder he had seen her with that young fellow in the

cart! The sort of chap her family would approve of, too. Alex jammed his helmet on again and went out on to the street. He was entitled to half an hour for lunch, but he didn't take it; he went straight back on patrol. He couldn't bear to face Jenkins and his teasing after this – and fortunately he was working up Trevarnon way, which kept him as far as possible from Mrs Thatchell's house.

Two

Jenkins did catch up with him in the end, of course. He came in while Alex was lying on the bed that night, pretending to be engrossed in studying the police manual again by the light of the flickering candle on the bedside chest. Jenkins put his own nightlight down and gave his roommate a knowing leer.

'You'll wear that Black Book out entirely, if you don't look out,' he said, taking off his jacket and stripping to his vest. He went over to the wash-stand and poured out some cold water from the jug. 'If you don't know the rules of giving evidence by now, then there's no help for you.' He slipped his braces down around his waist and plunged his face and whiskers into the washing bowl. He came up sputtering and groped for the towel, saying as he rubbed his glowing skin, 'What became of you this morning, anyway? You got that letter and then you disappeared. What happened? Your Miss Pengelly write to summon you?'

Alex slammed the Black Book firmly shut – he hadn't succeeded in looking at it anyway. 'No, of course she didn't. Quite the opposite! As it happens we've decided not to meet – for the present, anyway. As if it were any business of yours.'

Jenkins gave a little whistle of astonishment – amazing how sardonic he contrived to make it sound! 'Well there is a turn-up for the book and no mistake. Given you your marching orders, has she, after all? Well, you'll have no qualms about riding and dining with your heiress now.'

'As it happens I am dining with Miss Caroline this week.' He had written after getting Effie's note, to confirm the fact. 'Though that has nothing at all to do with it.'

Jenkins grinned. 'So you won't be interested to know that the "unidentified" we had last year – the one who was asking for your Effie in the town – may have been in line for an inheritance himself, according to that Broadbent fellow who called in today. Pity he brought that letter when he did. You might be sorry that you've broken off with her.'

Alex sat up sharply. He could not help himself. 'What do you mean by that?'

Jenkins poured the dirty water into the waiting pail and took down a pair of scissors from the hook. 'It's rather a long story,' he began. It *was* a long story, made longer by Jenkins trimming his whiskers between sentences and pulling strange faces in the shaving-glass. When he had finished he examined the effect – with apparent satisfaction – and swept the hairs into a paper bag, before he turned to Alex. 'So there you are, old man. You can see what this might mean for Effie!'

Alex had been listening to the tale with interest, of course, but he found himself saying, quite impatiently, 'No I damned well can't. What's it to do with her?'

Jenkins was pulling on his nightshirt by this time and there was a pause until his head emerged from it. He grinned at Alex, looking, in the long white robe, like some comic spirit in a pantomime. 'Why, Dawes! Of course, you always were an innocent, but surely it must have occurred to you by now that she's probably the natural daughter of this Royston chap? So if it turns out that he really was the corpse, she might have a claim on this inheritance.'

Alex shook his head, determinedly. 'I have seen her father, and she's the living spit of him.'

Jenkins refused to be deflected from his theory by this inconvenient fact. 'But think about it. What else could it be – the girl is exactly of an age to have been Royston's child and Broadbent says that he was famed among his friends for his conquests among the fairer sex. "A weakness for fillies – with two legs or four – that's what ruined him" – according to one acquaintance, it said in the report. What could be more natural than for him to have a fling with some attractive woman that he came across down here?'

'What would Royston have been doing in these parts? And how would he "come across" poor Pengelly's wife, who lived out at Penvarris all her days? It would be a wonder if she ever came to town, except on market days.' Alex was unaccountably annoyed. 'Hardly going to meet this dashing Royston for a fling, when she's been tramping miles along the lanes and she's got a basketful of eggs and butter on her arm. Anyway, is there any evidence that he'd been here before – even supposing that the corpse was his?'

'We're still not positive it was,' Jenkins said, carefully answering only the last enquiry. He had taken his nether garments off by now and was padding in his stockinged feet across the floor to put his trousers underneath his mattress where he 'pressed' them overnight. 'Broadbent thought it might be, but he's changed his mind and now he thinks it was most likely one of Royston's friends – but even so, he might have been asking for your Effie around town because he'd heard she was in line for this inheritance. Hoped to beg or borrow some of it, perhaps, or lure the girl into a liaison of some sort.'

Alex stared at him in disbelief. 'Broadbent told you that?'

'Not exactly,' Jenkins said, sitting on his bed to brush his boots. 'He pretends to think that the enquirer simply latched upon her name because he heard it mentioned in the town – but I don't believe that for a moment. No,' he breathed on the leather and buffed it with his sleeve. 'This money is at the back of this affair – you take my word for it.'

Alex stood up and he too began to strip. 'Well, I don't believe your theory about Effie's parentage. I can't see that Royston would pick a country girl – with no city manners and no doubt married young – even if he had the opportunity.'

Jenkins had got into bed and blew his candle out, pulling the bedclothes up around his neck. 'Why not? I expect she was pretty, like her daughter is!'

Alex pulled his shirt off. 'Well, where would he meet her, even if she were? A girl like that would likely have started down the mine as soon as she was eight or nine years old. And how would he ever have learned that she'd borne his child? I doubt if she could write, except perhaps her name! I don't suppose she ever went to school – it wasn't free in those days and times were very hard.' He splashed fresh water from the jug and rinsed his face and neck.

'Only a penny.' Jenkins was in a stubborn mood tonight. 'Hardly a fortune for her parents, even then.'

'That just shows how little you understand! It was a lot of money for a miner, then – and it's most unlikely they'd have scraped it up, especially for a girl.' If Jenkins could be dogged, Alex could be, too. 'And she'd be brought up strictly Methodist – just like Effie is. What would a handsome roué see in somebody like that?' He rubbed his teeth with a dentifrice and rinsed his mouth.

'He might have done it out of devilment.' Jenkins still refused to let the matter drop. 'According to Broadbent he was notorious – his friends say he could charm the witches from the waves.'

'Well, he would have to cast a spell or two himself, to be Effie's father!' Alex was quite vexed. He climbed into his nightshirt. 'I told you, she's a Pengelly through and through, the very image of her father and her aunt. Well, of course she is. What else would you expect? You're inventing mysteries where there are none. Anyway, I don't know what it's got to do with you. It isn't even much to do with me, now that we've decided not to meet again. So will you let it rest?'

He blew out his nightlight and got into bed, turning his face towards the wall, although it was a long time before he got to sleep. Perversely, when he did, he dreamt of Caroline.

Walter was sick and tired of lying uselessly in bed. It had seemed like a week of Christmases at first, staying lazy, tucked up in the warm, while the house and street were full of other people going to work. But that had quickly palled. Now when he heard the footsteps and the daily grumblings – 'Mornin' Arry – damty cold and wet today!' – instead of revelling in the chance to rest, he found he was wishing he was out there with them, in the rain, with a mine to go to and a job to do.

He stared at the embroidered text hung on the wall. 'Count your blessings.' Well perhaps he should – if you knew exactly what your blessings were. How many times had he complained, across the years, of having not a minute where he could sit and think – and now he was cursed with quite the opposite! He'd become a useless thing, a stick of furniture: that was the worst of it. Even small children had their chores to do, and the white-haired old men who hobbled round on sticks, too old and sick to work, at least had company – they met up every day, either in the Miner's Arms or on the bench outside – and he could hear their high-pitched cackles as they shared their memories.

He could not even read. There were no books in Madge's house, not even a text on mining like he had at home; only a huge Bible – far too big to read in bed. He had counted the different patches on the patchwork quilt, read that damty text until he was in danger of wearing out his eyes, and set himself a hundred sums to do (mostly concerning rocks and dynamite) but it was no good at all. He was chafing to be up and doing and he told his sister so.

'If I 'ad some crutches I could come downstairs a bit. Sole the shoes or something – like you said before.'

'Don't be so silly, Walter. The doctor said that it would be another week at least. Count yourself lucky and try to get some rest.' She picked up his cup and saucer and looked down at him. 'Though if you're really fretting, I could find some chores for you.'

And she had done her best: bringing him onions to thread onto a string, a heap of washing to fold and damp for ironing and today – more humiliating still – standing a wooden chair beside his bed, and showing him how to loop a skein of wool across the back to keep it taut while he wound it inexpertly into a ball. 'And when you've finished that one, you'll find a dozen more inside that paper bag. Save me no end of time when I am knitting socks.'

He nodded. It was mind-numbingly tedious and he wasn't sure it saved her anything – it took so long to bring things up and show him what to do – but at least it was better than staring at the wall. But it was woman's work, and he was not sorry, a little later on, to hear her calling cheerfully upstairs. 'Walter, can you hear me? You've got a visitor. Fellow from the mine. I've got the soup on boiling and I can't leave the stove. Is it all right if I send him up?'

Dear Heaven! That would be Captain Maddern, calling round again, as he had done several times this week. He couldn't let a fellow-miner find him winding wool, like a great girl. 'Half a minute!' Walter took the current wool-skein off the chair and stuffed it in the basket out of sight. He would likely cause a tangle, he realized that of course, but that could not be helped. He dropped the basket down beside him on the floor and leaned back on his pillows in a manly pose, before he called back down. 'All right, Cap'n, I'm ready for you now.'

But it wasn't Jack Maddern who came up the stairs: it was Artie Kellow's boy. He had obviously just come from the mine, although he was dressed in 'walking-home' clothes now and he'd clearly taken pains when washing and changing at the 'dry' – even his boots were dusted as he stood there at the door, turning his grey cap nervously between his big scrubbed hands, his broad, good-natured face the colour of his newly slicked red hair.

'Evenin', Mr Pengelly, sir,' this apparition said. 'Or I should say, "good afternoon". I was on the early shift today – thought I'd call by and see how you were getting on.'

Walter murmured, 'Kind of you, I'm sure,' but his mind was working overtime. What on earth was this young miner doing here?

Kellow coughed and made a gesture towards the empty chair. 'Is it all right if I . . .?'

'Of course, young fellow. Sit down, sit down do!' Walter said with sudden guilty heartiness. It occurred to him that something must have happened at the mine to bring Peter Kellow calling, so he added anxiously, as the young man pulled the chair up closer to the bed, 'News then, is there?'

Peter shook his head. 'Nothing in particular. Just thought you'd like a call, keep you up to date with how things are down there. Jack Maddern told me he'd been in once or twice – did he tell you that there'd been another fall along that seam? No one hurt though, that time – which is just as well. On the look-out for it, I suppose, after what happened to you and poor old Tom.'

'How's the Richards boy then?' Walter heard himself enquire, though he tried not to think about that eyeless socket more than he could help.

Peter made a doubtful face. 'Sad business that was. Lost that eye of course, and the other one is damaged, never be the same, though they think he'll have a bit of sight in it – enough to work up at the shaking-tables, perhaps, or even fetching for the carpenter. Don't know what will come of the poor lad otherwise, but they had a whip-round for him at the mine, in any case – and the Miners' Friendly has made a contribution too, so that will help the family manage for a little while.' His ears had turned an even brighter shade of pink. 'I saw Mrs Richards in the street, in fact, when I was coming here tonight. Says she means to come and have a word with you herself.'

Walter gave an inward sigh. I'll bet she does, he thought. And I have no excuse to offer her. All those years of training and experience – and what do I bring her family, but injury and loss? He shook his head. 'Poor woman, she must blame me for drilling where I did.'

Peter stared at him. 'Course it was devastating for her, losing Tom like that, and she blamed everyone at first – but what she said to me was, when she thought it out, if it was not for you she would not have Jimmy either. Wanted to come and thank you, is what she said to me – and as for the bad rock, don't blame yourself for that. Everybody knows that was an accident. If you didn't spot it no-one could have done. Cap'n Maddern told me once that I should study you, because you could read rock better'n anybody else he ever met. You remember that new stope that they were going to cut . . .'

And they were still talking mining when Madge came up the stairs. 'Walter Pengelly, are you still chattering? I declare, you've got less sense than Farmer Crowdie's goose! Supposed to be resting, that's what the doctor said, and here you are, holding an audience like the King and Queen.'

Peter Kellow had turned pink again. 'I'm some sorry, Mrs Martin, I don't mean to wear him out,' he said earnestly. He was already on his feet and edging to the door. 'Only thought he might like a bit of gossip from the mine.'

'And so I did,' Walter retorted, sticking up for him. 'It's my ankle that I'm resting, not my tongue. Won't hurt my leg to have a bit of chat. In fact, I do believe it's done me good. Give me something sensible to think about.' He smiled at Peter.

'Some glad to hear it!' Peter pulled his cap out and seemed about to jam it on his head. 'Well, I'll be off then!' But he didn't go. Instead he hesitated for a moment at the door, then seemed to pluck up courage and turned back again. 'Be all right if I came again, some time?'

Madge looked at him coldly and replied, as though Walter wasn't there, 'That's kind of you, I'm sure. But I can't see why you'd want to do a thing like that. 'Tisn't as if you were working in his pare. Young man like you – haven't you got a family of your own, will want you home?'

Peter had turned scarlet but he held his ground. 'Thing is, Mrs Martin, I feel involved in this. I was the one they sent into Penzance to tell Miss Effie about the accident and bring her back out here on Crowdie's cart. Didn't seem right to come in with her then, but stands to reason that I wanted to enquire.'

Walter looked thoughtfully at him. Effie, eh? And today was Thursday, by his reckoning. Was that why Peter Kellow was so interested in his health, all of a sudden? Well, it had to happen some day – Joe was right in that. And if it did happen, Effie could do worse. Nice boys, the Kellows, all hard-working like their dad. He said, casual-like, 'Well it's nice of you. Matter of fact, Effie generally belongs to come herself on Thursday, but she couldn't do, this week – cause she took that time off to come and see me and so she had to work this afternoon in lieu. Be here next week, I should think, and I'm sure she'd want to thank you, if you happened to look by.'

Young Kellow had turned the colour of iron water from the mine. 'I'll come in again then – let you know what's happening down the mine. If Mrs Martin doesn't think I'll wear you out, that is.'

'I suppose so!' Madge gave a doubtful sniff. 'Since Walter says you can. I have to say you've brightened him a bit. A bit of company won't do him any harm.'

So she hadn't put two and two together, like he had, Walter thought – never saw that it was Effie that the boy had come to see! Just as well, or Madge might have forbidden him to come, and it had been nice to talk to someone who knew life underground, for Joe only brought home news that reached the surface-men. He said, with feeling, 'I would be glad to see you, Peter, any time at all! Enjoyed our bit of chat.'

It was enough to make his sister say, a little grudgingly,

'Well, come back if you want to, but keep it short next time. I don't want him exhausted. I've got enough to do, to keep him occupied, without him wanting nursing all the time.' She turned to Walter. 'And that reminds me, what's happened to my wool? I thought you were going to wind it up for me.'

You would think that she would have more sense than to say that right out loud, in front of company! But Peter Kellow – mercifully – had felt himself dismissed, and had already pulled his cap on and tiptoed down the stairs.

Blanche Weston was just walking past the Anchor Inn when she saw the familiar figure coming out of it.

'Why, Mr Broadbent, what a happy accident!' she cried, waving her folded umbrella in salute. (It was not entirely an accident, in fact; she had timed her arrival for the sort of time he might have finished breakfast and be ready to go out and she had already walked round the block three times.)

He saw her approaching and doffed his bowler hat. 'Miss Blanche!' He seemed delighted, making her turn pink. (Pity, when she had purposely picked out her dark-red gown and coat; she must look like a petunia!) But he looked quite approving as he went on, affably, 'To what do I owe the pleasure? Did you have something you wished to say to me – some information that might be of help?'

She had been practising her answer all the way from home – a tiny detail or two that she could offer as excuse – but now that she had actually met him face to face her wits deserted her. Instead of the pretty little speech that she'd prepared she found herself stammering, 'Well, not really, no. I simply happened to be passing this way, that is all.' As soon as she had said the words she wished devoutly that she could call them back.

It was absurd. The Anchor Inn was right beside the sea and apart from rope-makers and riggers and that sort of thing there was nowhere in the area she could be heading for.

Broadbent must have known that but he swept a little bow. 'Well, I shall count myself most fortunate. Indeed if you've completed your business hereabouts perhaps I could escort you back into the town?'

It was more than she had dreamt of; all she had envisaged was a brief, polite exchange. But to walk her back into Penzance! What a thrilling thought! She was torn between the guilty temptation to agree and the near certainty that they would be observed and someone would mention her foolishness to Pearl. However, Mr Broadbent – 'Josiah' as she called him to herself – would be returning to London very soon, and having spent such pains in running into him she could not let him go without regretting it. Pearl could be dealt with later.

She gave him a smile, painfully aware of her enormous teeth. 'That would be delightful – though perhaps we could walk up through the alleyway, rather than the street? That way we are less likely to be seen – people talk so in a town like this!'

He twinkled at her. 'In that case, may I tempt you to some tea instead? There is a little tea room up there on the way, which will just be open at this time of day. I have frequented it once or twice before – and can recommend the tea and toast. Perhaps you would care to step inside where we can talk without being subject to so many prying eyes?'

'Really, Mr Broadbent! That's very kind of you. But do you think it wise? On such short acquaintance?' Blanche was all aflutter. She had never taken morning tea, alone in male company, in all her thirty years. But sadly propriety must be observed, so she added, 'After all, we've scarcely met. I should not care to give the wrong impression if my sister – for instance – should come to hear of it.' She knew that she had gone that ugly pink again. 'I am quite sure that she would not approve.'

He looked at her shrewdly. 'Then we must take care it does not come to her attention,' he replied. 'The tea shop is the very place. If you would care to take my arm . . .?' She thought his touch would brand her very flesh as he guided her gently up the alleyway she'd been referring to. In fact it was a good thing that she did have his support, for it was cobbled under-foot and rather treacherous, though obviously she had not known that when she spoke – it was so dark and narrow it was not a route she'd ever used before.

Halfway up there was a junction where it crossed another lane, and there, indeed, stood a little tea shop, though it seemed that it was closed. There was a printed notice saying so, but the door was half-open and through the window-glass you could see a waitress in a black uniform getting down the chairs, which had clearly been placed upside-down on tables overnight.

The girl saw them looking and said politely, 'I'm sorry, we don't open until half past ten. That's five minutes yet.'

Blanche was disappointed and about to turn away but Mr Broadbent was made of sterner stuff. He smiled at the waitress in his most winning way. 'Now that is a pity – since I've been here before, and I was strongly recommending your buttered toast and jam.' He kept on smiling but did not move an inch.

The girl looked at him with more interest. 'Oh yes, sir, I remember.' She glanced around, as if someone might observe, then gave a skittish laugh. 'Well, seeing that it's you, sir, and you've been before! The owner isn't here till later on, but I could make an exception for a few minutes I suppose.'

And a moment later he was guiding Blanche into the shop. 'Thank you, young lady!' he murmured to the girl. He looked around the room. 'Would it be possible – that table over there, in the little alcove at the back?' He dropped his voice. 'This lady and I have business to discuss – a tricky matter of an inheritance – and naturally we should prefer to be discreet.' He tapped one pudgy finger against his fleshy nose as though the waitress was a co-conspirator. 'I am sure that we can rely on you to see that we're not overheard?'

The girl was clearly flattered by this show of confidence. She coloured prettily and led the way towards the table he had specified. She got the chairs down, set them round and spread a table cloth. 'Will it be tea and buttered toast and jam for two, sir?' she enquired and when Josiah told her that it would she pottered off to get it straight away.

Blanche looked at her companion as he hung up their outdoor coats. He was not handsome – very far from that – but it was obvious he had a way with him. 'Charm', that was the word that she was looking for. No doubt in his profession it was a requisite but it was pleasant all the same. A charming male companion who was buying her some tea. It was quite the most exciting moment of her life – especially sweet, because she knew that Pearl would disapprove.

Her host had sat down opposite by now and was smiling at her across the table cloth. 'What did I tell you? They're most obliging here. Now then, my dear Miss Blanche Weston, what is it you sought me out to say? It's obvious that you must have had something on your mind; I can't believe you merely desired my company.'

Oh but I did, Josiah, she murmured inwardly, but aloud she said, 'There was a little matter which occurred to me. The man you came about. I believe there was a railway ticket in his coat. I don't know if you were aware of that.' There! She had remembered something new to offer him.

He received it gravely. 'Ah, yes, the ticket! We did know that, in fact. It was part of the information that the police sent on to us, and it was even mentioned in the papers, I believe.'

She nodded. 'That's where I learned of it. The return half of a ticket, so they said, but so damaged by the rain that it was impossible to see where it was issued from.'

'The police did not have much hope that it would lead us anywhere,' he agreed, 'but working on the assumption that it was Royston or his friend and that they were likely to have come from Paddington third-class, I had my own enquiries made.' He leaned forward and murmured confidentially, 'And I understand that a guard has now been found who thinks he may have seen the passenger. The early train, third-class carriage, the day before the death.' He paused for her approval, leaning back again.

She obliged him by saying, admiringly, 'That was clever of him. There must have been scores of people on that train.'

Josiah looked decidedly gratified at this. 'He noticed him because he looked so frail and ill, appeared to have no luggage with him, sought the last compartment, spoke to nobody and seemed to take no refreshment of any kind throughout the trip – though the guard could not be absolutely sure of that because the third-class compartments were non-corridor and he could only look in from time to time when the train was at a station. However after Plymouth the man appeared to be asleep, so he left him to it and thought no more of it – until our agent spoke to him, that is. I got a wire from London only yesterday. It's in my pocket now.' He pulled back the collar of his jacket so that she could glimpse the yellow telegram within, but at the moment the waitress reappeared from the kitchen at the rear carrying their tray of tea and toast.

The toast was excellent: fresh, hot and buttery and there was a little glass container full of home-made jam. Blanche was almost in an ecstasy. This was so different from their tea-time toast at home – which Pearl insisted on making personally on a toasting-fork beside their meagre fire, so it was generally tepid, undercooked and served with just a scrape of butter or of jam – never both, of course, because 'these things don't grow on trees'. It made Blanche feel like a naughty child to take a bit of each.

Her host however seemed delighted by her pleasure in his treat. He even urged her to another slice, but she remembered that a lady did not ever eat too much and that polite conversation was expected at the tea-table. Besides a dreadful thought had just occurred to her. 'So no doubt you'll be returning to London very soon?' she murmured, stickily.

Josiah shook his head. 'On the contrary, my dear Miss Blanche,' he said. 'It makes my task here more pressing than before. If it can be proved that it was Royston on that train, it is quite certain that he outlived his wife and therefore was entitled to inherit her estate. We can be fairly certain of the date. With all the recent railway strikes, there was a change of schedules, and it was the first day that the guard had ever worked that route. This could have implications for Miss Pengelly too – if we can discover why he wanted her. But you are quite certain that this was not the man who called?' He had pulled out the famous photograph again – though it was getting rather creased and was no longer in the envelope.

She took it from him and gazed more closely at the bewhiskered young hussar, smiling so proudly into the camera. Perhaps she could summon up some faint resemblance? Something that would keep Josiah here in town, to ask more questions? 'Well, I suppose it could be,' she said reluctantly 'There is an outside chance.' She found that she was shaking her head though, without intending to, so she forced herself to stop and added carefully, 'This fellow is roughly the right height, perhaps.'

'You think so?' Josiah had a sudden look of hopefulness which made her gulp.

She could not deceive him, she decided ruefully. 'Perhaps a little shorter, it is hard to tell. But if so, he must have changed an awful lot since then.'

Josiah put the picture carefully away. 'Thank you for your honesty, my dear Miss Blanche.'

There it was! He'd called her 'dear' again. She could hardly pretend that he meant anything by that — it was just avuncular friendship and concern — but it made her heart beat faster all the same. But Josiah was still speaking. She forced herself to pay attention to his words.

'That young Pengelly woman told me just the same — though her mistress was displeased with her for taking time to tell me anything. It seems I'm fated to cause problems when I call.' He gave a conspiratorial grin.

Blanche turned scarlet. He was talking about Pearl; you could see that from his smile! She said, to cover her embarrassment, 'Did Effie tell you anything of use?'

He nodded. 'One or two leads that I must follow up. She has a friend for instance, who is maid at a large house, I understand — I shall have to find her, though after my experience calling at Mrs Thatchell's house I am not disposed to seek her out at work.'

'That will be Lettie Pearson!' she exclaimed, delighted to have real information to impart. 'If you want to see her, you could find her at the shop — she comes in on a Tuesday with her mistress's books to change, and she'll be in uniform.' Why did she turn scarlet all the time, when she was talking to this man? It was a perfectly sensible suggestion, after all. 'Or perhaps it would be better to talk to her nearby,' she amended hastily. 'My sister . . .'

He looked at her gravely. 'Ah, yes! Your sister Pearl. You think she would object if I came in the shop?'

Blanche said feebly, 'She keeps a very close eye on me, of course — she always has. As the elder sister, she feels responsible though sometimes I think she treats me like a child.' As soon as she had said it, she realized what she'd done — made it clear that she had a personal interest in seeing him again. She wished for a moment that the tearoom floor would open up and swallow her alive. 'I mean . . . that is . . .' she trailed off in dismay.

But Josiah was smiling. 'My dear Miss Blanche, do I understand aright? I'd thought of suggesting that we might meet again – that you'd come and have another cup of tea with me perhaps, but I wasn't sure that you'd agree, bearing in mind your sister's attitude. Do I dare to hope that I was wrong?'

She was turning that unbecoming shade of red again. 'I would be very pleased to see you, Mr Broadbent,' she mumbled awkwardly, though Heaven knew how she was going to deal with Pearl. 'Merely for a cup of tea of course,' she added hastily.

He put on a comic, disappointed face. 'But I was hoping to buy you buttered toast and jam!'

She saw that he was teasing and it made her laugh, which helped to stifle her embarrassment. 'Shall we say tomorrow morning, if I can get away? Or the next day perhaps, since you want to talk to Lettie tomorrow when she comes.' It occurred to her that she might see him then in any case.

'Wednesday morning, then.' He was getting to his feet, reaching for his wallet to pay the bill. He walked over to the counter where the waitress was arranging a display of home-made buns. He dropped his voice and murmured something to the girl. Blanche found that she was straining both her ears to hear, but all he said was, 'Wednesday morning, at about this time of day. Could you reserve that table for us, do you think?' Then he was back to help her with her coat and walk her up the alleyway towards the town. At the top he left her and she walked home in a dream.

Pearl was waiting in the doorway of the shop, her mouth pulled downwards in a disapproving frown. 'Good heavens, Blanche, wherever have you been? You only went to buy a pack of matches, I believe.'

Blanche looked at her sister, arms akimbo on the step, and something in her gentle soul rebelled. To her own astonishment, she heard herself reply, 'And so I did, Pearl. Here they are.' She produced them from her bag. 'But it was a pleasant morning and I chose to take a stroll. Surely at thirty I am old enough for that?' And leaving her sister open-mouthed, she walked into the shop.

Three

'My dear life, Effie! Stop a moment, do! I've been chasing after you all the way down Causeway Head.'

Effie spun around.

It was Lettie, panting down the hill. 'Didn't you see me? I was just across the road. I called out to you, as you were leaving the Westons' shop.'

Effie shook her head. It was true of course, the street was full of people, but she'd not seen anyone – especially not Alex, whom she had been looking for! It was quite peculiar – a month or two ago he had been on constant duty near Mrs Thatchell's house, yet now it seemed as if he'd vanished from the earth. She'd kept a constant eye out but she'd not seen him for days. Of course, it was probably just a change of beat – she knew the roster altered all the time, he'd warned her about that – but she couldn't help wondering if he'd ever got that note.

Suppose that Broadbent fellow had forgotten it and Alex had spent hours waiting in the rain, wondering where she was and why she hadn't come? He might even have supposed that she was a heartless jilt, and had not turned up on purpose – especially after what she'd said to him a month or two ago about the difference in their families.

But she could not confide her fears to Lettie, who would only laugh and say that she should never have sent the note at all, let alone trust a stranger to deliver it. So she forced herself to give a cheerful smile and say, 'No, I didn't hear you. Too much on my mind. I'm in a proper rush-about today. Mrs Thatchell wants a pair of boots resoled – though the Lord alone knows why. She never uses them except to go to church.' She lifted the cloth cover from the basket on her arm, and showed the brown-paper parcel lying there, under the silks and newly borrowed books. 'And I want to pop into the butcher's while I am in town, pay half a crown off Aunt Madge's bill

– shouldn't really do it, on Mrs Thatchall's time, but if I leave it till Thursday, I shall miss the horse-bus home. But I'll have to look sharpish if I'm going to do it now, 'cause I'll be wanted back.'

Lettie gave her an old-fashioned look. 'Haven't got time to hear my news about your Alex then?'

Effie was about to say, as usual, 'He's not my Alex!' when it struck her that this time it might be true, so she changed it to, 'I thought I might have seen him somewhere roundabout, but he's obviously not on duty in this area today.'

Lettie chuckled. 'Won't be on the beat much longer anyhow, if I am any judge. Friends in high places, that young man has got. The Major's going to put a word in for him with the Chief of Borough Police – I heard Miss Caroline tell her mother so.'

Effie sniffed. 'Well that's as may be, but it isn't who you know – or not entirely. It goes on examination nowadays. He's got to sit one very soon to go up in rank a bit: Constable First Class if he does well in it. And he's very clever so I expect he will. Came top of all the new recruits the last time round in written work – though another lad just beat him at the marching drill, when they were judged on that.'

'Pity they don't give awards for riding horses, then.' Lettie gave a knowing little flounce. 'He's marvellous at doing that, or so the Major says. Let him have his best horse when he came last week – and sent a carriage to bring him up for lunch.'

Effie found that she was nodding, without being certain when she'd trust herself to stop. Last week – that meant Thursday, or she supposed it did. The day that Alex should have been with her! When she was sure that she could control her voice she said, as blithely as she could, 'I haven't seen him for a week or two, of course, with my Pa being bad.'

'How's that then?' Lettie took a step backwards in surprise, and almost collided with a passing cart. 'Drat,' she murmured, brushing down her skirt, 'I'll be all over coal-dust if I do not look out. Why do we have to put up with that thing in the street?'

'You ought to be pleased to see him,' Effie said. 'There was a time last year, with all those strikes and things, when coal was near impossible to get.'

'But he could control it better!' Lettie said, dabbing at the imaginary stain. 'He's not even bothering to hold the stupid reins!' She frowned at the coalman as he plodded by.

'Doesn't need to lead his horse, that's why! It stops at every customer of its own accord!' Effie said crossly, rather irritated by the fuss. She had been talking about how Pa was ill. Wasn't that more important than a bit of dust?

Her irritation must have been quite obvious, because Lettie said hastily, 'But you were saying . . . what about your Pa? What happened? Was he taken with a cough?'

'Oh, of course. I forgot you didn't know! I haven't seen you since the accident.'

'Accident?'

'There was a bad rock-fall, one man died in it and my Pa hurt his leg – proper performance it has been. Splinted and all sorts, though it's getting better now and the doctor's going to come and tighten it, once he thinks the swelling has gone down. So naturally I've been down there every chance I got, and I couldn't have met Alex if I wanted to.' She tried to make her voice sound casual. 'When did you see him? Thursday gone, I suppose?'

'It is always a Thursday when he lunches at the house – fits in with his roster, it appears, though now and then he sends to say that he's got other duties that week and he can't get away.'

Effie swallowed. 'Other duties' she thought bitterly. Was that how he'd come to think of her? Well, it obviously didn't matter now. She said, too brightly, 'Well, good luck to him. I hope that he does well in that exam, that's all.'

'If he gets promotion, will he earn enough to wed?' Lettie was looking arch.

'How would I know!' Effie snapped. 'We never talked of that. It wasn't really as if he was my beau. But speaking of admirers, how is your friend Bert?'

Lettie coloured. 'He is very well.'

They had been walking very slowly down along the street and she stepped aside to let the coalman past again, this time carrying a sack of coal across his back. He lifted the lid of the coal hole at the tailor's shop nearby and began to empty the sack into the chute.

The falling coal made a sudden roaring noise, and Effie had to shout. 'You're still walking out with him, I suppose?'

Lettie leaned across and giggled, saying skittishly, 'I'll let you into a secret if you promise not to tell.'

'Of course I wouldn't!' Effie forced a laugh. 'Who do I know that I could talk to anyway?'

'I haven't even told my Fayther yet,' Lettie said. 'Lord knows what he will say. Declare he's glad to see the back of me, I 'spect!'

'You never mean to say you're going to leave Penzance?' The coal stopped rattling halfway through her speech and Effie found that her voice was suddenly too loud and a delivery boy on a bicycle turned round to look at her.

Lettie put a warning finger to her lips and dropped her voice till she was almost whispering. 'Not Penzance exactly,' She gave a little laugh. 'But I might leave Miss Knight – and serve her right. Bert and me are likely getting wed, what do you think of that?'

'My dear Lettie!' Effie was truly delighted for her friend. 'Just what you always wanted! When's it going to be?'

'Sssh!' Lettie looked up and down the street. It was full of shoppers but there was no-one nearby, and even the coalman had moved across the road and was delivering opposite, but Lettie still whispered, as if the horse might hear, 'Don't talk so loud! I told you – it's secret, for now at any rate. We haven't told a soul yet – apart from you – so nothing's been arranged. Course, when it happens, I'll be sure and let you know.'

Effie was flattered to be the first to know. She made a rueful little face. 'Not that Mrs Thatchell would let me come, of course – not if you was marrying the Prince of Wales himself.'

'Prince Edward?' Lettie giggled. 'I wouldn't mind, at that! He's how old now? Eighteen? And some handsome, by his photographs. Coming back to England, so the Major says, going to study at the university.' Her sharp little elbow dug Effie in the ribs. 'That would be something, wouldn't it?

Walking out with him? The girl he takes a shine to will be the Queen one day.'

'Lettie!' Effie was laughing, but she was a little shocked. 'You can't talk about the Prince of Wales like that! He's royalty – you should have more respect. Besides, you're a married woman, or you're about to be – you are supposed to keep your mind on Bert.'

Lettie was unrepentant. 'A cat may look at a king, they say – and I aren't married yet. But when I am, there'll be a vacancy – that's what I wanted to talk to you about. You've got some experience as a maid, how don't you apply? You could give your notice and get a character. Miss Caroline can be a devil when she tries – but she's no worse than Mrs Thatchell, and the pay is good. Better than you're getting where you are, I'm sure.'

Effie shook her head, decisively. 'The Knights would never have me – I'm not trained for that. General duties, that's all I've ever done. Besides . . .' She trailed off. The truth was she could not bear to work up at that house and have to witness Alex coming to and fro, dining and riding with Miss Caroline. Though she wouldn't tell Lettie that for all the world.

'Besides what?' Lettie challenged.

Effie thought quickly. ''Tisn't certain, is it?' she replied. 'You told me so yourself. And look, we've been 'ere chatting for so long, the blessed coalman's nearly done the road!' She gestured to where the horse was ambling down the street. 'If I don't get these boots in for soling and get back double-quick, I'll be looking for a new position on my own account!' And without waiting for an answer she hurried quickly off.

Lettie stared after her departing friend and made a little face at her retreating back. She was rather regretting taking Effie into her confidence. She had expected something more like gratitude – some girls would have been thrilled to death, being the first to hear about a vacancy – but Effie had not even seemed particularly pleased.

She gave a little sniff as she set off down the street. She'd know better than to make the offer for a second time. Not that her friend was even really suitable. The Knights weren't

people to take just anyone: they advertised all over if they were
wanting staff, but you really needed a recommendation from
somebody they knew, like she'd had herself. She would have
been prepared to put in a word for Effie, she thought – though
whether Miss Caroline would listen was another thing, especially when Lettie was about to 'let her down'. And that did
look very likely: she was two months overdue and Bert would
have to make an honest woman of her soon.

Not that he was likely to object! He must have told her
scores of times how much he thought of her and how he
wanted to be with her all the time. No, it was the thought of
what their families would say that was causing her alarm. She
knew his parents slightly from the grocer's shop – his Da was
small and wiry and apt to be quite sharp with anyone who
got on the wrong side of him, while Ma Symons was so skinny
she was practically a stick, with a tongue that could cut pieces
off you, if she chose. And probably she would do when she
heard of this!

The whole family lived above the shop, of course – not just
Bert but there were younger brothers too. The Symonses had
leased the place since Noah built the ark. What would they
think about her moving in? Which is what it would come to,
to begin with anyway – she and Bert could not afford to rent
a room elsewhere, not with a baby to provide for too! She
could see that there were likely to be problems about that –
but there wasn't any choice. Fayther's present landlady had a
notice up: 'no infants, animals or Irishmen allowed'.

Not that Fayther would have had her anyway! In fact she
hardly dared to think what he was going to say. He wouldn't
take his belt to her, like some men would have done, but he
was likely to be simply furious – declare that she was nothing
but a terrible disgrace and refuse to see her or let her come
into the house. Course, she could hope to win him over, once
the child was safely born – as long as she was married before
it really showed. When you had a wedding ring, people soon
forgot, and there wouldn't be a scandal, or so she had to hope,
else Fayther would cut her off and leave her not a groat,
although she was the only living child he had.

She side-stepped a ragged woman with a baby in her arms,

a sight which almost made her catch her breath. If she wasn't careful, that might one day be . . . But she would not think like that!

Perhaps her stepmother might help talk Fayther round: the woman had never had children of her own, so she might like a baby to coo over at last. She might even be willing to have it now and then, so Lettie could go scrubbing or something by and by and try to bring a bit of money in. It didn't need a fortune-teller from the fair to see that the sooner she and Bert could get away from living with his folks and have a room somewhere that they could call their own, the happier their future life was apt to be.

They hadn't intended to rush it all, like this. She'd dreamt of getting married in a pretty dress and hat, with flowers and ribbons and a pair of brand-new boots, but none of that would now be possible, of course. Bert would be disappointed, too. When she had broached the subject of marriage once before, he'd been sure that they should wait and get a bit put by. 'Want to do it proper, if I marry you.' But circumstances had altered and he would have to change his mind.

Mrs Lettie Symons. It sounded very nice. She walked on down on the street, letting the words go rolling round her brain, so busy with her thoughts that she was blind to everything and everybody else. Several times she almost blundered into a passer-by but she just said, 'Sorry!' and walked on in a dream. It might have led to trouble when she came to cross the street, but a loud voice at her shoulder, calling her by name, forced itself suddenly into her consciousness.

'Be careful, young lady. Miss Pearson, isn't it? Mind where you put your feet! There's been a horse about!' Funny sort of accent − not from anywhere round here. She looked up in surprise to see a stout man in a bowler hat and Ulster overcoat, mopping his red face as if he was too hot. He smiled and swept the hat off. 'Perhaps I ought to introduce myself. The name is Broadbent. You might have heard of me?'

Lettie stared at the stranger in surprise. 'Not that I know of. How did you know my name?'

He tapped his nose as if to indicate that there were lots of things that he could tell her if he chose. 'It is my business to find things out.' He smiled again. 'For instance, I know that you're a friend of Mrs Thatchell's maid, Effie Pengelly – I believe I saw you with her just now in the street – and I understand you've talked about her with the grocer's boy. Isn't that the case?'

This was alarming. Lettie stifled a wild desire to run. 'Well, I might have done. There's no law against that, is there?' she retorted, stung. Rudeness seemed the only method of defence.

Mr Broadbent – whoever he might be! – only smiled and mopped his brow again. 'Of course not, Miss Pearson. But I am down here to make enquiries and this may be relevant. You may remember that there was an unclaimed body last year in the town?'

Making enquiries! And about the corpse! Was he a policeman then? They did have plain-clothes policeman up in the capital. Perhaps she had better mind her P's and Q's. 'The one who asked for Effie?' she asked, politely now. 'Yes, I remember. How could I forget?'

He looked at her intently. His eyes were shrewd and searching but they were not unkind. 'I know that after all this time it might be hard to say, but can you recall what you were doing the day before he died? In outline, anyway?'

She nodded doubtfully. 'I suppose so – though, as you say, it was a little while ago. That would have been the Monday, wouldn't it? Then – apart from normal chores like sweeping, dusting and putting out the outfits for the day – I would most probably have been washing lace and cleaning jewellery. One week's much like another, when you're a lady's maid.'

'I understand all that. But this might be important. Think before you speak. Were you talking to this grocer's boy of yours on that day at all? Mentioning Effie anywhere where you might be overheard?'

Lettie felt her cheeks turn burning red. 'Shouldn't think so for a moment!' She snapped out the reply, then – remembering that he might be someone in authority – she added, 'See, me and Bert had hardly started walking out by then . . .' She gave him her most winning girlish smile. 'We weren't talking about other people much.'

Mr Broadbent surprised her. He threw back his head and

laughed. 'I can imagine that. Well, that seems to be conclusive. Thank you very much. Though you might just check that with this Bert of yours, when you see him next. Are you likely to run into him today? If so, I could come with you and speak to him myself.'

'Oh, I shouldn't think we'll find him at this time of day. He'll be out about his rounds.' That was not true at all. Bert would have his bicycle all right, and there would be an order in the basket on the front, but he'd be waiting for her by the bandstand on the Promenade – she had told him last week that she'd meet him there today, on the excuse of taking letters to the post. Of course she had been hoping that things would be all right by now, but nothing had happened and she'd missed another month. She was simply going to have to talk to him – and she did not want any policeman interrupting that. 'Anyway,' she added, 'he'd tell you the same thing.'

Broadbent smiled at her so knowingly that she was almost sure he guessed, but he just said, 'In the meantime, if you think of anything, would you let me know? I'm staying at the Anchor for a day or two – or Miss Blanche Weston would take a message, I am sure. So, Miss Pearson, I will wish you a good day.' And he put his bowler hat on and went strolling down the street.

Lettie waited till he was out of sight, then hurried to complete the errand at the post office and hastened off towards the Promenade. She didn't have a lot of time – she was already late – but it was absolutely urgent that she should talk to Bert.

It was surprisingly windy on the Promenade today. Alex was glad of the chin-strap to keep his helmet on, otherwise it might have gone the way of the child's bonnet which was even now bowling merrily over the railings and out into the sea, while a hapless nursemaid watched it in dismay. If he had been a little quicker he might have rescued it, in proper constabulary fashion, but he had been too absorbed in his own thoughts to notice what was happening until it was too late.

He nodded at the nursemaid and her charges as they passed. 'Morning, miss!' but she was too busy scolding the culprit to respond. Pretty girl. She reminded him of Effie – though she did not have the smile, or the figure either really. He gave himself a shake. Every woman under forty-five seemed to remind him of Effie nowadays. It wasn't sensible. He must think of something else.

He devoted his attention to a pair of bicycles, in case either of them matched the description of a stolen one, and to the appearance of a ragged urchin lad, pushing a barrow piled with rabbit skins, who looked about seven and should have been in school.

'Doing an errand for me Ma before I go!' the child protested and Alex let him go, though he had his doubts, both about the school attendance and whether the skins had been honestly obtained or conveniently lifted from behind the butcher's shop. He would keep his eye out for the boy another time, he thought, and woe betide him if he caught him doing it again.

The wind was getting stronger all the time and there was beginning to be a hint of rain in it. People were scuttling for shelter as he watched – even the nursemaid had ceased to scold her charges and was leading them somewhere firmly by the hand. In a minute it would start to pour. Alex tutted. He should have brought his waterproof, not just his shoulder-cape. Perhaps he would take shelter in the bandstand for a while – at least it would keep him in the dry.

He was hurrying towards it, lowering his head against the wind and rain, when he realized that it was already occupied. There were two people in it, with their backs to him, and they seemed to be having some kind of argument.

'And I tell you that it is, whose else's would it be!' A woman's voice, quite loud and angry. Tearfully angry, by the sound of it. Surely it was a voice he recognized? He looked a little closer and of course it was – it was that friend of Effie's and her grocer friend. 'You wait till I tell Fayther, he'll be after you. He will tell your parents.'

'You think they would believe you? Don't you be so daft.' The boy was talking softly, but in an angry hiss. 'You can't prove anything. It could be anyone. I'll tell them that I never had to anything to do with it.'

Alex was close behind them by this time. He could not help but overhear and he felt embarrassed at interrupting them.

This was clearly something personal they were arguing about – he did not think to question what it was. Well, he wasn't going to let their squabble keep him in the rain. He cleared his throat loudly to warn them he was there.

Lettie and her companion swung around at once. When she saw Alex she let out a cry.

'Well, here's a policeman and he'll speak up for me. Constable Dawes, you've seen me walking out with Bert? You remember, up Mount Misery?'

She looked so intense that Alex was alarmed. 'Well of course I remember. Bert Symons, isn't it?' He smiled at the fellow who was scowling back. 'I'm sorry to disturb you for a second time, but I wanted to come under the bandstand from the rain; I think there's going to be a deluge before long.'

Lettie turned back to her beau, exclaiming, 'There, what I did tell you! I've got witnesses. Not just any witness, but a constable. So you can't go claiming that you've never heard of me. And what about all those promises you used to make? I never expected that you'd be overjoyed but I never dreamt that you would carry on like this.'

Alex found that he was frowning. This wasn't making sense. 'Witnesses to what, exactly?' he enquired.

Bert Symons raised a sullen face to him. 'Witness to the fact that she's got me in a trap and now I suppose I'll bloody have to marry her – though the lord knows what my parents are going to make of that. I expect my Da will beat the living daylights out of me – and hers will very likely do the same.' He glared at Lettie as though he wished her dead.

Lettie looked at Alex. 'That's only thanks to you. But at least he's agreed to marry me – that's something I suppose.'

Alex had just made sense of this. He felt an utter fool. He muttered, 'Well, I must be getting back. Congratulations, Mr Symons – if that's appropriate. Lettie, I wish you every happiness, of course.' And he left them to it as quickly as he could – just as the serious rain began to fall.

Four

It was taking simply ages in the butcher's shop. There were queues of people in front of her and most of them seemed to want their order cut in chops. It seemed they required every awkward sort of cut, so the owner was kept busy fetching down the different carcasses off hooks and chopping pieces off them on his butcher's block. Effie was almost tempted to leave her errand till another day but it would have to be Thursday if she did and then – as she'd said to Lettie – she would more than likely miss the midday bus. There wasn't another one to Penvarris for hours so it would take her half the afternoon to walk, and with Pa awaiting her she didn't want to get there and have to come straight back. So she stuck it out and waited while the folk in front of her requested brawn or trotters or suet in a piece.

But at last she reached the counter and handed in her two and six, and watched while the butcher wrote it in the book against Aunt Madge's name. She glanced through the window at the watchmaker opposite, who had a large clock mounted on the wall above his door. Dear Heaven, it was very nearly half past ten! She'd better get those boots delivered mighty quick!

She was in such haste to leave the shop that she almost collided with a portly gentleman who was standing in the queue. He caught her eye and smiled as though they were acquaintances – and his face did look familiar, somehow, though she couldn't for a moment remember where they'd met.

There was no time to stop and think about it now. There were still those boots to deal with and she'd be wanted back. She was almost tempted to break into a run but she restrained herself – and fortunately there was no-one waiting at the shoemaker's.

She reached into the basket on her arm and gave the cobbler Mrs Thatchell's Sunday boots to sole. 'See you make them dainty,' she said, unwrapping them. That was what her mistress had instructed her to say.

The shoemaker seemed to know it. He spat out the hobnails he was holding in his teeth and turned to smile at her. 'But she'll be wanting segs, I s'pose?' He gestured to the pile of assorted iron heel and toe plates he kept beside his last.

'I expect so.' Effie nodded.

'She generally does.' He picked the shoes up, marked a number on the soles in chalk and put them with the piles of others on the shelf. 'Ready by Tuesday,' he said breezily, tearing off a numbered chitty from the book and giving it to her with a grin. 'Seeing how she wants them "dainty" – and with segs as well.'

'Tuesday, but that's ages! She might want them for church,' Effie protested. 'I can't imagine what she's going to say.'

'Tell her that miracles take a little time.' He gave a wicked wink, took the pencil from behind his ear and scribbled the name Thatchell on the ticket-stub.

Effie grinned. It was not really proper, him poking fun like that, but he always made her laugh. She was still smiling as she turned to go, but the smile faded when she saw who was standing near the door. It was the fellow from the butcher's shop! And he wasn't moving towards the counter in her place – he did not even seem to have a pair of shoes to mend – he was simply standing watching with his hat between his hands.

It took her a moment, even then, to work out who it was. 'Mr Broadbent! What are you doing here?' This could not be mere coincidence. 'Were you wanting me?' she asked uncertainly.

Mr Broadbent shook his thinning ginger head, and answered in that up-country voice of his, 'I came to see the shoemaker, in fact, but it did concern you, in a way. It's in relation to that business that we talked about before. You mentioned that you sometimes brought your boots in here to mend.'

She said, in horror, 'And you've been watching me?' The idea of being spied on was not a pleasant one.

She must have sounded thoroughly upset, because the shoemaker came round the counter, with his cobbler's hammer in his hand. He frowned at Mr Broadbent and then turned to her. 'Do you know this gentleman, young lady?' he enquired. ''Cause if you don't and he is troubling you, I will call the police.'

Effie was almost tempted for a moment, but she had visions of Alex rushing in. Besides, she remembered what Mr Broadbent was trying to find out. She shook her head. 'Thank you, but there is no need for alarm. I have met this gentleman before and I am sure he means no harm – although I do not like his methods very much. However, I believe he wants to talk to you and I am wanted back at work, so if you will excuse me . . .' And with that she left the shop.

When she paused for breath, however, half a block away, she was surprised to find that Mr Broadbent was not far behind. He was out of breath and panting and his face was very red, but he was still smiling as he caught up with her.

'My dear Miss Pengelly, what must you think of me! I did not mean to cause you such embarrassment . . .'

She cut him off. 'I thought you wanted the shoemaker!' she protested, angrily.

'As I was attempting to explain, I was interested in the process when shoes are taken in. I wondered if that was how the dead man might have heard your name the day before he died, but I've observed the whole procedure and I don't see how. Everything is written and it is quite discreet.' He dabbed his flustered face. 'That was the information which I hoped to ascertain. It was the purest accident I found you in the shop, though it was useful in one respect at least – even when the cobbler spoke to you direct he didn't use your name.'

'So what were you doing at the butcher's shop?'

'Very much the same. I asked him outright if your name was written down where someone could have seen it, and he told me it was not – and according to his records you did not come in that day to make a payment on your aunt's account. So that disposed of that. Which left Miss Pearson. I spoke to her as well – shortly after you had met her in the street.'

Effie stared at him. 'You *are* following me about!'

He shook his head. 'I assure you I am not. It was Miss Pearson that I was looking for; Miss Blanche had told me that she usually comes into the shop today and I was trying to meet up with her. This is not London, Miss Pengelly, it's a small place after all, and running into someone that you know is not so much a possibility as a likelihood.'

Effie was ready to retort that Penzance was the biggest place for miles and you could walk the streets for hours without meeting friends, but she remembered that she had an interest in this mystery. 'So have you worked out how the dead man came to hear my name? It must have been from Lettie, from the sound of it.'

He shook his head. 'I should confess that I've made no progress on that score at all. Miss Pearson persuades me that she did not talk about you to her grocer friend. Several people remember having seen the man here in Penzance before he died – I got their addresses from the police – but they swear they didn't speak to him at all. In a small place like this I thought it was a possibility, but I can't find anyone who might have mentioned you – or at least, who remembers doing so. I am beginning to doubt my theory about how Royston knew your name – or Royston's friend, if that is who it was.'

Effie looked at him. 'So what happens now?'

'I might try a few enquiries at Penvarris, I suppose, but there is no evidence that he was ever there.'

She shook her head. 'If he'd been up Penvarris I would have heard of it, especially if he'd been enquiring for me. A stranger in a place like that is quite a rarity – people would have talked of nothing else for days.'

Mr Broadbent twinkled. 'You are a sharp young woman, Miss Pengelly. Yes, of course you're right. In a small place like Penvarris everyone would know.' He chuckled. 'Well done, young lady! I've got a junior up in my London office training in the trade – I wish he were only half as sharp as you. Pity you're a girl and live so far away, or I would be tempted to offer you his place!'

'I'll be needing a new one, if I don't look out!' Effie muttered, looking at the clock again. 'And I'm darned if it isn't begin-ning to rain on me besides! And I've only got a shawl. If I'm not careful, I'll be soaked through to the skin! Excuse me, Mr Broadbent, but I've really got to go!'

'Of course!' he murmured apologetically, 'I could fetch you

a brolly!' But she had already turned away. She hurried back as fast as she could go, but the rainstorm caught her and she got sopping wet.

'Good lord, Effie,' Mrs Lane exclaimed, when she came in, dripping, through the kitchen door. 'You're half-drowned! Get upstairs this instant and change into your other uniform, and dry your hair before you catch your death. You've just got time before you take the mistress up her tray.'

Effie did as she was told and managed to make herself presentable before she carried up the tea, but she didn't half get an awful fussing later on, when Mrs Thatchell found her library books and silks were slightly damp.

Blanche had been hovering at the window half the day, on the pretext of changing the display, but although she was certain that she'd glimpsed Josiah walking past – shortly after the Pearson girl had left – she hadn't managed to catch sight of him again.

'Oh, leave that now, Blanche, do for heaven's sake! You must have rearranged those gloves a dozen times,' Pearl said impatiently. 'I don't know what you think you are trying to achieve. It was perfectly satisfactory as it was before.'

'It's a new idea, Pearl dear,' she answered, mildly. She'd been expecting this, and had rehearsed a plausible excuse for why she was lingering where she could see the street. 'Liberty's have started doing it. I saw a feature in the Drapers' magazine. The prettiest new colours are put right at the front, with a little notice saying what they are – see I have written "new for the summer – taupe and misty fawn" – so much more attractive than saying "beige and tan". In London they have little stands to show them off, but I've just draped them on those boxes on the shelf and put out some hats and ribbons and bits of lace to match – instead of everything being jumbled, like it was before.'

Oh dear! She had called it 'jumbled' and Pearl had put it there! She hadn't meant to be so blunt; the word had just slipped out. She had got very daring since the morning of that walk when she'd defied her sister for the first time in her life and declined to say anything about where she had been. The results had been surprising: Pearl had stormed a bit, and then it had blown over and had not been mentioned since. But she hadn't meant to go as far as this and seem to criticize.

She braced herself for serious protest but it did not come. Pearl just pursed her lips into her 'disapproving' face. 'I don't know why you bother. It's a waste of time. People will come in to buy the gloves they always buy – beige ones for young ladies and black for older ones, and occasionally a pair of white ones for brides and christenings.' But she didn't order Blanche to change the window back – and Blanche did not dismantle her display or even offer an apology, the way she would once automatically have done.

Indeed she almost did the opposite. 'It does look rather pretty, doesn't it, Pearl dear?' she ventured timidly.

Perhaps Pearl thought so, because she didn't disagree. 'Well the proof is in the eating. I suppose that we shall see. If we sell a lot of extra gloves in consequence, nobody will be more pleased than I am, I assure you, Blanche! But I doubt we shall. Now, I can't stand here discussing these fancy modern games, there is old-fashioned stock to check and it won't do itself.' And she stalked off into the back room and began to move the boxes noisily.

Blanche breathed a sigh of real relief. She'd stood up to her sister once again and there hadn't been an argument, as there might well have been. It was still quite possible to go too far, as she'd discovered just the night before when she'd suggested that they might have sardines for tea for once, instead of the usual slice of half-cooked toast and jam. Pearl had got very waxy about that – demanded if she thought that these things grew on trees, and lectured her for hours about the price of fish.

But the question of the window had not caused a rift. It did look quite different from their usual cramped displays and Blanche decided that she was pleased with it – though the whole idea had only been a ruse so that she could look out for Josiah on the street. But it seemed to be having an effect, drawing lots of attention from the passers-by, and several people had even paused to look.

In fact there was someone stopping now to stare at it – that

Lettie Pearson girl – not that she was likely to become a customer for gloves! But perhaps she wasn't really looking at the display at all, because she didn't seem to notice when Blanche tried to catch her eye. The girl was simply staring into space and looking so stricken that Blanche was quite alarmed – and she thought she knew what had occasioned it!

This was the person that Josiah had been looking for – and it was almost certain that he'd caught up with her. The girl had been quite cheerful when she was in before, and now she had been crying, that was obvious. What had Josiah Broadbent said to her that could have upset her in this way?

It was ridiculous, Blanche was aware of that, but she could not help feeling responsible herself – after all, she had told him where to find the girl. Gone down especially to tell him, she remembered with a blush. She glanced around the shop. Pearl was still busy in the office and would not notice if she slipped outside.

She tried to move as gently as she could but she could not stop the bell from tinkling slightly as she went through the door. The girl outside the window looked up as it rang and seemed about to move away, but Blanche prevented her.

'Whatever is it, Lettie? I can see that you're upset. Did that fellow find you? Did you talk to him?'

The girl looked at her dully with swollen red-rimmed eyes. 'Yes, I did. And I wish I hadn't had to – he was simply horrible. You wouldn't believe the awful things he said! If it wasn't for that policeman, he'd have washed his hands of me and heaven only knows what would have become of me. Gone and drowned myself, I shouldn't be surprised.'

'My dear!' Blanche put in gently, but she was horrified. This was all her fault. She should never have taken Broadbent into her confidence and told him that Lettie would be coming here today – after all, as Pearl had pointed out, they did not know anything about the man. 'Surely it can't be as bad as that?'

Lettie gave an unbecoming sniff and rubbed her eyes. 'Yes, I suppose I'm lucky when you think of it like that. He has agreed to take me, so I will be all right – though he didn't really want to, and that's what makes me cry.' She raised her head and stared suddenly at Blanche. 'But how do you come to know about it anyway? I haven't said anything to anyone – excepting Effie, and she swore she wouldn't tell.'

Blanche was hardly listening. This wasn't making sense. Josiah taking Lettie – whatever did it mean? Not to London, by the sound of it. She felt as if the pavement was moving under her. 'What exactly did Mr Broadbent say?'

Lettie looked astonished. 'Don't tell me he's the one that found it out? He told me that it was his business to discover things, but I never thought he meant about me getting wed to Bert. What has it got to do with him?'

'You are getting wed to Bert? That's the grocer's boy I've sometimes seen you with?' The pavement had returned to its accustomed place and Blanche was beginning to get the sense of this. 'I think there's been a little misunderstanding here. I only meant to ask you if Mr Broadbent had caught up with you, as I knew he wanted to have a word with you.' She saw Lettie's look of horror. 'But you needn't worry. I will keep your secret, now I've surprised it out of you. Though for a girl who's getting married, you don't seem very pleased.'

'I might as well tell you, since you already know. It's a relief to talk to someone, to tell you the truth.' Lettie shook her head. 'Bert isn't really willing, that's the worst of it. I told him what we'd come to and in the end he said he would. But he didn't want to – you could see that clear as day – and if I didn't have to, I wouldn't marry him.'

Blanche was faintly puzzled. 'But surely you don't have to marry anyone? The law would take your part. We don't have forced marriage in this country any more.'

Lettie gave a little bitter laugh. 'Well, let's just say that sometimes things work out that way – you do what you have to, and put up with it. And as I say, it could have been much worse. Miss Caroline won't like it – she's got used to me – but she'll just have to find another maid, that's all.' She rubbed her eyes and face. 'Well I'd better go and face her, now I've dried my eyes. I can rely on you to keep this to yourself?' And when Blanche nodded she walked slowly off along the pavement, with her head thrown back and her chin jutting upwards as if defying fate.

Blanche watched her go in mild bewilderment. What a

peculiar attitude to have! *If someone was prepared to marry me,* she thought – not that it was likely at her time of life – *I would be only too delighted to accept and, what is more, I would want the world to know!* Though naturally she did not have any particular prospective groom in mind.

She gave a casual glance around the street. Mr Broadbent was nowhere to be seen so she went back into the shop again. Perhaps she would catch sight of him a little later on.

But she didn't have time to look out for him again. That afternoon there was an unexpected little run on gloves.

Walter was clinging to the bedposts with both hands, gritting his teeth and trying not to make unmanly sounds. The mine doctor was tightening the splint again and it felt for all the world as if the leg was catching fire under the pressure of the bandages.

'One more turn, Pengelly, and we shall be done.' The doctor stood up, looking satisfied. 'It must be done, you know, to keep it good and firm, otherwise it would give you no support at all. And it's coming on quite well now; there's an awful lot of bruising, but the swelling is going down – that's why the splint was getting loose – and there doesn't seem to be infection round the break at all, and that can be a killer if it starts. So it looks as if you're lucky, and in a week or so we'll have you on crutches and walking round a bit.'

'You said that last time! Another blessed week!' Now that the wretched fellow had stopped his tinkering the pain was less intense, and as it ebbed into a burning ache Walter found that he could trust himself to speak. 'A chap could go demented lying here all day.' He let go of the bedposts guiltily.

The doctor nodded briskly. 'I think we might agree that we can start to get you out – get you in a chair for an hour or two a day. It will make a change for you and stop you getting bed-sores, which otherwise it looks as if you might.' What gave him the right to look self-satisfied as he said this? 'But you'll have to keep your leg up for the first few days at least. We don't want to undo all the good work we have done. And if you start feeling giddy, it is back to bed at once. I've not forgotten that you took that knock as well.'

'Thank you, Doctor; it will make a change, at least!' Walter remembered to sound grateful. It wasn't what he'd hoped for, but it would be a relief. Perhaps he could get Madge to move the chair across a foot or two so that he could look out of the window to the street, and take an interest in the world outside instead of staring at that wretched text all day. 'You'd better tell my sister.'

'I'll do that all right. And I'll see the crutch is ordered for next time that I come. Then perhaps we can have you on your feet and after that I won't have to call again.'

And a damty good thing too, in Walter's view, but of course he did not say that, just forced himself to grin. 'You'll be as glad as I am when you've seen the back of me,' he said, in an attempt at pleasantry. 'Still can't take it in that I don't have to pay you every time.'

The doctor did not look at all amused, just put his equipment back into his bag and walked round to the door. 'We shall have to hope the system doesn't bankrupt anyone,' he said. 'I'm not at all convinced that it will work for very long. But in the meantime, make the most of it. If you'd had to pay for everything, it would have cost you such a lot that it would either have driven you to ruin or you'd have decided against it and would not have walked again. Or both if you had really been unfortunate.' He gave what looked like an ironic little bow. 'So count your blessings. I will say good afternoon.'

And he clopped off down the stairs. Walter could hear him in the kitchen, saying things to Madge, though he could not at this distance make out what they were.

It was not difficult to work it out, however, because a moment afterwards he heard the front door close and Madge came bustling upstairs, wiping her hands on her apron and looking cross as sticks.

'Well, he says that we can get you out into a chair – he's taking about tomorrow afternoon – but how he thinks I'm going to do that on my own I cannot think. You will simply have to wait till Joe comes home and that won't be till six – won't be what you're hoping, but it will have to do.'

Walter stared at her. 'Why ever would we have to wait for

Joe? I aren't helpless, broken bones or no. If I've got you to lean on, I can get my damty self into a chair. Only a matter of standing up and turning round.'

She shook her head. 'Well that's just where you're wrong. The doctor says you'll be as weak as water for a bit. It's one thing to half-sit propped up with pillows like you're doing now, but trying to get out of bed is something else, when you've been lying down for weeks. Might come over funny the first time, so he says – and if you fell over, what would I do then? I couldn't lift you back, with your splint and everything – to say nothing of the fact that you could hurt your leg again. I aren't risking that. No!' She held her hand up as he started to protest. 'We will simply have to wait for Joe – the first few days at least. So leave it go at that. Now, I've put the kettle on the hob. You want a cup of tea?'

He nodded glumly and she went downstairs again. It was her idea of consolation, but it did not help him much. He listened glumly to the noises in the street – a horse and cart, two women gossiping – fretting that he could not sit out and watch it all. The street would be half-empty by the time that Joe came home, and even then the man would want his tea before he came to help the damty invalid. Pity he wasn't on the early shift this week, like the men that he could hear approaching even now. And that was when he had his good idea.

He was actually smiling when Madge came back again, bringing him his tea and a slice of still-warm hevva cake she'd made.

'What's up with you then? I thought you'd be wild. I hope you're not intending to try to sweet-talk me and make me change my mind about letting you sit out? Well if that's what you're hoping, Walter, you can think again. I really mean it – I aren't willing to risk it on my own.'

He took a sip of sweetened tea and smacked his lips. 'Well how don't you ask one of the early shift to help? Young Peter Kellow now, he's a willing lad, and he's been here to see me of his own accord. I do b'lieve he would be tickled to be asked.'

She shook her head. 'Can't go asking favours of a lad like that. Why would he want to help?'

Walter had a very shrewd idea but he did not tell Madge. 'Give him a morsel of your hevva cake and that would pay him more than 'andsome, I should say! Nobody living makes hevva cake like you.' He knew that it was flattery, but the cake was very good and his Susan was dead so it was almost true.

'Get on with you!' Madge muttered, but she did not demur.

He had judged correctly. Peter Kellow was delighted to be asked and volunteered to come in every day – though Walter remained privately convinced that it had more to do with Effie than with any hevva cake.

Part Four

October – November 1912

One

Effie was delighted to find Pa out of bed and in the chair, with his bad leg propped up before him on a kitchen stool. He was sitting by the window with a rug across his lap, and he was balancing a saucepan on the top of it so he could string and slice a pile of runner beans which had been heaped conveniently on the chest of drawers nearby.

He waved the knife in greeting. 'Making myself useful. At least I'm trying to. But I keep on dropping half the damty strings.' He gestured to the floor. 'Be an angel, Effie, and pick them up for me. There's a bucket down there I'm supposed to drop them in, but they keep missing when I let them fall.'

She came over to plant a kiss on his cheek then knelt down to collect the fragments, which were scattered all around the pail. 'Can't be easy when you can't bend over. How's the ankle coming on? Aunty Madge says they are going to let you walk on it next week, but I see you've got a pillow underneath it on the stool. Not very comfortable otherwise?'

He shook his head and gave a rueful laugh. 'Not very comfortable anyway. Dratted splint's so heavy that it makes me thighs ache holding it like this. But don't you go saying that to your Aunty Madge or she will have me back in bed before you can say Jack Robinson. I've had a job to make her let me stay here as it is — she keeps on saying it will tire me out. I only kept her quiet by offering to do the damty beans. And I insisted that the doctor said an hour, so Peter Kellow isn't coming back till then.'

She had collected half of the errant bean strings by this time but she sat up in astonishment at this. 'Peter Kellow? What has Peter got to do with it?'

Pa was smiling at her with his eyebrows arched. 'Oh, he's been very good since I've been laid up in bed. Been to see me of his own accord and talked about the mine. Did me a power of good. And when he heard Madge needed help to

get me in and out the chair, he was only too happy to give a
bit of a hand. Nice boy is Peter. Don't know if you ever run
into him these days?'

She felt herself turn scarlet and she turned away again,
pretending that she was busy hunting beans. She said, in a
carefully casual tone of voice, 'I have come across him lately
once or twice – they sent him to fetch me when you had
your accident – though I hadn't spoken to him, up to then,
for absolutely years.' She crawled away to reach another fragment of a pod.

'Came to fetch you, did he?' Pa said, in a way that made
her think that he had known that all along. 'That was nice of
him. You'll want to thank him when he comes back here,
then, I'll be bound.' He dropped his hand on to her head and
ruffled up her hair. 'And don't think I haven't noticed. It's
clear he's sweet on you. And you've got my blessing if you're
thinking to walk out with him.' He gave a rather rueful sort
of laugh. 'Without you've got admirers in town I haven't heard
about. Joe's certain that you have, but I said you'd have told
me if there was anything.'

Effie shook her head. This was the last thing she wanted to
discuss with Pa today. She thought a moment before saying
carefully, 'Well there was a young fellow I took a fancy to, but
that's all over now.'

Pa was silent for a moment and then said in an altered tone
of voice. 'Don't you tell me that he's led you up the garden
path, or leg or no leg I'll go after him.'

It was clear he meant it, but it sounded comical and Effie
was actually able to give a little laugh before she answered,
quite light-heartedly, 'No, nothing of the kind. More the other
way about. I thought a lot of Alex but it would not have done
– and in the end I had to tell him so.' She had simplified the
story but that was the gist of it.

She was avoiding looking at her father all this time but she
could tell from his voice that he was staring searchingly at her.
'What do you mean exactly, "it would not have done". What
was it? He was twice your age? Some artist type or something,
who was not respectable?' She shook her head at each suggestion as he spoke but finally he voiced what must have been

his great anxiety. 'You're not going to tell me that he was a married man?'

It was a relief to Effie to be able to laugh his fears aside. 'No, 'course I wouldn't get mixed up in anything like that! Alex was nothing if not respectable. That was the trouble really, he was too well-off. You should have heard him talk about his family — servants and stables and that sort of thing and his father something important in the army once. I couldn't very well have brought him home to this! He wasn't really suitable for somebody like me.'

'And you never told me?' Pa sounded really hurt. 'I would like to have met him, any road, if you really cared for him.'

'Well actually you did meet him,' Effie said. 'Though I hardly knew him then. He was that young policeman who came out to the mine. There, I've said it, but it doesn't matter now in any case. It never came to being serious — he was only just a friend — and after what I said he saw the sense of it and he has started seeing someone else.' She straightened up and put the bean strings in the pail. 'So let's not talk about it any more.'

He reached across and took her hand in his. He was not given to such gestures and there was a moment of special closeness before he murmured in his gentlest voice, 'I'm some glad you told me, Effie, though I can see it gives you pain. I don't like having secrets between the two of us.'

She sat down close beside him on the corner of the bed. 'And no more do I.' She paused to squeeze his fingers apologetically, then added with a little laugh, 'But don't for pity's sake go telling Uncle Joe. You can just imagine what he'd say if he knew! Consorting with a policeman — and a wealthy one at that! I would never hear the last of—' She broke off at the sound of footsteps on the stairs. 'But let's change the subject — here comes Aunty Madge. Why don't we let her find us talking about how much you're enjoying your change of view?'

But it wasn't Aunty Madge who tapped the door a minute later. It was Peter Kellow, dressed up for visiting, his face and neck still glowing where he'd scrubbed them red and his ginger hair still damp with washing. He had even scraped the mine-dust from underneath his nails, and had clearly made an effort before coming here tonight, quite different from the day he'd come to get her from Penzance. You would never call him handsome, even now, but you had to admit that he did look quite nice when he cleaned up a bit.

He coloured with pleasure when he saw that she was there. 'Miss Pengelly – Effie!' he exclaimed at once. 'I was hoping you would come. How wonderful to see you. And you too, sir, of course.'

It was a bit discourteous in a sick-room, but Pa didn't seem to mind. In fact he chuckled. 'Don't mind me, young man. I don't need glasses to see what interests you!'

Peter was instantly contrite. 'I came to help your sister put you back to bed, but she's putting jam tarts in the oven for your tea so she suggested that Effie could lend a hand instead – it's only to help steady you, sir, after all.'

'Call me Walter, boy, for heaven's sake!' Pa said gruffly. 'You've seen me in me night-shirt and bare feet and knees – you can't call me sir for ever more.'

It was a great concession for a person of his age to somebody who wasn't in his family or his pare. Peter knew it too. He turned a brighter ginger than his hair. 'Thank you, Mr Pengelly, sir. I mean Walter, sir,' he muttered in confusion and made everybody laugh.

It was Pa who really brought things back to normal, though. 'Well, come on, you two. I've done these damty beans. If you'll just take the saucepan and the knife . . .' He handed them to Effie, who put them safely down. 'You can help me to my feet and get me into bed before Madge comes and makes a fuss.'

Effie took her place on the left-hand side of Pa while Peter went around towards the window side and they pulled the rug back while Pa swung his leg down from the stool and then leaned on their shoulders as they heaved him to his feet. It was the first time that Effie had seen him try to stand and she was not prepared for how unsteady he appeared to be. But she did manage to support him as they helped him turn around and manoeuvre himself a little further up the bed. Peter had the wit to turn the blankets back and Pa was able to lean back on the bolster and put his good leg in before they helped him raise the splinted one.

Effie saw him wincing and she bit her lip. It was going to be a good few days before he walked, she thought, and she almost told him so, but Peter caught her eye. He gave her a look which told her what she should have seen herself – that she wouldn't help her father by saying things like that. She nodded, gratefully.

'Well, there you are again!' She made her voice sound bright. 'Tucked up cosy and ready for your tea. I'll just take these beans downstairs for Aunty Madge – she will be wanting to salt them for Christmas I expect, so I can give a hand and leave you two fellows to chat about the mine.' She seized the pail and saucepan and the piece of newspaper on which the beans had stood, and suited the action to her words.

Peter was looking at her with dismay but she shook her head at him. It was not that she wanted to get away from him, as he appeared to think; it was simply that the tears were standing in her eyes and she didn't want her Pa to realize.

She explained that to Peter when he came down again and he was very nice. Said that he'd noticed and completely understood but that her Pa was waiting for her now. So she hurried back and talked to him herself, fifteen to the dozen – all the funny things that she could think of telling him – until it was time to catch the late horse-bus back into Penzance.

Major Knight seemed determined to be especially genial today. He had not only sent the carriage down, as promised, but as soon as the butler had taken Alex's coat and hat, the Major had come out to greet him warmly in the hall and invite him into his private study for a brandy before lunch. 'The ladies won't be joining us for half an hour or so. Titivating themselves up as usual, I suppose, eh what?' he said, expansively, leading the way into the room.

Alex had never been invited in there before and he wondered to what he owed the privilege today. It was obviously the Major's personal retreat, with leather easy chairs, an enormous bearskin rug, crossed African spears above the fireplace, and a collection of sporting trophies and regimental photographs on all the other walls. The Major sent the manservant away and poured the drinks himself, from a glass decanter in a sort of wooden frame device which unlocked with a key, saying as he did so, 'You like my little sanctum, eh? Well, bottoms up – good health and all that.' He raised his glass and sank into the deepest chair.

The brandy was absolutely excellent, far better than anything usually offered after lunch. This was another unaccustomed honour and Alex felt more and more uneasy as he took the other armchair on the far side of the fire, shadowed by a gigantic fern plant in a huge brass pot. All this affability was not the Major's general style. He was leading up to something, Alex felt quite sure, and he had an uncomfortable suspicion that he might know what it was.

He braced himself for an embarrassing exchange. He wasn't ready to be asked what his intentions were towards Miss Caroline. He didn't really have any, if the truth were told. He found things satisfactory exactly as they were: an undemanding conversation over a pleasant lunch followed by a gallop on a splendid horse. But how could he explain this to his host – or indeed to Caroline, who was no doubt entertaining other hopes of him?

The Major put his glass down and cleared his throat a touch. 'I wanted to have a quiet word with you, before we went in to lunch.'

This was it, then! Alex gulped more brandy than he'd intended to, and almost ended up by spluttering. But he managed to contain it and murmur – though his voice came out unusually hoarse – 'Of course, sir. What was it about?'

The Major surprised him by broaching something else. 'Fact is, I happened to run into Old Broughton yesterday – you remember I mentioned that I saw him now and then?' He made that little throat-clearing noise again. 'Found myself sitting next to him at some charity affair. I took the opportunity to put in a word for you.' He leaned back and looked at his guest expectantly.

'That's extremely . . .' Alex said, and let the sentence lapse. Here was another dilemma he wasn't ready for. If he expressed undying gratitude, as the Major was obviously expecting him to do, he might invite the same thing to occur again. And the truth was that he did not welcome it. He had fought for years to stand on his own feet, without his parents pulling strings for him behind the scenes, and now here was someone else's father doing it. Or trying to at least; it was possible that it would have the opposite effect. The Borough Chief of Police (Alex could not think of him as 'Old Broughton' even now) had never been a military man and was said to have delivered a famous diatribe against 'these ex-army johnnies trying to pull rank and interfering with the running of the civilian force'.

But Alex could hardly say that either. He would offend his host, so he sought words that seemed decently polite. 'That was so unlooked for, Major, I don't know what to say,' he settled on at last, which had the advantage of being true at least.

The Major took it as an expression of delight. 'Oh, don't bother to thank me. It's of no account at all. It was the least that I could do. After all, I've known the chap for years. Caroline's been urging me for weeks to speak to him.'

Alex took another gulp to stay his nerves. He felt the liquid fire running through his veins and it emboldened him. 'It was kind of you to think of it, Major Knight, of course. But I doubt that the Borough Commissioner would even recognize my name. He does not have much to do with us junior constables.'

Knight tossed back his brandy with a practised hand. 'But my dear fellow, that's just where you are wrong. Old Broughton knew exactly who you were – especially when I pointed out that you'd topped the entrance test. Said oh yes, you'd done exceptionally well and he had been keeping an eye on your progress ever since. Apparently your training sergeant speaks very well of you in his regular reports.'

Alex murmured something deprecating in reply.

'Asked him outright what future prospects were and he told me, if you kept on doing well, you could expect promotion in due course and even have a village station of your own, with its own accommodation, within a year or two.' Knight warmed his brandy in his hands and slowly drained the glass. 'No doubt that's the sort of thing that you were aiming for?'

'That was my ambition, certainly.' Alex saw where this was leading and made a bold attempt to parry the attack. 'But you appreciate that it would take me several years before I could think of . . .'

The Major waved a hand to cut him off. 'A little police house in the country with perhaps a maid to help? And perhaps a sergeant's posting somewhere after that? It sounds idyllic in the abstract, I agree. But it's not the sort of life my daughter is accustomed to and I warn you that I think that she would find it difficult – though she will be of age quite shortly and wilful enough to defy my judgement I am sure.' He leaned forward sharply in the chair. 'No, my boy, we'll have to find another route for you. And that's where I can help. I hear from my contacts in the regiment that they are particularly keen to recruit qualified policemen nowadays, especially anyone who is handy with a horse – apparently the training and drill is excellent – and a proper commission would be well-nigh guaranteed. Now, young fellow, what do you say to that?'

Alex did not have anything to say to that at all, so he said nothing – which was probably as well.

Knight hurrumphed. 'Of course I realize that all this will take some time. You'd have to finish training and all that sort of thing. But if you did decide to make the switch, I promise you I would be generous for my daughter's sake. Though for the moment, this is just between ourselves. May I take it this is something you're prepared to think about?'

Alex squared his shoulders. 'I'm sorry, Major, I can't promise that. I've put my shoulder to the ploughshare and I don't want to change horses in the middle of the stream.' Panic was making him jumble up the images, so he tried to sound a little more decisive as he said, 'I like to finish what I have begun.'

He was expecting a verbal drubbing for his ingratitude, but strangely this seemed to be the right response, because the Major laughed. 'Good for you, my boy. Perhaps my daughter's right. There is more about you than the other weak-chinned lads her mother's brought here and had straggling after her. You stand by your principles and you won't be bought. I like that in a man – it shows decisiveness. We shall make a soldier of you yet.'

'But . . .' Alex muttered, but the Major cut him off.

'The army is the place for men of character. That's what Old Baden-Powell used to say. Served with him briefly in South Africa. Picture of me with him somewhere over there . . .' He gestured vaguely at the rows of photographs with his now-empty glass. 'Good times they were, too. So you think carefully about what I have said. There isn't any rush. A long engagement is quite the fashion nowadays and in a year or so you might be ready for a move.'

Alex said, in desperation, 'I'm not looking to rush into anything.'

'Good man! Let's drink to that.' He went as if to pour more brandy out when there was a sudden commotion in the hall outside: what sounded like a violent scuffle and men's voices raised in a way one did not associate with a house like this. Knight put down the decanter. 'What the devil's that?' He frowned at Alex, who had started to his feet.

'Do you need assistance? I am a policeman, after all.' Alex knew it sounded pompous, but he said it all the same.

The Major shook his head. 'Some disgruntled tenant, by the sound of it. There won't be any real trouble I am sure, but I'd better go out and investigate. I told the servants I was not to be disturbed. Help yourself to cognac.' He strode towards the door and opened it.

Alex had just time to glimpse the most amazing sight: a large man in boots and leggings and a workman's smock, waving a battered billy-cock hat in one enormous hand, while with the other he held the struggling, angry butler at arm's length – with about as much effort as if the man had been a fly.

The butler was protesting in a strangled voice, 'I've told him, sir, he can't just come in here . . .' He broke off as the hand around his throat began to shake him violently.

'And I say I want to see her. She's my blasted . . .' The newcomer had a bellow like a bull.

'Now listen here!' The Major roared, marching out and slamming shut the study door behind him. Alex found that he was left alone. He could still hear the bellowing, but it was muffled now to a distant wordless roar. How embarrassing! What the deuce was a man supposed to do when he found himself in a circumstance like this?

Lettie was arranging Miss Caroline's hair — for what seemed like the umpteenth time that day — and now her mistress was looking in the glass and saying discontentedly, 'I'm still not certain that I don't prefer it down. I'm afraid the chignon makes me look severe. What do you think, Lettie?'

And Lettie, who knew that her opinion would matter not a jot, tried not to look impatient and answered dutifully, 'Ah, but the chignon is very *à la mode*. And they will be sounding the gong for luncheon very soon. You don't want to be . . .' She stopped. There seemed to be a sudden fracas happening downstairs.

Miss Caroline had heard the noises, too. 'Whatever's that? That's not a visitor, that's a workman's voice! One of the estate workers perhaps, who's had too much to drink and burst into the house? Lettie, go and have a look and see what's happening.'

Lettie was curious herself. There was not much excitement in a well-run house like this, and the promise of a scandal gave her a secret thrill — besides, it would be something to tell Effie, next time that they met. She hurried to the balcony that overlooked the stairs and leaned over the banister to get a better view. What she saw below her made her exclaim aloud.

'Fayther! What the dickens are you doing, coming here! And in your carter's clothes, as well!' She could not believe her eyes. 'And let Mr Wilson go. You can't go treating the Major's butler in that way, holding him up and shaking him like a sack of beans. You'll lose me my position. What are you thinking of!' She was already running down the stairs.

Fayther had let Wilson go when he caught sight of her and the butler was muttering and straightening his clothes — she would never be able to think of him as dignified again. But this was no smiling matter. Major Knight himself had burst out of the study now, and was sounding absolutely furious. 'Now look here, my man, I don't know who you think you are, but you can't come stalking in . . .'

Fayther whirled around to face him. 'Can't I? Well, it seems you're wrong because I damty have. This is a family matter, an emergency. I am Ernie Pearson, that there is my daughter, and I want to talk to her.'

Lettie closed her eyes in horror. She knew what this must be about – though she hadn't said a word to anybody yet. She tried to rescue a little dignity. 'But Fayther! Can't it wait until I'm free? You can see that I'm in the middle of my chores. Miss Caroline—'

He cut her off. 'I don't give a tinker's fiddle for Miss Caroline. And as for your position, what difference does it make? If you're so blessed fond of working here, you should have thought of that before and not got yourself in this disgrace.' He reached up to where she had halted on the stair, grabbed her by the arm, and pulled her roughly down the last few steps to him.

'Now, look here my good fellow!' The Major had put on his blustering tone of voice. 'You can't just force your way into this house and demand to talk to my servants when it pleases you. Wilson, escort this fellow to the servants' stairs and see that he leaves the premises at once. And you, sir, will go quietly – or shall I ring for help? Some of my outside staff are hefty chaps and as it happens there's a policeman in the house . . .' He had gone over to the bell-pull and had one hand on it.

This threat had an immediate effect. Fayther quietened down and stopped his hollering, but all the same he didn't let her go. 'Oh, I'll go and welcome – but Lettie comes with me.' If anything he tightened his grip upon her arm.

'Fayther!' Lettie almost squealed. 'Let me go! You're hurting! And I can't just go with you. I'm supposed to be on duty . . .'

Fayther gave a bitter laugh. 'On duty, is it? I'll give you "on duty" when I get you home.' He had been drinking, she could smell it on his breath, and ale had made him reckless, like it always did. He turned to Major Knight. 'She hasn't told you then? I didn't think she would have. Well, I'll save her the trouble. She won't be coming back. She's going to be married, aren't you, dirty little cow? I've just had Bert Symons come and tell me so – though he wanted money to go through with it, young scoundrel that he is! I nearly had to bruise my knuckles knocking sense into the boy.'

'Lettie? What's the matter?' That was Miss Caroline, coming from her room to look down from the balcony herself, with her afternoon dress still all unbuttoned down the back. 'Don't you know I'm waiting?'

Fayther looked up at her. It must have been the drink, because he said – as though she were of no account at all – 'Well, you'll be waiting a long time then, 'cause she's coming home with me. I'm going to keep her under lock and key until we get a special licence through. You'll have to learn to dress yourself, miss, like the rest of us.'

'Papa? What is going on here?' Miss Caroline was shocked, as well she might have been. Nobody ever spoke to her like that.

The Major cleared his throat. 'It seems that Lettie is leaving us, my dear. This is her father and he's come to take her home and, if I understand aright, then it is just as well. It seems she's got herself in terrible disgrace, so I could not possibly have kept her on, in any case.' He looked at Lettie. 'Well, girl, you have caused us all embarrassment, at a moment when we have a luncheon guest as well, to say nothing of leaving my daughter in the lurch without a maid. I hope that you are proud of what you've done?'

Lettie made an effort to protest. 'It isn't my fault that Fayther came bursting in like this. I didn't know . . .'

The Major cut her off. 'From what I understand, it is entirely your fault. If I found my daughter – god forbid – in the same predicament, no doubt I'd feel equally incensed. Now I am not a harsh man; I shall see that you are paid what you are owed this week, despite the fact that you have forfeited your post – but you may take your notice as of now. You need not even go upstairs to fetch your things. I will have them sent over – just give Wilson the address. Wilson, see these people out and let the kitchen know that lunch will be delayed until one-fifteen. Caroline, go back and ring the parlour maid to help you dress. I'll put an advertisement into the press today for someone permanent.'

And he turned back to the study, went in and closed the door.

There was a silence, broken by Miss Caroline who called

down tearfully, 'Now look what you've done, you selfish, thoughtless girl! Left me without a proper maid — and at a time like this! When I am going to sit by Alex Dawes at lunch! And just when I'd got used to you, and trained you properly! Now what on earth am I supposed to do?' She turned on her heel and flounced angrily away — though because of the buttons her exit was a little less impressive from the rear.

Wilson did his best to take control of things. 'Then Mr Pearson, is it? If you'd care to come this way? The servants' entrance is downstairs at the back.'

'It's not the servants' entrance this time, it's the exit,' Fayther said. 'And the last time you go through it either way, my girl!' He still had hold of her and bundled her along. 'And after all the trouble that your stepmother went to, pulling strings to see you got the job! Well, I hope you're pleased with what you've brought us to! Having to bribe the grocer's boy to marry you and threaten him with all sorts if he didn't get a special licence before your trouble starts to show — I suppose he took advantage, though he swears you led him on.'

Lettie said nothing; she was too full of tears, though there was a good deal more angry shouting to be endured as she was hustled home. But as her stepmother told her firmly, as she locked her in the box-room without anything for tea, Lettie Pearson was a lucky girl. It could have been the work-house for her and the child, but it hadn't come to that.

Bert had obviously changed his mind again and would have wormed his way out of this wedding if he could, but — however cross he was — good old Fayther had stood up for her, so she would still be married and it would be all right.

Two

Alex was in the study, completely at a loss. The sounds from the hallway had subsided now but there was no sign of his host returning, even so.

He thought of pouring another brandy as he'd been invited to but the decanter was almost empty and he did not like to take the little that was left. Instead he found himself walking around the room pretending to be interested in the photographs. There were a great many portraits showing Major Knight when young – looking quite dapper in his uniform – and pictures of him dressed for various physical pursuits (cricket and riding in particular), a few shots of him posing with the big game he had shot, and one extraordinary photo showing him in shorts, looking knock-kneed and scrawny in a tug-of-war.

Alex was embarrassed by the knees. He moved away towards the other wall where there were more formal photographs of groups. He found the Baden-Powell one, and lots of others showing men lined up in serried ranks both with horses and without them. Perhaps his father would be in one of them? He ran his eye along the lists of names: Bellwether, Hinton, Selwyn, Royston, Knight . . . He paused. Royston. Why did that ring a bell? Surely he had heard it somewhere, recently?

He looked more closely at the individual in the photograph – a rather dashing fellow with a curled moustache and handsome side-whiskers, whose thick hair was combed backwards in a fetching wave like Bronco Billy in the poster outside the picture house. He was still staring at it when Major Knight came in.

'Storm in a teacup about one of the maids,' the Major said. 'I've given her her marching orders, so that's disposed of that. Sorry to have to abandon you like that. Found someone in your family?' he added heartily, coming over to look at the photograph as well.

Alex shook his head. 'It's this fellow Royston I was looking at. It's not a common name and someone was enquiring for a Royston recently at the police station. Called him Captain Royston; could this be the one?'

'I suppose it's possible.' Knight had turned away, taken a bottle from a drawer and was refilling the decanter as he spoke. 'Though he was a London man; don't know why they would be looking for him here. Lieutenant when I knew him, but no doubt he rose. Brave as a tiger − though headstrong as a charging elephant when he chose to be.'

'But you did know him?' Alex asked, aware that this was sounding like an interview. 'He was in the Devonshires?'

'Only on secondment, as I remember it.' Knight came across again and peered at the photograph again. 'That was taken outside Paardeburg. Dickie Royston was seconded as my aide de camp − my usual fellow had taken a bullet in the foot. He was moved on shortly after; I don't know what happened to him then.' He paused and frowned, waving the decanter vaguely in the air. 'Though come to think of it − didn't I hear he was cashiered? Can't remember at this distance. Brigade would tell you, if you wrote to them. Why do you want to know?'

Alex took refuge in a vague official stance. 'Concerns a missing person, that's all I can say. Police business − confidential as I'm sure you'll understand. But this man may be relevant. Cashiered, did you say? In which case he would not be entitled to use a rank at all. What would that have been for? Cowardice? Desertion?'

Knight had gone back to the table and refilled his glass. 'Shouldn't think so for a minute. Not his style at all. Conduct unbecoming in an officer, I expect you'll find. Attacking a superior, perhaps − I can imagine him doing that when he was in his cups. Can't remember now.' He barked a laugh. 'Stealing the regimental silver, I wouldn't be surprised, and selling it to put the money on a horse.'

'That fits with what we know about the missing man,' Alex said, too eagerly. He was trying to remember Jenkins' account of his interview with Broadbent − and wishing heartily that he had paid a little more attention at the time. 'We were told he liked a flutter.'

Knight swallowed his brandy in a single draught. 'More than a flutter, in Dickie Royston's case. Bet on anything – two drops of water on a window pane if there was nothing else. And he never seemed to learn. Even when he lost (which he generally did) he was always convinced that the next one was "cert" and if he didn't have the stake money he'd try to borrow it – and with his looks and charm it is surprising how often he got away with it.' He put down the glass. 'Tried to touch me for a shilling once – wanted to bet on which of two red ants would cross the compound first.'

'When you were his superior?' Alex was amazed. He tried to visualize himself asking 'Old Broughton' for a loan to gamble with, but his imagination failed.

Another snort of laughter. 'That's the sort of feckless fellow Dickie Royston was. Of course I didn't come across with it – and just as well, he would have lost the lot. All part of his love of taking risks I suppose. Mentioned in dispatches several times. I was sorry when I heard that he had been cashiered, but I was not surprised. He was always rushing in where wiser men would pause. Haven't thought about the chap for years. As to what became of him, I have no idea at all.' He was locking up the decanter in its wooden frame again and Alex realized that the subject was being closed as well.

He made a last attempt. 'But I can tell my superiors what you've just said to me? It may turn out to be significant.'

'Oh you're welcome to tell them anything you like – I only wish that I could help you more and I wish you better luck with your enquiries elsewhere. Might do your promotion prospects a little bit of good.' He favoured Alex with a mighty wink. 'And now it is time to join the ladies, what? But not a word to them about all this, of course.'

And Alex was obliged to sit beside Miss Caroline at lunch, making small talk and enduring the Major's private smiles, while the unexpected information he had gleaned burned like an impatient fire in his brain. In the end he could not bear it any more. He excused himself from going out riding after all (on the pretence that there was a threat of coming rain) and

– to the evident disappointment of his hosts – hurried back
to tell Sergeant Vigo and Jenkins what he knew.

Walter got his crutches and a proper curse they were. He hadn't
imagined it would be so difficult. The doctor had fitted a
much lighter splint by now, but his foot and leg were still
swathed in bandages and he had been warned that his bad
ankle would not yet bear his weight, so he was reduced to
virtually hopping everywhere, supported by his arms.

'If we'd had you in plaster of Paris, like they would have
done in town, it would have held you better. But it will come,
in time. Though mind you take it easy for a day or two – just
around the house until you're used to it.'

The man had spoken as if Walter was likely to have set off
for a stroll, but it was a major undertaking just to hobble down
the stairs – and he had to sit down for an hour and recover,
even then. It was ridiculous. He had always been so strong!
But now his arms were aching from merely doing that – though
he was profoundly grateful for the change of scene.

There was one ambition that he had managed to achieve.
When he got his breath back, and Madge was busy upstairs
putting right the bed, he went out to the yard and visited the
privy on his own – it wasn't easy, dealing with your clothes
when you were trying to balance on a crutch and half a leg
– but it gave him a feeling of dignity after all these weeks of
struggling to use the wretched chamber-pot (and having to
ask his sister to help him, even then).

Madge was furious when she found out, of course. 'You
could have fallen over, and where should we be then!' But he
refused to promise that he'd wait for her to go out with him
next time.

'I'm not a damty child, Madge. I managed this time, and I
will again. You watch, now I'm up and walking I'll get stronger
every day. Now hand me that tea cloth and I'll help you wipe
the cloam. Make myself a bit more useful than I've been till
now. Don't make that face at me. I can dry up while I'm
sitting here, on the settle by the fire.'

And so he did. But the effort of walking all that way had
taken more out of him than he supposed and he must have

nodded off, because he only woke up when the rest of them came in, and were clamouring round the kitchen table for their tea.

'You had a visitor a little while ago,' Madge called, from the scullery where she was slicing bread. 'But when she saw you sleeping she went away again. Wouldn't disturb you for the world, she said.'

Walter paused in the act of spearing a pickled onion to join his slice of home-made brawn. 'Never Effie?' He could not keep the disappointment from his voice. 'She don't belong to come on Monday as a rule.'

'Don't be so bally daft! As if I'd let her go without you seeing her!' His sister came in with the laden plate and put it on the table with the butter pat. The younger children all reached out at once, but Madge said sharply, 'Cheese or butter, you can take your choice. Not you, Walter; you and Joe can have a bit of each. Menfolk need the extra to keep up their strength.' She doled out the little cubes of crumbly cheese, which she must have got from Crowdie earlier in the day. 'No, it was Mrs Richards asking after you. Tommy Richards' widow,' she added, as if Walter might misunderstand. 'Came with Peter Kellow — he says they'll call again. Asked to be remembered to you, by the way.'

''Spect it will be Thursday that we see him then,' he muttered with a grin, then — before anyone could ask him what he meant by that — he added, 'So I'll make sure that I'm managing these crutches a bit better before then. Though p'raps you'd better give me an 'and to get upstairs first time, Joe, old lad.'

It was an awful struggle, worse than getting down — largely because Joe had no sense at all of how to help, let alone hold the candle up to light the way — but they managed in the end and Walter was quite glad to settle into bed again. But he meant what he had said: he would walk a little further every single day. Tomorrow would be better and the next day better still. Perhaps he could even get back out to the shed — with a stool to sit on he could use his tools a bit, re-sole those shoes that Madge was on about and maybe even do a bit of whittling. Imagine if Effie could find him doing that!

Full of these happy thoughts he fell asleep, before he'd even had the time to blow the night-light out. Madge must have looked in later and snuffed it out herself.

Effie had lingered at the haberdashery for longer than she should, but there was no sign of Lettie anywhere. She was rather disappointed, for she had hoped to see her friend – not only to hear more details of the wedding plans (Lettie would surely have begun to make them now), but also because she wanted to ask her for advice.

About Peter Kellow. What was she to do? Even Pa was in the know about him, it appeared, and kept on dropping hints – what a nice boy Peter was, how the two families had known each other for years, and what hard-working, honest fellows all the Kellows were. And it was true; she was aware of that. Peter was everything a girl like her could want – except he wasn't Alex. She gave herself a shake. What difference did it make? Alex wasn't walking out with her these days, giving her half-accidental kisses in the lane; he was off courting that Miss Caroline! It didn't help Effie's state of mind to know that she very likely had herself to blame – she was the one who'd said that it would never do, because of the difference between their families. But he didn't have to take her so quickly at her word, she thought indignantly.

Well, it was no good standing around here any longer, pretending to be having trouble matching silks. She'd already taken half a dozen to the door 'to see them in the light' but actually to look for Lettie up and down the street, and now there was no further possible excuse. She went back to the silks she'd started with, and had intended to purchase all along, and took them to the counter for Miss Pearl to wrap.

Miss Pearl was looking particularly sour. 'Made up your mind then, have you?' she enquired, stretching her thin mouth into a mirthless smile. 'That's one and ninepence, after all that time.'

Effie fumbled in the pocket of her cape and pulled out the necessary coins. 'It's always difficult to match the greens,' she offered, apologetically. 'If I could ask Miss Blanche—'

Miss Weston cut her off. 'Well unfortunately, that isn't possible, because she isn't here. Found some new errand to take her into town. She's taken to doing that almost every day. I've told her we could pay an errand-boy, but no! Claims that exercise is beneficial to her health. Leaves me on my own like this to man the shop – just when we are having an enormous run on gloves. And when I remonstrate it seems to make her worse. I don't know what's got into her – it's not like Blanche at all.'

Effie had the wit to realize that this complaint was not really addressed to her at all, but that Miss Pearl simply needed to let off steam a bit, so she just said brightly, 'Yes. I saw her this morning walking down the street. And she was looking blooming, so perhaps she's right. They do say that exercise is good for you these days – even if you are a lady like Miss Blanche.' (She did not add that when she'd glimpsed her near the post office, Miss Blanche had been engrossed in conversation with a man – that Mr Broadbent who had called at Mrs Thatchell's house the other day. Perhaps she was helping him with his enquiries.)

Miss Pearl pulled her thin mouth thinner still. 'I never heard such nonsense. Exercise indeed!' She pressed the buttons on the cash register and made the price come up, while she put the florin in the open drawer and took out a threepenny bit. 'And threepence change.'

Effie took the tiny coin and slipped it in her purse, while Miss Pearl put the silks into a paper bag. 'Well, I'll have to hurry,' she said aloud, to no one in particular. 'Mrs Thatchell will be wanting . . .' She broke off as she heard the shop door ring.

It was Miss Blanche returning, and she was not alone. It was not Mr Broadbent opening the door and standing back to let the lady through, instead it was a man in policeman's uniform.

'Alex!' Effie could not believe her eyes. 'What are you doing here?'

'Looking for you, Effie,' Miss Blanche replied. Her horse face was radiant, and she gave a girlish laugh. 'I told him that I'd seen you walking up this way and that you usually came on Tuesday to the shop. I was on my way myself, so I came back with him.'

Miss Pearl had set her face into a frown. 'Bringing the police into the shop again! My dear Blanche, what on earth will people think!'

Alex gave her his most disarming smile. 'They'll think exactly what you would hope they'd think — that you two ladies are on good terms with the police. But I won't cause you any more embarrassment. I'll speak to Miss Pengelly outside in the street.' He opened the shop door. 'Miss Pengelly, if you wouldn't mind? Official business; it won't take very long.'

Effie, who had been listening to all this with dismay, found her tongue again. 'Official business? What's this all about?' But he had grasped her gently by the arm and was propelling her outside. On the pavement she turned to glare at him. 'And why am I "Miss Pengelly", suddenly?'

He shook his head at her. 'It's all right, Effie. Don't disturb yourself. I just did not want those two to overhear. But I have some news I thought that you should hear. It's about that man who died.'

'Captain Royston? If that really was his name.'

'I believe it was. I found a photograph at Major Knight's. I think it's the same man. You saw a picture of him, didn't you?'

She nodded. 'Good-looking fellow with a big moustache and wavy hair, smart as all get out in army uniform. Didn't look much like the corpse I saw, but as I said to Mr Broadbent, it just might have been — if you took off the whiskers and thinned out the hair and face. The picture must have been taken years and years ago. If he was old and poor and hungry he'd get thin, I suppose.'

Alex nodded. 'It's possible. And your picture does sound very much like mine.'

She looked up at him — then turned away again. She didn't want to look into his eyes. 'How don't you go and talk to Mr Broadbent then? He's got the photograph.'

She wasn't looking but she could feel him smile and his voice was gentle as he said, 'Of course, I'll have to do that. I always knew I would. But I wanted to see you, if the truth was told. This gave me an excuse. I promised I'd tell you if I discovered anything.'

She did look at him then. 'I thought that you were seeing someone else.'

'And so are you,' he countered. 'I saw you riding with him on that cart. And then you sent that note, saying that you wouldn't meet me, because of some incident at home. And when I remembered the way that fellow looked at you . . .'

She interrupted. 'Incident?' She wrinkled up her nose. 'I wrote no such thing. I said that there had been an accident. My poor Pa has been laid up in bed, with his leg all splinted and his ankle broke – there was a fall of bad rock in the mine. One man was killed and another boy was hurt – I'm surprised you never heard.'

He shook his head. 'Not a police matter, I suppose. I did see something mentioned in the press, about there being a fatality, but it was not a name I knew. It just said that two other members of the team were hurt but were not in any danger of their lives. I never imagined it would concern your Pa. I'm sorry to hear that. I know how much your father means to you. How is he managing?'

She made a face. 'Not as well as I would like him to – though he's got his crutches now and should be beginning to get around on them. So I hope to find him better when I next go home.'

'Which will be on Thursday?' Alex said.

She nodded. 'And before you ask, I shall be doing that. Obviously I can't be meeting you, with Pa the way he is.' She realized as she said it that Alex had not suggested that she should.

He grinned, the grin that always made her knees go weak. 'Wouldn't expect otherwise, Effie. But you'll be catching the noon horse-bus I expect? Suppose that I was there to see you on to it? I know you think it isn't sensible but I have missed our little chats.'

'And what about Miss Knight?'

'Miss Knight can do without me for one afternoon.'

He said it so bitterly that she was moved to say, 'You mustn't hurt her feelings, not on account of feeling sympathy for me. Lettie says Miss Caroline is very fond of you.'

He gave a scornful laugh. 'I don't think there's any danger that it will break her heart. What Caroline is really fond of is herself. I should be more sorry to offend her family. The

Major, in particular, has been good to me. He has even unwittingly brought me back to you – if it were not for him I never would have found that photograph at all. Dicky Royston was his aide-de-camp.'

'Whatever is an aidy-camp?' she asked, and then realized what he'd said. 'Dicky Royston?' She emphasized the word. 'Then it isn't the same man after all. Mr Broadbent said that he was Arthur, I am sure.'

He stared at her. 'You are quite sure of that?' He frowned. 'Might be a brother or something I suppose. But you're sure that he said Arthur?'

'Well I think he called him "Artie", but isn't it the same? Peter Kellow's father is called Arthur, I am sure, but they always call him Artie down the mine.'

Alex slapped his thigh. 'Not Artie!' he said suddenly. 'It's R.T. Don't you see? It must be his initials. And you see the possible significance of that?'

She thought for a moment before she got the point. 'You mean it might have been the same with me? Maybe it wasn't Effie that he wanted after all? It was F. E. Pengelly he was looking for?' She let out a long sigh. 'Be some relief to me, if that was true. But who on earth is that? I don't know any Pengellys with names that start with "F". Though, come to think of it, there might have been a second-cousin Frank who went abroad. Australia or something. But that was years ago. Why would anyone be looking for him here?'

Alex was grinning. 'It is a lead, at least. The shipping offices have lists of all their passengers. I'll put Jenkins on to it. He has already written to Army Lists and Records to enquire about Lieutenant Richard Royston and his subsequent career.' He made a wry face. 'Apparently he had a glittering record in the field but Knight says he was dishonourably discharged.'

The words brought Effie to her senses, suddenly. 'Dear Lord! And so shall I be, if I don't get home. Mrs Thatchell will be having vapours as it is.'

'Then I won't delay you longer.' He gave her a shy smile. 'But I'll see you Thursday?'

She nodded silently and hurried off but the promise gave her wings and she was not as late as she had feared she would be. But she got an awful jawing from Mrs Thatchell anyway, for having left the bag of sewing silks behind her in the shop. She had to do without her lunch and scuttle back for them.

Three

'Well, I trust your urgent errand was a success?' Pearl demanded sourly, when Effie and her policeman friend had gone and Blanche was alone with her sister in the shop again.

Blanche pulled out her hatpins and removed her hat – her very best one, with the tulle and roses on. 'It was. I caught the midday post,' she said.

'Though why you had to take that order letter down in such a rush, I simply do not know. It would have done quite well another time, without your leaving me on my own to run the shop for more than half an hour!'

Blanche swallowed. Where she got the courage was a mystery that she would never understand, but she found it from somewhere. She took off her nice beige Sunday coat and said, quite mildly, 'Would you come into the office for a minute, Pearl? I need to speak to you.'

It was such a reversal of their usual roles that Pearl looked quite affronted and amazed, but she said stiffly, 'I suppose so, if you must.' She led the way, stiff-backed, into the little room and stood by the fire like a sentry at his post, ready with a challenge. Sure enough, it came. 'What is it this time? Some other modern nonsense that you've read about in the Haberdasher's Weekly magazine? I grant you that the business with matching up the gloves has proved to be a moderate success. But enough's enough. We're not in London here. Our customers like things as they are, they don't want us trying to fancify the shop.'

Blanche had been trying to signal all this time that what she had to say was nothing to do with haberdashery, but without success. So she turned away to hang her hat and coat up on the rack, and when her sister paused for breath, she murmured quietly, 'The fact is, Pearl, you'll have to know – I've met a gentleman.'

'A gentleman!' her sister said, in a tone which suggested that

it was preposterous – as if Blanche had remarked that she had
met a hippopotamus. A pause, and then 'I knew it!' though it
clearly wasn't true. 'That's why you've been gallivanting round
the town like this! Whatever would our father have had to say
to that! It isn't decent at your time of life. I tell you now,
Blanche, it will simply have to stop.' She had turned a brilliant
shade of puce. 'Who is it anyway? Someone inappropriate, I
have no doubt at all.'

Blanche cleared the boxes off a chair and sat down cautiously
– anything was better than a confrontation eye-to-eye. 'His
name's Josiah Broadbent,' she began.

'Not the wretch who came . . .?'

'The very same,' Blanche countered. 'And not a wretch at
all. He's a very pleasant person when you get to talk to him
– as you might have discovered for yourself if you had not
been so determined to order him away.' Pearl seemed about to
protest, but Blanche found inner strength and waved the words
aside. 'As to his being inappropriate, that is a matter of opinion
I suppose. He has a decent business in the capital, and has
inherited a little house – he lived there with his mother and
nursed her till she died, which is why he never married. But
he's done me the honour of asking for my hand. That makes
him seem very appropriate to me.'

Her sister sat down abruptly, on the chair opposite – apparently oblivious to the pile of socks already on the seat. When
she spoke she sounded shaken to the core. 'Blanche, you are
such a foolish innocent. You hardly know the man. Most likely
he has seen these premises and is only hoping to gain a share
of it. No, this is nonsense; put the thought away. I would not
permit it anyway. And you have never set foot outside Penzance.
What would you do in the capital?'

'It's not a foreign country, Pearl. You talk as if Father did
not come from there. I'll do what Mother did, I suppose, and
learn to be a wife.'

Pearl made a scornful noise. 'You talk about it very glibly
now, Blanche dear, but you're not fit to marry anyone. You've
never run a household in your life. You haven't the first idea
what married life is like.'

Blanche felt an unexpected wave of sympathy. 'Neither have

you, my dear,' she murmured, in her gentlest voice. 'I know
that's been a sorrow to you half your life. And I grieved for
you when your beau let you down. But this is my chance to
grasp a little happiness – probably the only chance I'll ever
have – surely you would not deny it to me now?' She'd hoped
to see Pearl soften but there was no reply so she said, with a
sudden courage in her tone, 'Not that you *could* deny it, so
Josiah says. I am of age and I don't need your consent. I've
given him my answer and he's already making arrangements
for the banns.'

Pearl turned away, her face as blank as stone. She still refused
to speak.

'Though I would like to have it, and your blessing too, if
you could find it in your heart,' Blanche said plaintively. She
leaned forward and tried to take her sister's hand, but it was
snatched away. She tried a different tactic. 'But if you can't,
we will have to do without,' she said more coldly, getting to
her feet.

Pearl snapped her head around to glare at her and Blanche
was startled to see the glint of teardrops in her eyes. 'Do
without!' Pearl muttered. 'It's me who'll do without! How am
I supposed to live here on my own, manage the shop and run
the library and everything besides? Did you even give a thought
to things like that?'

Blanche sat down again. 'More thought than you suppose.
Josiah says we'll come down once a year and he will try and
help you balance the accounts – I know that's always been a
trial for you. And I will try to find suppliers for you in the
capital.'

'We don't need new suppliers!' Pearl burst out, petulant.
'We've always used the ones that Father chose.'

'And though we have been customers for years, they still
charge us full price for everything. Josiah thinks that we could
get a discount if I tried – especially if we threatened to move
our trade to somewhere else. We have talked it over and Josiah
says—'

'Josiah says!' Pearl echoed mockingly. 'I'm tired of hearing
what Josiah says. What does he know about haberdashery?
Only what you've told him, and what good is that? You've

never been the slightest good at ordering, or keeping stock or making up the books.'

'Only because I never had the chance!' Blanche was rather stung. 'But it's true that you have always seen to everything yourself – which means you really do not need me anyway. Though I shall keep a modest interest in the shop, of course – and try to help from London, as I said before.'

'And am I expected to run the place alone? I can't afford to pay an extra pair of hands.'

'You could take a lodger – there will be an empty room. That would help pay the wages for a girl. After all you won't have me to keep – and it would prevent you from having to live here on your own.' This time she caught the hand and held it in her own. 'And of course you must come and visit us – just as we shall come and visit you. I couldn't bear it if we were not friends.'

Pearl snatched the hand away and stood up suddenly. 'You've thought it all out, haven't you – you and your precious friend? Well, since I can't prevent you, I must make the best of it. But don't blame me if it all ends in tears.'

Blanche understood her sister. She was on her feet at once. 'Then you won't object too much? You'll come to the wedding? It will be very small – hardly more than just the three of us.'

Pearl said, tightly, 'What good would it do me if I did object? You've already told me that you'd do it anyhow. But I decline to spend a fortune on a wedding coat; the one I have will simply have to do.' Two tears were gently spilling from her eyes, but she did not try to wipe them from her cheeks – as if by ignoring them she could pretend they were not there. She went on in a strange unsteady voice, 'And if I'm to be related to this wretched man, you'd better arrange to have him come to tea, I suppose.' She turned and picked up the socks from the chair. 'Now look what you have gone and made me do – these have got all creased, and we haven't even put them on the shelves!'

It was the nearest to a blessing that Blanche was going to get.

Alex walked back to the police station in a sort of dream and almost collided with Jenkins in the entrance way.

'Look out, young Dawes! What are you playing at?' Jenkins had almost dropped the pile of papers in his hand.

Alex shook his head. The truth was that he hardly knew himself what he was 'playing at'. He had set out to find Effie, to tell her his news, but he had not planned to promise to see her on the bus – that had simply seemed the natural, proper thing to do when he was in her presence. But now he had the problem of dealing with the Knights: he would have to let them know that he would not be there, and they would doubtless be a bit offended, as it was, by his premature departure on his last visit there. He heaved a heartfelt sigh.

'Good God, man, what's the matter?' Jenkins had dropped his teasing tone and sounded genuinely concerned. 'You look and sound as if the problems of the world are on your back.'

Alex shook his head. 'Oh, it's nothing really. Just given myself a problem for Thursday afternoon. I'm wondering if I ought to try to change my duty-shift that day.'

'Ah!' Jenkins gave a would-be friendly leer. 'Women problems, is it? Wish I had your luck.' He tapped the pile of papers with a forefinger. 'Which reminds me – there's something here that might just interest you. That "unidentified" that we were dealing with – wasn't there some connection with that maid-servant you used to squire about, before you started consorting with the gentry every week?'

Alex was unnerved by that description of events. It made him sound a cad. Perhaps he was, he thought. He said, in a rather priggish tone of voice, 'No connection had been proved at all. Unless you've got something there tells us otherwise.'

Jenkins raised an eyebrow. 'Steady on, old chap! I'm only pursuing information which you gave me yourself. I wrote as you suggested to the Army Board and I've just had a reply. Come to the desk a minute and I'll let you see.'

He led the way and Alex followed him into the room.

Jenkins rifled through the papers. 'Here it is. "Re: Richard Thatchell Royston. I have the honour to reply to your enquiry . . . Blah, blah, blah . . . Mentioned in despatches, served South Africa . . ." Yes, here's the bit we want: "Returned to England September 1903 . . . Court-martialled in December of that year . . . conduct likely to bring the service into

disrepute, evidence of general moral turpitude and two days'
absence without official leave. Stripped of his rank and dishonourably discharged . . ." There's quite a lot, but that's the gist
of it. You'd better read it through and let me have it back.' He
handed the document to Alex as he spoke.

Alex stared at it. 'Richard Thatchell Royston?' Surely that
could not be a coincidence. It was not unusual for people to
carry their mother's maiden name. There must be a connection. And it would make sense. Effie had told him the story
about the former maid called Efigenia. They had even laughed
about it at the time – how Mrs Thatchell had preferred to go
on calling her new maid 'Effie' too (rather than Ethel, as she'd
wanted at the time), because it was easier to remember that
– although it was impossible for Alex to think of Effie as ever
having any other name.

'What's in a name?' He'd learned that play at school and
quoted from the speech before he'd realized it.

Jenkins frowned at him. 'What do you mean by that?'

Alex put the papers back down on the desk. 'I think you
might have solved our little mystery. I don't think it was my
Effie that he wanted after all. We may have been searching for
acorns up a linden tree. But I suppose I ought to check. I'm
quite sure that Miss Weston told me that he'd said "Pengelly"
too – I wonder if he did, or if she just supplied that when
trying to recall?' He nodded to Jenkins. 'I'll go and talk to her,
and if I learn what I expect to learn I'll go and see what Mrs
Thatchell has to say, and find out if this fellow was a relative.
And I think I'll call in on that Broadbent man as well. I hear
he has a photo that might be relevant.' He jammed his helmet
on his head and made as if to leave.

Jenkins called after him, 'But what about the letter?'

Alex paused a moment and then went back for it. 'On
second thoughts, I'll take it with me after all. It might help if
I am carrying what evidence we have.'

The administrative police clerk handed it to him and went
on fossicking. 'And there's another letter for you, somewhere.
A personal one this time – from your mother, by the look of
it. Judging by the post-mark anyway. Yes, here it is.' He produced
the monogrammed envelope with a knowing smile.

Alex glanced at the distinctive, spidery handwriting. It was Mater's hand all right, no doubt complaining that he'd upset the Knights. He stuffed it in his pocket, as it was. He'd deal with all that later; just for now it seemed imperative to go and sort this other business out. The worry had caused poor Effie lots of sleepless nights.

Jenkins was saying, 'Not going to open it?'

Alex shook his head. 'Not at the moment. I want to follow up this information that you got for me.' He was about to move away, but it suddenly occurred to him that if he did not answer her letter by return, Mama might try to telephone him here – she would not care what people thought. He turned back to Jenkins. 'If she rings here asking for me – which she might, although I've warned her that it's not appropriate – just tell her that I'm on duty and not available, but I will write her when I can. It will be true enough. There's a lot to do in connection with this case. And I'd better do it quickly. There's no time to spare.'

He was not sure why he felt such urgency, but he genuinely did. He wanted to prove that he could solve this thing himself, and it also seemed important to free Effie from her doubts. Clutching the Army document he picked up his cape and baton and, almost neglecting to salute the Station Inspector who had just come in, marched out into the street, leaving a startled pair of policemen staring after him.

Effie was astonished when she got back to the shop to find a policeman's bicycle propped up beside the wall. She positively rushed round to the kitchen door.

Mrs Lane looked up at her as she arrived. 'Well here you are at last, and just in time as well. I'm in a quandary what I ought to do. We've had a policeman and a gentleman arrive and insist on seeing Mrs Thatchell straight away. I tried to turn them off, but they made such a fuss that in the end she came out of the morning room herself – and to my surprise she made me let them in. Well I came and made a tray of tea, of course – well, you would do, wouldn't you, when there are visitors? But it's been twenty minutes and she hasn't rung for it. I don't know if I should take it up or no.' She gazed at

Effie, who was taking off her cloak. 'But you're here now, so you had better go.'

'Me?' Effie was alarmed. She didn't relish the idea of barging in, if Mrs Thatchell didn't want the tea. She knew how her employer treated people who interrupted her.

'Well, you got those silks to take her, haven't you? I heard her tell you to bring them straight away. Besides it's your job – if it's anyone's – to take the tea tray in.' She gave Effie a funny sideways look. 'What's more, it's your two gentlemen who are up there with her now.'

'My two gentlemen?' Effie cried, amazed. 'What gentlemen are those? I don't know any gentlemen at all.' Then she remembered the police bicycle outside. 'You don't mean Alex? The young constable that came?'

Cook looked triumphant. 'If that's his name, then that's exactly who I mean. And that bowler-hatted fellow that you talked to on the step. Don't think I didn't see him, 'cause I've got eyes, you know – I saw you when I was taking out some scraps, to leave for Mrs Mitchell when she came.'

'Mr Broadbent? What's he doing here again?' Effie felt uneasy suddenly. 'Here, it isn't about that blessed corpse again, I hope? I've told them till I'm sick of saying it that I had never seen him in my life before.' She turned to Mrs Lane. 'Well there is only one way to find out. Let's have that blooming tray. She'll have my guts for garters, but at least I'll know the worst – and if I take the tea up, it will give me an excuse.'

'You're a good girl, Effie.' Cook looked quite relieved. 'Let me freshen up the tea.' She took a cloth and seized the kettle from the hob as she suited the action to the word. 'There, that's better. You can take it up. And if she's nasty, tell her you was sent.'

'I'd better take these damty silks to her as well.' Effie slipped them in her pocket as she spoke. 'Though I'm bound to be wrong, if I do or if I don't. You know what Mrs Thatchell can be like.' She picked up the heavy tray.

Cook came up and held the swing baize door for her, and Effie sidled to the morning room. Her heart was beating like a drummer at the fair as she balanced the tea-tray on the what-not in the hall, and tapped softly on the door.

Mrs Thatchell did not answer her and Effie stood a moment, wondering what to do. But then the door swung open and to her surprise she found Mr Broadbent smiling down at her. 'Ah, Miss Pengelly. And you've brought some tea. I think your mistress might be glad of it. You had better come inside.' He stood aside to let her walk into the room.

Mrs Thatchell was sitting in her normal chair, but that was the only normal thing about the way she looked. Her hair was half-dishevelled, as if she'd had her hands in it, and her face was all contorted and red and streaked with tears.

'Madam?' Effie put the tray down and went across to her. 'Is something the matter?' It was a stupid question – there obviously was.

Her mistress looked up dully. 'Oh, tell her, someone, do. She'll have to find out sometime. What does it matter now? For years and years I've tried to live it down, but it's come back to haunt me. I thought that I'd be safe here, but I shall have to go. I can't stay in Penzance once this has got about.'

'Why, what is it, madam?' Effie cried. This was not the Mrs Thatchell that she knew at all.

'Effie!' It was Alex. She hadn't noticed him, standing by the window with his helmet in his hand. 'This concerns you slightly. It is best you understand, though there isn't any need to spread the news outside this room. You understand?'

She nodded.

'Mrs Thatchell is understandably upset . . .'

But he couldn't finish because Mrs Thatchell was saying, inexplicably, 'Please don't call me that. Miss Borlaise will do me very well. It is what I was born with, and it's all that I deserve.'

'But . . .' Effie started, but Alex raised a hand to silence her.

'It's an unhappy story. Not Mrs Thatchell's fault. And I'm sorry, madam, but I'm going to call you that, because you deserve a title of respectability. The thing is, Effie, she was married once—'

'Only I wasn't!' Mrs Thatchell snapped.

Alex went on as if she hadn't said a word. 'Or she believed she was: there was a proper wedding ceremony and she had a ring, though she married a man of whom her family did not much approve.'

'They said he was a gambler,' Mrs Thatchell said. 'But he was worse than that. He was already married – if I only knew – and with a child as well. Of course, I knew he often went away, but he told me it was army business and I never questioned it. And then he was posted to South Africa. I missed him terribly, but he wrote me every month and I thought that I was lucky – can you imagine that! And when I heard that he was coming home, I went up to meet him – but I was not the only one! This other woman and her child were there, and when I asked for Ricky Thatchell, I was told there wasn't one. It wasn't even his proper surname – as I soon found out.' She buried her streaked face in both her hands.

'His name was Royston,' Mr Broadbent said. 'Thatchell was his mother's maiden name and he reverted to it, for the second wife. I suppose he thought it would be hard for anyone to trace. And he might have got away with it for years, if it hadn't been for that decision to go and meet the ship. Of course the women met. The Army tried to hush it up – these things are not good for the reputation of the force – but they court-martialled him. He made it easy for them, it appears, by escaping custody and following your employer to beg her to have him back.'

'So he was absent without official leave,' Alex put in. 'Cashiering matter, for an officer, so they were able to be vague about the other charges on the sheet. But that was the end of Royston's military career. He had to go back to his legal wife, of course, though to do him justice I believe that if she had agreed to give him a divorce he would have preferred to marry Miss Borlaise.'

'I would not have had him,' Mrs Thatchell said. 'After a divorce! And he wasn't just cashiered. Afterwards they put him in prison for a week, for bigamy! Imagine the disgrace! I'm only glad my parents did not live to learn how right they were and what a mistake my so-called marriage proved to be.'

Effie was shaking her head in disbelief. 'But I don't understand. What was he doing here? I suppose it was him who was found dead in the court – though you would not have known it from the photograph.'

Alex nodded. 'We're satisfied it was. His second wife was

able to identify a certain – shall we call it – identifying mark.'
He looked at Mrs Thatchell.

'He had a strange-shaped mole,' she said, reluctantly. 'Low
down on his . . . on his lower back.'

Alex nodded. 'The sort of thing that only a wife or mother
would generally know. And the notes record a similar marking
on the corpse. So it appears that we do have an identity. As
for why he came here, that seems clear enough. As Mr
Broadbent told you, I believe, Royston had been living in a
state of penury and had long been estranged from his legal
wife – ever since this incident in fact – but she died of a fever
together with the child. So since she had adamantly refused
to grant her husband a divorce, and there were no other relatives, the estate would have come to Royston in the end. He
had probably found out. He had been trying for months to
contact Miss Borlaise – presumably to beg her to have him
back again, now that he was in a position to provide for her
and make her properly his wife.'

Mrs Thatchell nodded. 'He kept sending letters through my
bank – he knew the branch I used. I kept replying that I could
not forgive and I did not want to see him and forbade them
to continue forwarding his messages to me. I suppose he came
here looking as a last resort. He must have gleaned from them
that I was living in Penzance.'

'And it wasn't you that he was asking for at all, Effie,' Alex
said gently, coming to her side. 'It was the former Effie – the
maid that Mrs Thatchell used to have when she was first
married. He tried the haberdashery, because he knew that his
lady loved embroidery and when he mentioned "Effie" Miss
Blanche thought of you. He thought the maid would plead
his cause, perhaps.'

'She would have done, as well,' Mrs Thatchell snapped. 'It's
one of the reasons that I was glad to see her go. She was always
begging me to let him contact me and saying that the whole
unhappy thing had only happened because he'd loved me much
too well. Ricky could always charm a girl as soon as look at
her. Well, I was not going to let him try his charm on me.
I'd fallen for it far too much before. That's why I didn't trust
myself to let him come.'

Effie looked at Mr Broadbent. 'So what will happen now? Who will inherit the dead wife's estate?'

Broadbent shook his head. 'It doesn't seem that Royston left a will at all, so I suppose that it will go to Chancery. Mrs Thatchell might be able to submit a claim to it, but she says she doesn't wish to anyway, and it is doubtful whether that would hold in law. Pity, because it means that I won't get my fee – but there are compensations for my having come.' He smiled. 'No doubt Miss Blanche will tell you, if she has not done so yet?'

Effie had had sufficient puzzles for one day. She shook her head. 'I only saw Miss Pearl when I went back and she was all peculiar and hardly said a word. But I was only worried about bringing back the silks. I've got them, Mrs Thatchell.' She produced the little bag. 'And what about this cup of tea? It will be getting cold.' She looked at the three faces staring back at her. 'Well, I mean to say, the story you just told me is very, very sad, but it doesn't really alter anything at all. And you said you didn't want the news to spread outside this room. Mrs Lane will think it's odd if you don't drink some tea.'

It was oddly reassuring to hear Mrs Thatchell say, in something much more like her normal tone of voice, 'Very well, Effie. You may start to pour.'

Four

Alex did not ask to change his duty roster, after all. Instead, he wrote a little letter to the Knights, thanking them profusely for their hospitality but explaining that – between a complicated case that he was dealing with and the necessity of studying for the forthcoming exam – he was not in a position to avail himself of their kind standing invitation. He read the missive through a dozen times, then added a scribbled 'for the present anyway'. It was prevarication, but it didn't sound so bald.

He felt like a weasel as he sealed the envelope but he had already put off writing this missive several times and it was already close to being impolitely late. He got it stamped in time to catch the early-morning post so that it would reach them by Wednesday afternoon.

Next day he went, as promised, to put Effie on the bus. He was there before her and he watched her come, pretty as a picture in her best cape and navy skirt, her neat boots tap-tapping on the pavement as she hurried up to him.

'My life, Alex! What a day it's been. I thought that I was never going to get away at all.' She looked around. 'Although the horse-bus isn't here yet, that's a mercy anyway. I was afraid we wouldn't get a chance to do more than say "hello".'

He made a sympathetic face at her. 'Is Mrs Thatchell being difficult? If we can still call her Mrs Thatchell, after what we know. I shouldn't be surprised if she was quite impossible. This must have been an awful shock for her.'

Effie shook her head. 'Not so much that she is difficult, it's just that she's made up her mind she's got to go, and she's got us clearing out the drawers and making lists of things to pack. I've told her till I'm purple in the face that no-one in the town is going to know a thing, but she won't believe it. Says that in a little town like this, gossip spreads like wild-fire and she could never hold her head up any more – I suppose she means in church, since that's the only place she ever goes.'

Alex was frowning. 'You mean she's really going to leave Penzance?' Then, as Effie nodded, he asked, 'So where's she going to go?'

'Back up to London where she came from, I believe. I think the fact that this Royston man is dead has given her a sort of freedom to do that – she says at least she won't be running into him. Or his wife and family either, come to that. It's strange. She's almost got more human, since it all came out. I thought she'd want to see the back of me, since I was the one that brought this trouble home, but it's quite the opposite – she's asked me to go with her.'

Alex felt as though his heart had missed a beat. 'And are you going to do that?'

She looked at him as though he were an idiot. 'Well, of course I said I couldn't – not with Pa the way he is. Anyway, I'd be frightened in the capital. I know that lots of it is marvellous – Miss Blanche was telling me – parks and palaces and all sorts of things. But all those crowds of people! And miles and miles of streets. They say that you can walk all day and still be in London at the end of it!'

Alex made a little joke to cover his relief. 'I can walk quite slowly in Penzance when I put my mind to it.' Then he added, more seriously, 'So you're going to lose your position? What are you going to do?'

She grinned at him – a grin of open-hearted simple joy, so different from the cultivated simper of Miss Knight. 'I shouldn't really tell you, because I promised that I wouldn't say anything until it was arranged. But there is a possibility of something else – an expected vacancy elsewhere – and a friend's put in a word to recommend me for the post. It's something that I'd love, though I don't really have the experience I'd need. But I think that there's a chance. Mrs Thatchell herself was asked and has put in a word for me.'

'Has she?' Alex said. He didn't mention that he had a fair idea of what this exciting vacancy might be. He'd never spoken to anyone at all about that embarrassing lunchtime at the Knights. 'That's very good of her.'

Effie smiled. 'She's not a bad stick, really, when you come to think. She was ever so good about giving me the time to go and visit Pa when he was bad, and Cook says that it was the same with her, when she had sickness in the family. It's just that she can be a Tartar when she tries!'

'I wonder if Miss Caroline is worse, though, all the same?' Alex said, but then rather wished he'd held his tongue. He grinned at her ruefully. 'I imagine that's the vacancy that you are speaking of? I know that your friend Lettie has moved on from there.' That was as tactful as he knew how to be.

But Effie was staring at him, perplexed. 'Oh that! No, that isn't what I am thinking of. I suppose I could apply for that, if this other thing falls through. But what I'm hoping for is something else. I suppose I could tell you . . .' She leaned over and almost whispered in his ear. 'Miss Blanche is getting married and will be going away. She wants Miss Pearl to have me in the shop – there's even a spare room that I could have, she says. All those lovely silks and the library besides – she says that I could even get to read the books, to make sure which ones are really suitable! And they would pay me four and six a week, with only a small deduction for my keep. Sounds like the sort of job I should pay them to let me have!'

Her eyes were shining with the thought of it and she would obviously have liked to tell him more, but there was the horse-bus clopping up the street so he had to help her into it and could only stand and watch as it bore her away. He wished he'd done what it had crossed his mind to do: put on flannels and a sports coat and catch the bus with her – and spring himself upon her family if it came to it.

And it would come to it. Sooner or later it would have to come to it. These weeks without her had taught him that, at least: one day he would have to meet her family and, what was more daunting, take her to meet his. And if the relatives did not approve, then he and Effie would have to brave the storm. Because he knew, with certainty, that he was going to ask her for her hand. It did not occur to him that she might not accept.

He was still turning over that resolution in his mind as he

walked back to the police-station, and his upstairs room. He would devote his Thursdays to studying his books and earn that promotion: if he could get a solo posting with a house attached to it, he could offer Effie marriage in a year or two.

So he was astonished, as he was making for the stairs, to be summoned by the sergeant. 'Ah! PC Dawes! I know you are off duty until six o'clock, but could you step into the inner office, please. There's someone here who'd like to speak to you.' He stepped back to usher Alex in.

Dear Heaven! Who was this now? Mater? She had done it once before, dropped in without warning and made him look a chump. But no – he couldn't see clearly through the patterned glass, but enough to know the visitor was certainly a man. Surely it could not be Major Knight? However offended Caroline's Papa might be, he would not seek a public confrontation in this way. Or would he? Alex walked in with a thumping heart.

What awaited him could hardly have surprised him more if it had been the King himself. It was 'Old Broughton', the Chief Inspector of the Borough Police in person, with his famous beaky nose and stone-blue eyes turned towards Alex as he came into the room.

'You asked for me, sir?' He had the wit to put his helmet underneath his arm and stand stiffly to attention as if on parade.

Broughton nodded. 'Stand easy, Constable.' He turned to the other policeman who was hovering at the door. 'You may leave us, Sergeant,' he said, while Alex did a text-book exercise of counting out the moves, as he shifted to the other regulation pose.

Broughton made a little steeple of his hands and rested his long chin on the central fingertips. 'I imagine that you know why I have sent for you?'

'No idea at all, sir!' said Alex, truthfully.

'Hmm! I've had my eye on you, young fellow, for a little while. Did well in your examinations up to now, I think – and your sergeant gives me a good report of you. Says that you managed to clear up an "unidentified" which had been on the books for better than a year, by keeping your eyes open and your mind engaged. Is that a fair assessment?'

Alex made a deprecating noise. Whatever else, he had not expected this.

'Thing is, young fellow, I am looking for a man – subject to the outcome of the next exam, of course – to work on attachment to a little country station out towards St Just. There is a sergeant out there who is getting on a bit and he's starting to find the duties are too much for him, especially in the evenings, when he's trying to patrol – the country's hilly, even though he's got a bicycle. Needs a younger fellow that he could train up a bit, who could take over in a year or two, when he's ready to retire. Would you like to be considered for the posting, Dawes?'

Alex took a deep, unsteady breath. 'Well, of course I'm very flattered, sir, and I would love the job . . .' More than the Commissioner could possibly suppose, in fact. It must be near Penvarris, which would be a dream come true. 'But honesty compels me to make something clear. I believe you may have selected me for this on the basis of a recommendation you received from outside of the force. Would that be correct?'

Broughton brought his beetle-brows into a frown. 'Well, yes, that is certainly the case. I have received the warmest commendation of your skill, from someone whose opinion I attach importance to. Quite unexpected too – someone I spoke to at a charity affair. He came up to me, entirely unasked, and wanted to tell me what an ornament you were . . .'

Alex shook his head. 'That's what I was afraid of. Sir, I am sure that it was kindly meant, but I cannot in good conscience permit you to believe that this was an impartial testimonial. I fear that the gentleman had hopes of me as a potential son-in-law. It is only fair to tell you that, since those hopes are false, it is unlikely that he would say the same again.'

Broughton looked puzzled. 'But I understood the fellow had no family at all. And he didn't even seem to know your name. But he was quite specific – he wrote your number down. He told me he'd had dealings with you in Penzance, and had been so impressed that he intended to write a letter commending you to me, though he hadn't managed to get round to it. He'd just moved into the St Just district, he was telling me, and when he heard that I was looking for a younger man to help the sergeant there, he thought of you at once – promised to send me your number, which he did next day. You'd be ideal, he said. Understanding and patient with a country way of life. Said you were most helpful when he lost his pig, when other people simply took no interest at all.'

It was so unexpected that Alex laughed aloud. 'Oh, the pig! In that case, I am happy that the owner thought so well of me. At least it's genuine. I thought the commendation might have come from . . .' He tailed off, in dismay.

'Major Knight, I take it?' Broughton leaned back in his chair and looked at him. 'He did go wittering on the other day about one of our recruits. I didn't pay too much attention, I'm afraid. Don't hold with these military Johnnies, trying to exert their influence on the civilian force.' He glared at Alex. 'So it was you, again? I see. He seemed to have some notion that we should train you up so you could go and join the Army afterwards. What do you say to that?'

'My father was in the Army and my two brothers are. I have every respect for them, of course, but if I had wished to join them, then I would have done,' Alex said simply. 'My family hoped I would – and of course, if there was a threat to England, that would be different. My father seems to think there might be trouble soon, with Germany re-arming and all that sort of thing, and of course if that happened I should enlist at once. But generally I have no thirst for shooting things – and people least of all. I'm much more interested in keeping Cornwall safe.'

For the first time, Broughton gave him an approving smile. 'Well said, my boy. In my case it was Navy – but otherwise my situation was very much the same! I chose the police force and it's served me very well.' He gestured vaguely at his insignia of rank. 'I think that my informant was correct. I think you would be an ideal candidate. I'll put your name forward when the time comes, then – depending on the outcome of the yearly test, of course. I think I made that clear.' He scribbled something on a notepad which he had in front of him, and then looked up again. 'Very well, Six-six-three, that will be all for now. You will be hearing from me in due course, I hope.'

Alex was dismissed. He floated up the stairs as if he had a bubble under him, and he could hardly concentrate upon his books at all. Promotion to a country station near Penvarris Mine, where there was accommodation and he could take a wife! That would be something to tell Effie, the next time they met!

In the meantime there was Mater's letter to attend to – he had forgotten it. He pulled it out and read it. It was full of recrimination and reproach. He had left a luncheon early, snubbed Miss Caroline and was suspected of involvement with that awful maidservant, who had seemed to know him and had now left in disgrace. Would he write back instantly and swear it wasn't true.

Alex was more than happy to oblige. There was a young lady he was fond of, he agreed, but she was not the 'awful maidservant'. She was a young lady of good character. He left it at that, this time – but wouldn't it be splendid to be able to report that his 'young lady' was not a maid at all, but a more socially acceptable assistant in a shop? He hoped with all his heart that Effie would get that position with Miss Pearl.

Mater would grumble that it was 'only trade' of course, and look down on them both – but haberdashery was the most respectable and ladylike of trades. Besides, if strait-laced Mrs Thatchell, all those years ago, had defied her family to marry the young man of her choice, and if Miss Blanche had found the courage to do something similar, shouldn't he be willing to stand up for his choice?

He grinned. He'd have to give Effie a few lessons on how to use a knife and fork, but she'd learn a few graces living with Miss Pearl. And Pater would approve of Effie's love of books.

Perhaps it would be possible to introduce them after all.

Lettie's wedding was a very hurried, small affair. Fayther managed to take the afternoon off work to lead her down the aisle, in last year's Whitson dress that was getting far too tight, and her stepmother and the senior Symonses were there to witness it. And that was all. They didn't even go back for tea and sandwiches because Reg Symons said he had to go and mind the shop, and if Lettie was going to be a Symons now as well, she had bally-well better come and start to earn her keep.

So Lettie spent the first hours of her married life weighing out sugar and putting it in bags. In fact, she found she didn't mind it very much and – since she was nicer to the customers than her in-laws were apt to be – she found that people were soon queuing up to have her deal with them. It very nearly caused a row, in fact, until the till was shut and trade was proved to be quite sharply up on what it generally was.

Effie had sent a pair of hand-embroidered pillow-slips, which she had made herself, and Lettie felt quite special as she put them on the bed, but when her husband came back from his round – which father had insisted that he did as usual – he simply took his boots off and rolled against the wall. She put her arm out to him, but he pulled away.

'Don't be so soppy, Lettie. My folks are through the wall. They could hear us breathing, let alone if we were doing you-know-what. I can't be doing with it; it puts me off my stride.' All this was delivered in a whispered hiss and it was clear that Bert meant every word he said. 'Anyway, in your condition, it might not be wise.'

Lettie was more than a little bit dismayed. It wasn't that she was especially keen on that sort of thing herself but it was expected of you, wasn't it, when you were a wife? This was supposed to be their wedding night, so where was the romance? 'Well, you could give me a little kiss at least,' she murmured, silkily, cuddling up to him in her most alluring way. 'That doesn't make a noise.'

But her new husband was already fast asleep.

It was Penvarris feast again and this time Effie was able to attend. Miss Pearl had let her have the whole day off from working in the shop – only a few weeks after she had started, too – though of course there'd be a shilling stopped out of her pay.

Effie had turned her navy skirt in honour of the day, and

made herself a brand-new blouse to go with it. She had time to do these little chores these days – shop hours were quite different from a servant's timetable. Of course there were lots of things to do, before and after they opened for the day – stock to be accounted for and orders to be made, and shelves to be dusted and all that sort of thing – but even so by eight o'clock or thereabouts, Effie found that she had time to call her own.

It was a wonderful experience – especially with a library of books downstairs to read. Of course, the meals were rather different from those she'd had from Mrs Lane: Miss Pearl had no idea how to cook at all. Her idea of dinner was a slice of ham and maybe a tomato if it could be had. Effie had plucked up courage in the end, and asked if she could fry a plate of sprats, provided that she bought them for herself, and Miss Pearl had surprisingly agreed. Not only that, but she'd deigned to sample some, and the whole experiment had been enough of a success for it to be repeated several times. On the last occasion, Miss Pearl even gave her sixpence for the sprats and let her clean the kitchen when the meal was done.

Effie was no great expert with a pan herself, but if she ever married – and she supposed one day she might – she would be grateful for this chance to learn to use a stove. Besides, she was beginning to tire of sprats by now, and was wondering what other culinary treats she could initiate.

Thinking of culinary treats, she looked around the street. Dozens of brightly coloured stalls were selling sweets and pies, or offering a chance to win a goldfish in a bag by rolling pennies down a chute. Any minute now the procession would come by. A brass band was already marching down the street, followed by groups of dancing children, dressed up for the occasion in their Sunday best, or imitating nursery characters – she counted three rabbits and a humpty-dumpty – in home-sewn costumes made from flour sacks in honour of the feast.

Effie felt quite like a child herself. She had three ha'pence in her pocket, kept back from her wages, and she was free to spend it any way she liked. There was even Peter Kellow at the hoop-la stall, making eyes at her and trying to win a

hideous teapot on a stand, which she suspected he would want
to give to her. It ought to quite be perfect. So why did she
feel that there was something missing from the day?

She gave herself a shake. She ought to be grateful. Things
were so different from the way they used to be. Mrs Thatchell,
who had packed up and gone with as much speed and as little
fuss as possible, had written just one letter to the shop (using
one of those browning envelopes) to say that she had safely
settled in, and that was the last that Effie heard of her. It was
as if that whole portion of her life had simply never been.

'What you doing, Effie? Going to let me buy you a piece
of gingerbread?' That was Pa, as agile as a monkey walking
with his stick, coming up behind her unexpectedly. 'Or would
you sooner have a bag of toasted nuts from that standing over
there?' He gestured to the stall. 'You still got time to get down
the other end and watch the children race. Your cousin Sammy
is in the egg and spoon.'

Effie nodded. 'Gingerbread, I think.' And he went off to get
it while she watched the parade. She was just applauding a
woman with a bicycle, who had woven coloured ribbon around
every spoke and turned the handlebars into a bank of flowers,
when she was interrupted by an unexpected hand upon her
arm.

She glanced across her shoulder, naturally imagining that it
would be her Pa. 'That didn't take you long!' But there was
her father, still over at the stall, deep in conversation with Mrs
Richards and her boy! She whirled around. 'Alex! What are
you doing here? And it isn't even Thursday!'

That sounded ridiculous, even to herself, and Alex was
grinning as widely as could be. 'Brought you some flowers,
Miss Pengelly!' He handed her a posy – a bunch of wild roses
mixed with Queen Anne's lace – one that he'd obviously caught
when the girls were tossing them from the decorated carts.
'Anyway, it's a public procession, isn't it?' he said. 'If I am likely
to be posted close nearby, I thought I better come and see
what sort of place it is.'

She gazed at him. 'You got the St Just position then?' He
had mentioned in passing that he might be in line.

''Tisn't certain, but the results of the examination came out yesterday. I topped the list, and there is a message on the board saying that Broughton wants to see me first thing Monday, so it is looking promising.'

His fingers were still resting on her arm, and she squeezed them to her, close against her side. 'I'm delighted for you, Alex. Did you come to tell me that?'

'To tell you the truth, Effie, I felt I ought to come. I've thought of coming out here with you several times before. I've never met your family, and it's time I did. The longer that we leave it, the harder it will be. I thought the feast day was an opportunity.'

She shook her head at him. 'I'm not so sure. Pa will be all right, but Uncle Joe is funny where strangers are concerned.' Alex did seem a stranger suddenly, not a part of this whole world at all. It disconcerted her.

But he was saying firmly, 'Shan't be a stranger if I come to work out here. And your Uncle Joe can say anything he likes, I'm not going to marry him.'

The band was still playing and the children sang and screamed and there was laughter and gossip everywhere around, but to Effie it seemed that a sudden silence fell. 'Meaning that you're going to marry someone else?' she said, in a voice that she could hardly hear herself.

'You, if you will have me, Effie,' he replied. 'I didn't mean to blurt it out like this, but you must have known that it was coming. You know how I feel – and I believe you feel the same way about me. I know you have misgivings but—'

'Your ginger fairing, Effie!' That was father's voice. He was standing close beside them with the sweetmeat in his hand, looking at Alex with a strange expression on his face. 'I think I recognize your face. And you clearly know my daughter. Should I know you from somewhere?' His voice was rather clipped.

'This is Alex, Pa,' she told him. 'The boy I told you of. And you have met before.'

Pa bit off a large piece of gingerbread, without seeming to notice what he did. 'Of course,' he murmured, through the crumbs, 'that young constable that came out to the mine. I didn't recognize you out of uniform.' He stuffed the fairings in his pocket and held out his one free hand. 'I am glad to meet you, after all this time,' he said warmly. 'Effie has mentioned you to me, but I'd had the impression that you two had agreed to part. If that's not so, I'm glad to know it – for her sake, at least. I know she thinks an awful lot of you.'

Alex said the best thing he could possibly have said. 'Sir, I am delighted to meet you properly. Effie holds you in such deep respect that I regret that we have not really met before. We did feel that our backgrounds were rather different, but we have decided – at least, I have decided . . .' He trailed off. 'I have just been presumptuous enough to ask your daughter if she would marry me. I should of course have asked for your permission first. May I request it now?'

Pa shook his head, but he was grinning ear to ear. 'Far too soon to ask me what I think. Got to see you in action a bit first. Now, I've seen you as a policeman, and you do all right at that. How do you get on with eating gingerbread? Test of a proper suitor, that is. Can I get you one?'

Effie let out a happy inward sigh. Alex was laughing. It was going to be much easier than she thought. She said, 'Pa, Alex walked out here to tell me that he's passed his last exam. Top of the whole course he came, now what do you think of that? And he's going to have a posting to a station out this way, and in a year or two he'll run it on his own – and there is a police house goes with it – just a little one, and . . .'

'Dear life, Effie! How you do run on. Let me get the man some gingerbread and you can tell me slowly, so I can take it in.'

Alex intervened with, 'Let me get my own, sir.'

Pa waved a hand at him. 'No need for that. I'm feeling flush today. And while I'm on the subject, I've got some news myself. Spoke to Cap'n Maddern a little while ago, while we were waiting for the band to start. Seems there's a job on the settling-tables coming up – one of the men is going to Canada to join his sons – and it's mine if I want it. So I said I would. 'Tisn't what I choose, and of course it doesn't pay like tributing, but it's money all the same, and it's something I could manage even with this leg. It's only standing, there's not much carrying or climbing round involved. So I can afford to splash out on some bits of gingerbread.'

It had cost him an effort to bring himself to this, and Effie knew it. But the prospect of being back at work again had given him more pleasure than she'd seen in him for months – and today, of all days, she was glad of it. However, she knew better than to make a song and dance. 'Well, in that case, buy some for Jill Richards and her son, while you're about it,' she said. 'She's been looking at it woeful, but she hasn't bought a crumb, so I suspect that she can't run to it.'

Her father looked thoughtful. 'Some nice woman she is, Effie, and I still feel responsible for what happened to the boy. Don't know whatever will become of him. I have been wondering . . . should I go and lodge with her? Give Madge back her bedroom and give that poor widow a hand to pay the rent? She has suggested it – but you know how people talk.'

'How don't you marry her, in that case?' Effie said. 'That would stop the talk. Give you a bit of company and all. Besides, it seems marrying is getting fashionable round here.'

'You wouldn't mind?' her father said. 'Madge thought perhaps you would. Your mother . . . you know . . . perhaps you might object if another woman seemed to take her place.'

Effie looked at him. 'Well of course I wouldn't mind! Better for everybody all round, I'd say, and save you feeling guilty all the time as well.' She laughed. 'Here, this is a turn-up, isn't it? You are asking my permission and we're asking yours. Tell you what – you give me yours and I will give you mine.'

Alex, who had been listening to all this, turned to her and broke in suddenly. 'You mean that you will have me, Effie? You haven't actually said so, in so many words.'

She grinned up happily at him. 'Well, I'll do it now. Since Pa has given his permission, I will marry you.' She wanted to catch the words and put them in a frame so that she could look at them for ever, like embroidery.

Pa looked at Alex sideways. 'No, I meant what I said. I want to see you eat that gingerbread before I agree to any marriages. After that, just you be sure that you look after her. Though you might find her Uncle Joe is harder to convince. But you had better go and tell him – he's down the Worker's Educational, helping to put out the chairs and tables for the tea.' He turned to Effie and gave a wicked wink. 'Tell you what, young lady, if your uncle gives you any trouble over this, you send him to me. Either that, or call a policeman.'

Effie laughed out loud.